D0052868

What Readers Are Saying about the Men of the Saddle Series

LORI COPELAND

MEN of the SADDLE

the Plainsman

Tyndale House Publishers, Inc.
CAROL STREAM, ILLINOIS

Visit Tyndale's exciting Web site at www.tyndale.com

TYNDALE and Tyndale's quill logo are registered trademarks of Tyndale House Publishers, Inc.

The Plainsman

Designed by Catherine Bergstrom

Edited by Kathryn S. Olson

Scripture quotations are taken from the *Holy Bible*, King James Version.

The Scripture in the epigraph is taken from the *Holy Bible*, New Century Version, copyright © 1987, 1988, 1991 by Word Publishing, Dallas, Texas 75039. Used by permission.

Library of Congress Cataloging-in-Publication Data

Copeland, Lori.
  The plainsman/ Lori Copeland.
    p. cm. — (Men of the saddle ; #4)
  ISBN-13: 978-0-8423-6931-2 (sc)
  ISBN-10: 0-8423-6931-7 (sc)
  1. Pioneers—Fiction. I. Title.
  PS3553.O6336P57 2005
  813'.54—dc22   2005020445

Printed in the United States of America

12 11 10 09 08 07 06
9   8   7   6   5   4   3   2

SO BE VERY CAREFUL HOW YOU LIVE.

DO NOT LIVE LIKE THOSE WHO ARE NOT WISE, BUT LIVE WISELY.

EPHESIANS 5:15

New Century Version

CHAPTER 1

Louisiana, 1865

Tyrone, Kansas, got hotter than a cookstove sometimes, but the town had never been ankle-deep in mud. Not to Trey McAllister's recollection.

His stallion plodded through standing water, its hooves heavy with Louisiana red clay. Thunder rolled overhead, and rain continued to come down in buckets.

Trey huddled deeper into his poncho and slowed the animal's pace. The horse was close to exhaustion; thick sludge impeded its progress. A glance at the sky showed no break in the thick gray cover. Trey reined up, his gaze searching for adequate shelter. A spreading oak, thick with hanging moss, caught his eye. It wouldn't be much, but it would be drier than sleeping in the saddle. No need to push his horse past its limits, and he was about done in himself.

When he'd left home, going to war had sounded exciting.

Not that he liked the thought of fighting and killing. He'd thought of it more as a chance to see some of the country and to strike a blow for what was right. He'd learned the hard way that there was nothing exciting about war, and as it turned out all of the country he'd seen was one battlefield after another.

He never dreamed he could be homesick for Kansas. Sure, the South was pretty with its moss-hung trees and antebellum houses, but it couldn't compare to riding across a Kansas prairie with a good horse under you and the wind in your face. He pictured the land of his birth: wide-open spaces with sunlit clouds racing overhead and the good, fertile soil stretching out to meet the sky. Here, while the land was flat enough, he felt hemmed in, the lack of space stifling to a man used to seeing for miles in every direction.

Trey took care of his horse first. Buck, the big, black stallion, had carried him many a mile. A man could get awfully attached to a horse. A woman, now, she might let you down, but a good horse never would. And he'd miss his friends: men who'd fought for their states but been separated from their companies by battles. Eventually the men had formed their own fighting group and stuck together closer than brothers.

He carried his saddle to the shelter of the low-hanging tree branches. Even the trees were different from back home. He dropped his burden and stood up to stretch, tired of the constant rain and the clinging red Louisiana clay. He'd had too many years of blood and death and fighting. Now that the war had finally ended, he was riding old Buck back to Kansas—God's country. If he ever got the urge to leave again he'd nail his boots to the ground.

Half an hour later Trey had made a wet camp and settled in.

Tonight's fare would be cold bread and meat. No hot coffee.
No fire.

It wasn't the first time he'd slept in the rain and later eaten a
cold supper. Three years fighting the Confederates had turned
him from a fresh-faced boy to a battle-hardened man. He knew
he looked older, tougher, but the biggest changes were on the
inside. You couldn't watch men die under the most brutal
conditions and be untouched. He had a stronger appreciation
for life now and a greater realization of how temporary it could
be. He'd heard men die cursing the Almighty for not sparing
them while others had met their Maker with a prayer on their
lips. He knew his own faith had grown stronger through it all.

But the war was really over this time, no cruel hoax like the
one attempted earlier last year when two New York papers
reported that President Lincoln had issued a proclamation
ordering that May 26 be a day of fasting and prayer. The proclamation further commanded the conscription of an additional
four hundred thousand men into the Union army on account of
"the situation in Virginia, the disaster at Red River, the delay at
Charleston, and the general state of the country."

There was not a word of truth in any of it, and to a
war-weary country the hoax was particularly cruel. The perpetra-
tors were found and dealt with, and the nation fought on.

On April 26, 1865, Confederate general Joseph E. Johnston
surrendered his army to Union general William T. Sherman. On
May 4, General Richard Taylor surrendered the last significant
Confederate force near Mobile, Alabama.

The news was slow to filter down to Trey's regiment, but
when it did a shout the likes of which hadn't been heard in
years marked the victory. Young men dropped their weapons

and grown men cried. By then the war had been over for
a month.

Men had packed their bags and headed home to families
they hadn't seen in far too long. Others who were missing limbs
and eyesight had been carried or supported by compassionate
comrades.

Trey rolled into his wet bedroll and closed his eyes, listening to the rain hit the brim of his hat. Thunder boomed in the
distance and he knew he wouldn't get much sleep—not tonight.
It would be another week of hard riding before he reached
home—home being a little town north of Olathe. Tyrone,
Kansas: population fifty-three, not counting the babies born
while he'd been gone.

A smile lit his rugged features. *Home* was a good-sounding
word. He pictured the faces of his four sisters—Ellie, Naomi, Sue
Ann and Beth—and he could practically smell chicken frying in
the skillet. Tyrone would celebrate when he rode into town.
Then—and only then—would his own celebration be complete.

He rolled deeper into the soggy blanket, trying to get
comfortable. The ground was soft enough, just mud and mire,
but it wasn't the same as a bed. He longed for freshly washed
and sun-dried sheets.

Must feel like heaven.

Sue Ann would make sure he'd have clean sheets and hot
biscuits and freshly ironed shirts. Trouble was she'd also make
sure his hair was cut every month, his boots were shined, and
his nails were trimmed. She might even go so far as to demand
clean socks and a bath twice a week.

Having four women to fuss over him was a downright pain.

While he was in a hurry to get home, he wasn't in a hurry to get back to all that bother. He'd missed the girls. Couldn't deny that, but he hadn't missed their infernal clucking. Being the only boy—and the baby to boot—his life had sometimes been an unholy nightmare. He occasionally still woke in a cold sweat when his dreams were invaded by childhood memories of those four girls dressing him in frilly dresses and bonnets. This had gone on until he was big enough to fight his way free.

They'd laugh and say what a "pretty baby" he was with that thick head of red hair and sky blue eyes. Said he was "pretty enough to be a girl."

Those were fighting words.

Around the age of five or six he'd started hiding out on the days the girls got that "play house" look in their eyes. One day he'd stayed away until long after dark, and Naomi had come looking for him with a hickory switch.

"We thought something awful had happened to you!" She'd given him a tongue-lashing harsher than lye soap.

He was being raised and maternally oppressed by four interfering females. He fought as best he could.

His grin widened when he thought about the women. Twenty-four years old now, he wasn't going to be intimated by their presence—or at least he didn't figure he'd be when he got home. He was a man, and a man ought not to have any trouble holding his own with dominating females. He'd been gone long enough for the girls to appreciate his individuality. He'd killed men, fought for his country, upheld the flag.

His sisters wouldn't likely try to control his life the way they had before he left. He wouldn't allow it. When he got home he'd get him a place of his own and visit the females for Sunday dinner.

He had no doubt that Beth would already have him lined up

with every single belle in Tyrone, which would amount to two women: Florence Williams and Peggy Stovall. Florence's buckteeth were so bad she could eat lettuce through a picket fence. Peggy wasn't hard on the eyes, but she didn't talk much. He'd gone through eight grades of school with her and he'd venture that he hadn't heard her speak more than a handful of words. "Mrs. Pruitt. Trey threw my chalk down the privy hole." That's about all he'd heard out of Peggy. She was his age; surely she'd be talking more and probably wearing those corsets women wore. But then again Peggy wasn't the sort who ever said or wore anything worthwhile.

He rolled to his side, pulling the hat lower. The past three years had taken a lot out of him, and for the next few months he planned to do what he wanted with no females to interfere. Peace and quiet. That's all he was looking for, but he had a hunch it wouldn't be that easy. Trouble waited for him in Tyrone. His sisters needed him, and he wasn't a man to turn his back on kinfolk in trouble.

Trey rolled onto his back again and the rain sluiced down. With the wet blanket tucked around his chin, he said what he said every night before he dropped off to sleep.

"Thank You, God, for seeing me through this war. I'm much obliged."

Trey set off an hour before dawn in a heavy downpour, tired, sore, and sleep deprived. Forked lightning lit the narrow roadway. Thunder boomed overhead. The stallion spooked and shied away from nature's rowdy display. Kansas rains were usually significant, but Trey had never seen anything like this. Louisiana was swamp country; some folks buried their dead above ground, and now he understood why.

By midmorning Buck was tiring again. Trey scraped layers of mud off the animal's hooves, hoping to get in another couple hours' travel before he stopped to rest. He'd ridden though mostly swamp for hours now, catching sight of a few gators and steering clear of the snakes that crossed his path. Two more good reasons to favor Kansas. They had snakes out there, but not like these. Cottonmouths as long as your arm with gray shiny skin and gaping white mouths. Imagine waking up and finding one of those varmints in your bed. Kansas copperheads and rattlers were bad enough, but he hated the looks of a cottonmouth.

Toward noon, Trey sat up straighter in the saddle, peering through a veil of heavy rain. Straight ahead he spotted a wooden sign:

Sassy Gap: Population 8½

He smiled. The ½ that had been burned into the wood must be somebody's way of announcing a new baby.

He clucked to the horse, urging the animal forward. Maybe he'd find a hot meal and a dry bed for the night.

When he entered the burg a few minutes later, he walked the horse down the middle of the street. Water stood in rising puddles; the road was nothing more than a marsh. His eyes scanned the line of the three nearest buildings. One looked to be a general store; the second was nondescript, but he spotted a livery in back. The third and smallest had—

Flames shooting out the roof.

Fire!

Black smoke rolled out from under the shingles of the roof.

Trey dismounted quickly and raced toward the building, where flames were shooting straight up. Mud sucked at his boots. Sparks, whipped by the wind, skipped across the wooden shingles.

Suddenly women rounded the corner, each carrying a bucket of some kind.

Trey watched as they quickly formed a brigade, passing water from the watering trough into the building. He counted. One, two, three—six—eight. Eight females. Where were the men? Why would they send women to fight fire?

A heavyset woman glanced up, clearly startled when she saw him running at her.

He hurriedly introduced himself with "I'm Trey," then grabbed the bucket from her hand and joined the fight.

Women raced back and forth, drenching the licking flames.

"The roof!" a woman at the trough yelled. "Save the roof!"

Minutes later Trey grabbed the rope from his saddle, propped a ladder against the outside wall, and hurriedly scaled it. Once on the roof he began hauling up every other bucket of water. It took twenty-two buckets and close to an hour for him to save the roof. Were it not for the heavy downpour, the building would have been in ashes.

Exhausted, the women collapsed to the ground, catching their breath while Trey smothered the last remaining embers with a thick blanket someone had handed him.

He sank down to the shingles and coughed, black smoke filling his lungs. Below him, he noticed the silence. The women sat with bleak eyes, staring up at the building. They'd managed to save the exterior, but inside the structure had major damage. Rolling to his side, Trey again looked around for the town's men. During the firefight, he hadn't spotted one man. Not one. Only women. One now carried a small child—a girl—on her hip.

He descended the ladder and faced the strange assemblage. The women's faces were black with soot. Dresses were soiled and bonnets trailed down their backs. His eyes moved to the sign he'd missed earlier and he winced.

Speck's Mortuary.

He'd stumbled onto an undertaker's parlor.

One of the women slowly got to her feet and adjusted her skirt before addressing him. "Much obliged, stranger. The name's Speck. Grandma Speck. This here is my place, and I'm sure grateful to you for helping save it."

Trey quickly removed his hat. Overhead thunder rolled and lightning lit the bizarre scene. "Ma'am."

The stench of smoke and burning rubble in the air made it difficult to breathe. The older woman looked like she was worn to a frazzle. The hand she offered him trembled.

Of the eight, Trey realized, she was easily the oldest. The others looked to be varying in age all the way from very young to this woman, who appeared to be in her later years. Way past the age to be fighting fire, to his way of thinking. He looked around again, expecting to see at least one man peering from the shelter of the other buildings.

Grandma Speck stepped back, assessing the damage. "Well, looks like the good Lord's blessed us mightily."

Trey lifted a singed brow. "Ma'am?"

She returned his look. "God's done gone and blessed us again! We still got part of the building."

"Yes, ma'am." Trey turned to look at the source of her blessing. Smoke curled from sections of the roof. Didn't figure he'd count the past hour a blessing, but he supposed some folks had a sunnier outlook than he.

He turned when a younger woman approached. She was pretty, with dainty features and jet-black hair hanging loose to her waist. Cajun, Trey decided. Native Louisianian.

"Grandma Speck looks on the bright side," she explained with a heavy French accent. She smiled and Trey's insides lurched. She was about the prettiest thing he'd seen in years. No bigger than a minute, cheeks flushed by the fire, soot covering the tip of her nose.

"Yes, ma'am," he repeated.

Another woman, the one carrying the child, came to stand beside him. "Please, won't you come inside where it's dry? Maybe you'd like a nice cup of hot coffee to ward off a chill?"

Now that the emergency was over, Trey remembered he'd been about to look for a dry place to sleep tonight. The heavy deluge appeared to have set in for the day.

"Thank you. A cup of hot coffee would be welcome."

The women clapped with glee and quickly dispersed in opposite directions. One hung back with Grandma Speck.

The older woman made another grateful declaration about God and Trey, which he passed off as being purely coincidental.

"I happened to be passing through," he said. "Saw the fire and pitched in to help."

The old woman's eyes narrowed. "You're not a man of God?"

"No, ma'am. I mean, yes, ma'am. I believe in the Almighty."

Trey wasn't sure what answer she was looking for, but he guessed any heathen riding through Sassy Gap would be asked to keep riding—that much he sensed in her tone.

"Everything happens for a reason," she said.

"Yes, ma'am."

Right now he hoped the reason was a hot meal and a dry bed for the night.

The young woman who'd stayed with Grandma Speck stepped in to help Trey stable his horse, then lingered while he dipped a scoop of grain and dumped it in the wooden feed trough. She was thin as a reed with brown hair tucked into a bun on the back of her head. Her recent bout of firefighting had pulled strands loose to straggle around her face. The acrid scent of smoke drifted from her clothing in an almost visible cloud.

She held out her hand. "I'm Helen. We surely appreciate you helping us out like that."

Her hand was rough and calloused, and he suspected she was no stranger to hard work.

Trey grinned down at her. "Wasn't anything, ma'am. Anyone would have done the same."

"I'm . . . not so sure of that."

She turned away and Trey felt a stab of curiosity. There was something strange about this town, but he guessed it wasn't any of his business. He wouldn't be here long enough to get involved.

Once Buck had been taken care of, Helen took Trey by the arm and led him across the street from the smoking undertaker's parlor to the entrance of the second building. The rain was still coming down like pouring water on a flat rock. When his eyes adjusted to the dim light, he saw that he was in some sort of communal room—a large area that served as a kitchen and sleeping quarters. To the rear of the room, he saw nine cots, each separated by a single curtain. A fire burned in the fireplace, and a pot of coffee steamed on the hearth. The women greeted him like a long-lost brother.

The black-haired one turned from the stove, her cheeks radiant from the rain and wind. She smiled. "Welcome to our town, Mr.—?" She waited for Trey to introduce himself.

"Trey McAllister. From Tyrone, Kansas."

She nodded. "Mr. McAllister. What brings you through Sassy Gap?"

Her voice was lyrical. Soft . . . the sort that could be real trouble for a man who hadn't seen a pretty female in a long time.

"Been fighting in the war, ma'am, but I'm going home now."

"But the war has been over for a while."

"Me and some friends stuck around to help a few wounded buddies get home before we left, Miss . . ."

"Please. My name is Mirelle, but my friends call me Mira."

Trey wasn't comfortable with the exchange of personal information. Clearing his throat, he acknowledged, "Coffee smells good."

"Sit down; I'll fill a cup."

Trey pulled a chair out from the large wooden table and sat down. Other women started to appear one by one, each doing her best to serve him.

Over coffee he learned their names. Grandma Speck owned and operated the only undertaker parlor for thirty miles around. Mirelle, the pretty French girl, helped her. Then there were Melody, Jane, Brenda, Helen—the one he'd met at the stable,

Vivian, and Dee. All had lost their husbands or betrothed in the fighting during the last two years. Melody had one child, a girl. Her name was Audrey and she was three. Trey had never seen a cuter child: round blue eyes, curly dark hair, and a sprinkle of freckles dotting the bridge of her nose.

"My mama planted freckle seeds," Audrey told him. "And they're growing."

"Indeed they are," Trey acknowledged, which seem to satisfy the child.

Dee wanted to dominate the conversation. Trey sensed the women hadn't been around men much lately, and he wondered why they chose to live in a town void of male companions. When he managed to get a word in edgewise, he asked. "Why are there no men in Sassy Gap?"

"Oh, one rides through every now and again," Vivian conceded. The women exchanged candid looks. "But he never sticks around for long."

Trey wondered about the significance of the looks but decided not to delve into the issue. For whatever reason, it appeared males had no interest in the strictly women-only town.

Draining the last of his coffee, he pushed his cup back. "Is there a vacant room in town?"

One or two women tittered.

Mira shot them a warning look. "No hotel. Did you want to spend the night?"

Trey glanced at the window, where thunder rattled the panes. "Thought I might try to find a dry bed and a hot meal before I head out in the morning."

Grandma Speck laid her knitting aside. "You can sleep in the parlor."

"Parlor?" Trey smiled. "What parlor?"

"I'll show you," she replied, getting up from her chair.

"That's real kind of you, ma'am."

"No bother." She paused at the door. "Suppose you might want to wash up a bit before supper. Follow me."

Trey followed her out of the building, huddling deeper into his poncho. They walked the short distance back to the charred building. He paused, looking up at the still-smoldering roof. Then it hit him.

Parlor.

She'd just offered, and he'd just accepted, the *undertaker's* parlor.

"I'll get some blankets and you can roll up in here."

She pointed to the small dais, which he suspected a casket occupied during services. A chill crept up his spine.

"Most of the fire damage is on the far end of the roof," Grandma said as she gathered up blankets and pillows. "The smell of smoke ain't pleasant, but I reckon it's dry in here and shore better than sleeping in a downpour."

Trey's mind raced, trying to think of a gracious way to decline the hastily accepted offer. He was used to killing and dying, but spending time in a place reserved for dead people was something else. But if he refused her offer then he'd have to say why, and he wasn't inclined to get into all that. He caught the blankets and pillows she tossed him.

"Rest up a bit. The girls will have supper on the table in a spell." She paused, her eyes scaling Trey. "We're mighty beholden to you, Mr. McAllister. If the parlor had burned we'd have no means of support. Burying folks is the only income we have."

Trey thought about the damaged roof and wondered who would make the repairs. It would take a month's work to restore the shingles. Water dripped into buckets the women had placed under the holes.

"There aren't any men around who can help?"

Grandma Speck laughed. "Lots of men around, but not a one has the guts to help us."

Trey thought that was an odd statement.

"It's a fact," Grandma said. "Mira's papa is Jean-Marc Portier, and he won't let them."

The situation was getting more bizarre by the minute. Mirelle. The pretty French girl. Her *father* wouldn't let them? What sort of nonsense was that?

As though she sensed his question, Grandma went on. "Jean-Marc is one of the richest, most powerful men around these parts. When Mira's husband, Paul, was killed last year, Jean-Marc insisted she come home. Mira refused, and now he is determined to make her go back. There's bad blood between them, though Mira won't talk about it.

"Seems to me their quarrel goes beyond the regular father-and-daughter spat. Their hatred is buried deep. Bone deep." The old woman clucked her tongue. "He's made our lives miserable trying to bring her to heel, but Mira's independent and a mite stubborn. She vows she'll never let Jean-Marc dominate her again." Grandma shrugged off any further exchanges on the subject. "We'll let you know when the meal's ready. Thank you again, Mr. McAllister. We're all much obliged."

With that, Grandma Speck left Trey alone, standing in the middle of the burying parlor.

Belatedly it dawned on him.

Fool!

He ought to have followed the example of other men and rode straight through Sassy Gap, raining or not.

He tossed the blanket and pillow onto the floor and eyed the dais.

A mortuary?

Jean-Marc Portier stood by the window, staring in the direction of Sassy Gap. Rain lashed the windows. It would have to rain. He hoped Curt Wiggins would have enough sense not to set the fire tonight. You'd think a fool would be smart enough to wait until it stopped raining before trying to burn down a building. But not Curt. He'd wager on it. The man followed orders to the last letter; he wasn't all that quick at thinking on his own.

A rosy glow reflected against the low-hanging clouds. Jean-Marc gripped the rich, burgundy-colored velvet curtains. Fire! At Sassy Gap. The old funeral parlor should burn like fatwood kindling once it got started, if the rain didn't put out the flames.

Even as he watched, the glow faded. He lingered for a moment before turning away from the window. Another failure. Those Sassy Gap women had more lives than the proverbial cat. They were too stubborn for their own good. He didn't particularly want to hurt them, unless it was necessary. But he needed the ground that town sat on, and he couldn't afford to let eight scrawny women—including Mira—thwart him.

A sardonic smile broke across his handsome features. Especially Mirelle.

The smile faded and hardness settled around his eyes. That girl would learn to heel or he'd know the reason why. He'd fought and won control over her spineless mother. Mirelle would be no different.

CHAPTER 2

Trey stood in the middle of the funeral parlor studying the situation. Blue velvet curtains hung at the windows, and oak benches with carved backs and seat cushions of the same hue had been shoved out of the way during the fire. Everything was soggy and reeked of smoke.

How could he have missed the coffins stacked against the far wall? Everything from plain pine boxes to the very finest crafted. A touch he could have done without.

He closed his eyes. An undertaker? His luck was running true to form. All he'd wanted was a dry place to sleep and look what he'd got. God surely had a sense of humor.

Trey ventured out in the rain again to check on the stallion. He'd needed a place for his horse, and he was grateful the livery was fairly dry and had plenty of feed. Buck would have a good night's rest, better than he'd been used to.

He tossed a couple of forkfuls of hay into the manger and filled a bucket with water. Before going back to the community building he lugged his saddle in from the stable, plodding through the wet one more time. He was so waterlogged that he squished when he walked.

Back inside the funeral parlor he picked a corner as far away as he could get from the coffins for his gear. They might be empty, but he had no false impression as to what they would be used for. Some folks might think less of him for his phobia toward being shut in with a dead body, but everyone had something that made them skittish, and he guessed his wasn't any worse than some things he could think of. He didn't believe in ghosts, just didn't like being in the proximity of a person whose spirit had gone on, leaving a solid part of himself behind.

Giving one last look around at what would be his bedroom for the night, Trey went back to the community building, where Granny Speck had said supper would be served. When he opened the door the chattering and laughing he heard pierced his ears. The women sounded like a flock of laying hens.

The room was crowded and Trey felt out of place. He hadn't been in the company of so many females at one time since he'd left home to join the war. Eight—plus a toddler, with her dark brown curls bouncing, her blue eyes shining with excitement— bustled around, straightening the room. The aroma of brown beans and ham coming from the corner woodstove reminded him that he hadn't eaten a hot meal in three days.

The women gathered around now, making him welcome. Grandma Speck, with her thin white hair pulled back in an untidy bun, looked him over. "Seems like you got burned a mite. I've got some ointment that will fix you up real good."

"Don't worry about me. I don't need any thing," Trey said. "I'm fine."

"Don't you 'fine' me, young man. I've forgot more about burns than you'll ever know. Let me get my satchel."

Mirelle lightly touched her hand to his arm, and he looked down into her dark eyes, noticing again the black waist-length hair and skin the texture of a magnolia petal. A smile curved lips that looked as sweet and red as ripe strawberries.

"You would do well to let her help. She does not take no for an answer."

Trey nodded. His sisters were the same way. He was feeling more at home all the time.

"Thank you for helping put out the fire. We appreciate it so much."

Trey broke out in a sweat when she touched his arm again. It had been a long time since he'd been near anything this winsome. "Glad I could help."

He waited a moment, trying to find a proper way to broach the subject before deciding to just ask. From bits and pieces he'd picked up he'd begun to understand why women ran the town. "I hear all of your menfolk died in the war."

Her expression changed, relaxing slightly. She nodded. "Yes. They are all dead."

"Fighting or guerrilla raid?"

"Fighting. All except one." Anger sparked her eyes. "Cantrell's raiders rode through here. Grandpa Speck was the only man in town." She looked away and swallowed hard. He could see the movement in her throat. "They hanged him."

Trey shook his head, disgusted. He'd seen worse things in the war, but hanging an old man was a cowardly act. People could be wicked and cruel. He'd known men who actually enjoyed hurting other folk. But he couldn't see it himself. God hadn't put him on this earth to make life harder for his fellow man.

Truth was, he didn't hold with the war. Hated the fighting, but he loved his country, and when he was conscripted he'd gone. But there had been many a day, month, and year when his heart had not been in the battle. War was sort of like women. Necessary but something he could do without.

Grandma Speck returned carrying a cracked brown-leather satchel. It was her husband who had been hanged? Trey felt a sudden spurt of sympathy. The war had been hard on women. He wondered how his own sisters had fared, though they'd put on the best face in their letters to him. Said everything was fine and for him not to worry.

A letter he'd received just a couple of weeks ago from Betty Hargrove, a neighbor, told a different story. Seemed like the girls were in danger of losing the farm. With him gone for three years there'd been no one to put in crops. No one to push a plow through the tough Kansas sod or mend fences to keep the livestock in. Some carpetbagger from up north had his eyes on the McAllister family homestead, and the fact that Trey had fought for the Union didn't appear to make any difference. He guessed greed was an overriding force these days.

Kansas was a border state, raided by both Union and Confederate troops, and Trey had seen enough marauding, out-of-control soldiers on both sides to know they didn't particularly care whom they robbed. No telling what hardships his sisters had faced. They needed him, and he was determined to get home as soon as he could. Once he got there, he'd figure out a way to save their home and maybe make it in time to put in some crops. Regardless of how it worked out, he'd take care of the four women who had raised him.

Grandma hobbled toward him, leaning heavily on her cane. "My rheumatism is acting up again. Agitated by all this running around fighting fire, I guess. I'm getting too old for these kinds of shenanigans." She motioned to a slat-back chair. "Sit down over here and let me see those hands."

"There's really no need, ma'am. I've been hurt worse."

Dee—tall, rawboned, and blonde, with a smattering of freckles across the bridge of her nose—put her hands on his shoulders and pushed him into the chair. "You just sit down there, honey pot, and let Grandma Speck take care of you." She winked at him. "I'm Dee. Don't believe I caught your name."

"Trey."

And that was all she was getting from him. Something in her expression made him think of a hungry dog eyeing a pork-chop bone. As soon as it stopped raining he was getting on his horse and heading for higher ground.

"Trey. That's a right nice name," Dee crooned. "Where you hail from, honey pot?"

Trey turned his back on the inquisitive female. He was not going to give this woman any personal information. "New Orleans."

He had just come from there. That should count.

Dee grinned. "I love New Orleans." Only she pronounced it *Nah Luns*. "Real romantic place, don't you think?"

Trey mentally sighed. Maybe he wouldn't wait for the rain to stop. Soon as he could sneak out, he was gone.

Long gone.

Mirelle stood at the stove dishing up supper, keeping an
eye on Dee flirting with Trey. She didn't blame her for being
so open about it. Women made good friends, but sometimes
one hungered for male conversation. Or as Dee put it, "A
yard full of hens ain't worth much without at least one
rooster." And this particular rooster was quite pleasant to
look at.

Grandma Speck smeared Trey's hands with a cool green
lotion that she had made with herbs grown in the porch boxes.
"There now. That'll do you. Those burns should be feeling
better soon."

Trey stared at the runny ointment. "That's powerful, ma'am.
The burning has almost stopped."

Grandma closed her satchel and, with a final pat on his arm,
walked away, stopping to scoop up a couple of cats. They snuggled close, purring, and the older woman nuzzled the furry creatures affectionately.

Mirelle smiled. "Grandma loves her kittens. They have been
with her for a very long time."

"I can see that she's real fond of the animals. I'm a dog man
myself, but a cat has its place. My sister Sue Ann thought so,
anyway. She had an old tom that looked like a mate to one of
these. Loved that cat—took even better care of it than she did
her brother."

Mira lightly touched his shoulder. "We have prepared a meal

for you in appreciation for your help. If you're through here, it is ready to eat."

She watched as Dee hovered near Trey, but another woman had approached offering a hand.

"I sure thank you for coming to our aid with the fire. I'm Vivian, and I'm proud to know you."

Viv had taken time to comb her flaming red hair and wash her face. Mira noticed that she'd even changed into her Sunday dress. She eyed the two women, each striving to claim Trey's attention. Grandma Speck wore a bemused expression, probably wondering which one would win the battle.

Melody approached with Audrey clinging to her skirts. "You're our guest of honor tonight, Mr. McAllister. Please be seated at the head of the table."

Color flooded Trey's cheeks. Mirelle grinned. Melody looked like a sweet young thing, but she was as sharp as a fresh-honed knife. She'd have Mr. Trey McAllister thinking he was the best thing since white sugar.

"We saved a seat for you." Vivian clasped his arm, elbowing Melody out of the way. "Right over here by me."

Dee grabbed his other arm. "Come on, honey pot. We'll take good care of you."

Trey looked hunted and Mira stepped in, hoping to avoid a confrontation. "I think Jane needs help in the kitchen. Could you two lend her a hand?"

Dee sighed. They turned to the kitchen area, but Mirelle knew they would be back. When it came to men, those two always came back.

Jane set a platter of crispy brown fried chicken on the table and Trey shook his head in wonderment. *Would you look at that?* He'd not seen anything that fine since leaving home. If it tasted as good as it looked, he was in for a meal to remember.

The ladies took their places around the table, Dee on Trey's left, Vivian on his right. As close as they were sitting, he felt like a pork chop sandwiched between two slices of bread. He reached for a chicken leg, and Grandma Speck eyed him over her glasses.

"We'll ask the blessing first."

"Oh. Right."

He dropped his gaze to his plate, feeling ashamed. A man sometimes forgot the niceties of life on the battlefield. He'd thanked the Lord every day for His care and mercy and gave God all the credit for bringing him through the war without a scratch, but when you had to grab a bite to eat between bullets skipping over your head something got lost in the process.

Grandma Speck clasped her hands and bowed her head. Her voice rolled through the room as she conversed with God in a tone that only one who knew Him could speak. "We thank You for sending Mr. McAllister our way when we needed him the most. He'll likely turn tail and run same way as all the others, but we appreciate what he did just the same. We thank You for this food we're about to partake of and for all of Your many blessings. I know You'll give that bullheaded

Jean-Marc Portier what he has coming, and we'll thank You for that, too."

Trey cracked one eye open at the mention of her last request.

The others joined in a final amen and started passing bowls around the table. Trey filled his plate with fried chicken, brown beans and ham, biscuits and gravy. He thought of his four sisters—all good cooks, every one of them—and felt disloyal because this looked like the finest meal he'd ever sat down to.

The unpleasant stench of smoke and charred wood nearly smothered the heavenly aroma of the food. He thought of the half-burned building next door.

"How are you going to rebuild the funeral parlor?" he asked conversationally.

Mirelle shook her head. "We cannot say, but we will manage. We have no choice. The parlor is our only income."

"Really?" He reached for the butter. "Must be a lot of bury-ing going on around here."

"We're the only parlor in this area. It's either here or folks' burying their own."

He didn't like the idea of women doing such hard work. Digging graves, seeing to the deceased. Seemed more like a man's job.

"My husband ran the parlor before he—" Grandma Speck stopped midsentence, eyes misting.

Trey nodded. *Was hanged,* he silently finished. That explained what the women were doing running a funeral parlor.

Viv nibbled on a drumstick. "We don't know anything else to do. We've tried to come up with ways to earn extra money but nothing seems to work out."

Trey turned to address Mira. "Grandma Speck said something about your father."

Her expression darkened. "Yes. Jean-Marc is determined to force me to go back home."

"Force you?"

Dee spoke up. "Ever since Mira's husband, Paul, died in the fighting last year, Jean-Marc has waged war against our little town. He wants Mira back home. She refuses. He's done just about everything under the sun to bring her to heel, but so far—" Dee flashed Mira a congratulatory smile—"we've been able to hold on. He started the fire, you know. Or one of his men."

"Can't know that for sure," Grandma Speck cautioned. "Could have been a lightning strike."

Viv shook her head. "Might have been made to look like an act of nature but it was Jean-Marc's men, all right."

The women around the table nodded.

Trey's gaze moved to each of the women in turn, and he thought of the charred building that would have to be rebuilt. "Wouldn't it be easier for Mira to concede?"

"Easy isn't always best." Melody turned her attention to Audrey, who sat beside her, urging the little girl to eat her custard pie. "Jean-Marc doesn't have Mira's best interests at heart. He wants to destroy her, and we won't let that happen."

Vivian elbowed Trey in the ribs. "You say you're from these parts?"

"I rode in from . . . New Orleans."

Dee grinned at him, and he mentally renewed his decision to clear out before dawn, before she, or any other female sitting at this table, started getting ideas. He took another biscuit, slathered it with butter, and bit down.

Maybe he'd wait until after breakfast.

Audrey dozed over her pie. Mira slid an arm around the child. "Are you weary, precious one?"

The little girl nodded and Melody started to get up, but Mira waved her back. "I will ready her for bed. You sit and rest. I know you must be tired."

"So are you."

But Melody sank back in her chair and picked up her fork. She glanced at Trey and he smiled at her. She was a nice-looking woman, quiet and soft-spoken, the way a woman should be.

"Were you in the war, Mr. McAllister?"

He nodded. "Yes, ma'am, I was. I've seen my share of fighting, and I'm glad it's finally over."

"As we all are."

She looked down at her plate, and he recalled that she'd lost her husband in the fighting. A lot of good men on both sides had died. He knew sometimes war was necessary, but he'd learned fighting rarely settled anything.

Mira came back to the table and started helping clear dishes. A couple of the younger women were already busy scraping leftovers into a large pan that Trey assumed would be the dog's meal.

Jane, medium height and hefty, poured herself a second cup of coffee and waved the pot in Trey's direction. "Refill?"

"Don't mind if I do." He held the cup toward her and she filled it to the brim with the hot, fragrant brew. Trey breathed deeply. He'd missed his daily coffee during the war. When he got back home he was going to have a cup first thing every morning for the rest of his life.

Mirelle kept an eye on the stranger. He needed a shave and a haircut. And a bath. Definitely a bath. But he was better looking—and had better manners—than the usual run of men who drifted through town.

She knew some of the men who rode through were Jean-Marc's spies, sent to see how the women were getting along and to report back on how they could cause the Sassy Gap females even more trouble. She understood perfectly why Jean-Marc carried on this insane fight. She knew too much about him, and that knowledge could be deadly for him as well as for her. Mira had the power to bring him down if only she could find a way to use that information.

The people here saw them as a squabbling father and daughter, each too proud to give in. What would they think of Jean-Marc Portier if they knew the secrets hidden deep within Mira's heart?

Grandma Speck laid a hand on her shoulder. "You aren't worrying about the fire, are you? thinking it's your fault?"

Tears welled up in Mira's eyes. "It *was* my fault. It wouldn't have happened if I was not so stubborn."

The old woman shook her head. "Foolish. Jean-Marc hasn't thrown anything at us we can't handle so far. It would be a sin to give in to a ruthless bully like your father."

Mirelle nodded, but she knew what they were struggling against. Jean-Marc Portier never gave up. Something in his nature wouldn't allow him to lose. He'd fight this battle to the death.

And quite likely it would be hers.

After supper, Trey excused himself. He needed a good night's sleep. He thought about the funeral parlor—his bedroom for the night—and wondered if he shouldn't leave now. But the sound of rain changed his mind. At least the parlor would be empty except for him, and he'd be long gone in the morning.

While the unexpected delay had been interesting, he wouldn't be spending a second night in Sassy Gap. He'd rest a lot easier when he got home and assessed the situation there. He appreciated the good food and a dry place to sleep, even if he wasn't all that fond of the accommodations, but there was nothing to hold him in Sassy Gap, Louisiana. Everything important to him resided in Tyrone, Kansas. He'd be glad to get home.

Mira noticed when Trey got up and said good night. She'd seen his troubled expression when the funeral parlor was mentioned, and she figured he wasn't happy about sleeping there. A lot of people had phobias about dead bodies. She found that strange. A dead body didn't cause any trouble. It was the live ones you had to watch out for.

Grandma Speck sat down beside her. "Mr. McAllister turning in?"

She nodded. "He said he was tired."

The old woman grinned. "A bit skittish about sleeping over there by himself?"

Mira laughed. "He did not mention it if he was, but I would not be surprised."

Running the parlor was Grandma and Mira's job. The others, though helpful in most ways, refused to lay out the deceased. That work fell to Grandma and Mira.

Grandma watched the door close behind the redheaded stranger. "He wouldn't. It wouldn't be manly. Won't anything bother him tonight except for the water dripping into them buckets we set to catch the rain."

The women had just finished washing the dishes when the door opened and three men and a woman entered. The female wore a bedraggled skirt and man's coat, both having been washed so many times that the color had faded to a dirty tan. Water dripped off the brim of the man's hat she wore. The men with her didn't look much better.

The woman stepped up, her voice loud and demanding. "I'm looking for Grandma Speck. We got a body for the burying in the wagon."

Grandma glanced at Mira. "Looks like Mr. McAllister is going to have company tonight after all."

After he left the community building Trey checked on his horse again before retiring for the night. If there had been room in the shed and he hadn't been afraid the women would laugh at him, he'd have slept there.

When he entered the parlor he lit the candle Mira had given him. A downdraft from the holes in the roof made the stench of burned wood even more unpleasant. Quickly stripping down to his long johns, he laid his trousers and shirt out to dry as well as they could, then laid his pistol beside his bedroll, although he didn't know why. Anything that disturbed his sleep in here probably wouldn't be stopped by a bullet. But he hadn't slept without his gun for three years, and he didn't see any reason to break the habit yet.

He rolled up in the blanket Grandma Speck had provided, breathing in a faint fragrance that made him homesick.

Lavender. His sister Ellie raised lavender in her herb garden to scent the sheets and blankets. The scent had been a part of his life for as long as he remembered. Fancy running across it here, in a charred relic of a burned-out funeral parlor in Sassy Gap, Louisiana. He guessed women were the same the world over, always trying to make a home no matter the circumstances, whether they were in a Kansas farmhouse or living in a run-down town in war-torn Louisiana.

He'd barely dropped off to sleep when the sound of the door opening woke him. Trey automatically reached for his pistol.

Grandma Speck entered, carrying a lantern. Three men and a woman filed in behind her.

Trey rose onto an elbow and watched the strange procession. Had they forgotten he was sleeping in here tonight? He would get to his feet but he wasn't dressed for company.

His movement caught the attention of the big, broad-shouldered man with the white hair and beard. The man shot backward, letting out a yelp.

Grandma Speck quickly allayed his fears. "Just Mr. McAllister. He's sleeping here tonight out of the rain."

The man calmed, but Trey caught part of the muttered conversation. "Might ought to warn a person. Scared the beans out of a body."

Sliding his pistol back into the holster, Trey watched the group move toward the dais. Was Grandma Speck going to bed them down in here with him? While he'd welcome the company, he didn't know if it was the proper place for a woman. Although after a second glance at the woman he got the impression this particular female could hold her own in any situation. The take-charge type. He'd seen her kind before. Get in her way and she'd walk right over you. He lay down and closed his eyes, trying to be inconspicuous.

Grandma led the group over to the coffins stacked against the wall, out of the way of any invading rain. "How much did you want to spend?"

"No more than necessary," the dark-haired man said. It was the first time he'd spoken since entering the room.

"Take a look at that one. It's not the fanciest we got, but it'll keep 'em dry."

The younger man ran a hand over the smooth top. "This is the one then."

The dark-haired man pointed to a pine box. "Is that one cheaper?"

The woman interrupted. "We ain't going to go for the cheapest in the lot, Slade. It's Grandpa and we're putting him away in style." She nodded at Grandma. "We'll take the nicest one."

"All right." Grandma Speck whipped out a small pad of paper and a pencil. "Now you got any preference in the music? Mirelle sings 'Amazing Grace' like an angel."

"That's right nice," the woman decided. "Maybe 'In the Sweet By and By,' too. Grandpa always favored that one."

Trey stared at the ceiling. He had company all right. The worst possible kind.

A raindrop penetrated the leaky roof and hit him on the nose.

"Now for the sermon," Grandma continued. "I'll do the honors there."

"No! I ain't for that," the white-haired man protested. "I don't cotton to women preachers."

Grandma drew herself up to her full height. "And why not, pray tell?"

He shook his head. "You can't find women preachers in the Bible. It's gotta be a man, the husband of one wife."

"Well, there isn't a man available. I've only had one husband, so we're halfway there. You'll have to make do with what we got."

The woman, completely in charge, stepped in again. "Stop it! We're going to give Grandpa a proper farewell if it's the last thing we ever do, and I don't want to hear no more about it!" She wagged her finger in the man's face and he fell silent.

She turned back to Grandma. "We got the music and you're gonna say the last words." She motioned to the men. "Boys, bring Grandpa in out of the rain."

They returned in a few minutes carrying a blanket-wrapped, human-shaped burden between them. The three men set the bundle on the dais and then stampeded toward the door.

Grandma and the woman followed at a leisurely pace. The door closed behind them.

Trey lay on his bedroll listening to the *plink, plink* of water hitting buckets.

Nice. Just him and Grandpa.

CHAPTER 3

Sassy Gap woke to a rooster's crow. Seemed like the thing must have taken roost right outside the undertaker's window. Trey brought the pillow up over his head.

The bird crowed long and loud, announcing a new day. Rain dripped from the building's eaves, but for once Trey didn't hear a heavy downpour. He lay still, eyes half closed, listening to the steady *plink, plink* of water dripping into buckets the women had placed last night—a soothing, although somewhat monotonous sound. Throwing off the pillow, Trey peered up. A patch of pale gray sky beamed through a hole in the roof.

It took a minute to orient his thoughts, and when he did he sprang to his feet, pistol gripped in his hand, an automatic reflex. Not thirty feet away lay the man they'd brought in the night before. Trey reached for his trousers, slowly backing away from the sight of the bundled blanket. The stench of wet, charred wood stung his nose. Though the heavy blue drapes and rose-colored lamps were pretty, the place gave him the willies.

As a boy he'd once been locked in the church with his deceased grandpa for a full afternoon before anyone, including his sisters, had thought to look for him. For years he'd had nightmares about that little oversight, and while the dead didn't scare him, he kept a respectful distance from them.

The women of Sassy Gap were buzzing with excitement when he stepped out of the building. First morning in over a week without rain, and his hostesses were taking full advantage of a pretty day. Several stood over steaming tubs, scrubbing dresses and pantaloons on washboards. Two others hung wash on a long line strung between two large hickories.

Trey pointedly ignored the women's unmentionables, while politely acknowledging the women's presence with a brief lift of his hat. He walked to the kitchen, more than a little aware that the pretty French girl, Mira, had turned from hanging wash to watch him pass.

For a second he felt sympathy for her and her problems. What father would go to such unreasonable lengths to torment his daughter? The women had mentioned a few childish tricks. It sounded to him like Portier needed to stay out of his daughter's business.

The man's attitude bordered on cruelty and that annoyed Trey, but he reminded himself that Mirelle wasn't his concern. A man could get into big trouble butting into a woman's business. Mirelle was a stranger, and Trey wasn't about to get involved in a family feud. He'd already done that, and once was enough.

Grandma Speck was parked in her rocker, knitting needles flashing, when he walked into the kitchen.

"Morning. Hope we didn't bother you overly much last night. Never know when business will pop in."

"No. No bother."

He hadn't slept much, but it was their place. And it was dry. He guessed they had a right to keep a dead body in a guest's bedroom if they chose to do so, but he'd rather they'd waited.

He made himself at home, pouring a cup of coffee from the big pot sitting on the back of the stove. Real coffee, not the bitter chicory he'd been drinking. He took a chair at the table and held the cup under his nose, breathing deeply of the fragrant steam.

"Sleep well except for our little visit?" Grandma never looked up from her yarn.

"Real well, ma'am. Nice to be dry for a change."

If she was waiting for a reaction from him, she wouldn't get it. A man had his pride.

She smiled. "We'll be prayin' for rains in these parts come August."

He'd heard Louisiana had two seasons: the rainy season and the hot season.

"Kansas can get pretty hot and dry along about then too."

"So you're from Kansas?"

"Yes, ma'am. Tyrone. Ever hear of the town?"

Old as she was, he figured it was safe to tell her the truth. He doubted she would be after a man like that Dee and Vivian were. If a man wasn't careful they'd have him standing at the altar before he even knew he'd proposed. Trey shuddered, determined to avert a close call.

Grandma shook her head. "Haven't traveled more than five miles from here since I was born eighty-two years ago."

Trey leaned back and stretched. The kitchen felt cozy this morning and brought back memories of home. His sisters kept a clean house. Picky to a fault, Beth would make him wipe his boots before he came into the house. He decided that the women of Sassy Gap were just as particular. Everything looked neat and in its place. Enough of Audrey's toys were scattered about to make it look like a home, but in general the room was orderly and clean.

He thought of the way he'd lived the past three years: sleeping outdoors in all kinds of weather, eating with his hands, bathing only when he could find enough water, wearing clothes for weeks at a time. His hand came up to touch his prickly beard, and Grandma Speck's voice drew him back.

"Did you wear that beard before the fightin'?"

"No, ma'am."

"Then I suspect you'd welcome a shave and a hot bath."

Trey closed his eyes, remembering the bath he'd taken several days ago. He'd stopped off in New Orleans and rented a room for a couple of days. He'd enjoyed a hot soak and then found the biggest steak fifty cents could buy.

Yes, a hot bath and shave would be welcome.

"Can't say that I wouldn't like that, ma'am, but I have to be moving along."

The old woman nodded. "Got kin expecting you?"

"Four sisters."

He'd written Naomi last month and told her that he was heading home. He hadn't heard back from her, but his sisters would be expecting him. They'd have the welcome mat shined up and ready.

"Sisters, huh? Folks gone?"

"Yes, ma'am. Lost both parents to cholera when I was six years old. My sisters raised me."

Grandma's needles clicked. "Shame. Must have been real hard on young girls."

"Yes, ma'am. It was." He swallowed the last of his coffee and set the cup back on the table. "I'd best be going. Sure appreciate last night's bed and meal."

He noticed the breakfast dishes were done. A plate of biscuits and butter sat on the table, but he hadn't been invited to partake. Maybe the women's supplies were running low.

"Anytime," Grandma said. "Glad to help." She laid the yarn aside and pushed out of her rocker. She wasn't a small woman—hefty in size. Looked like she'd put away her fair share of biscuits and gravy. "I'll see you off."

Trey held the door open and she stepped outside. The sky had brightened, but the sun was covered by thin layers of clouds.

"Think the rain's over?" Trey asked as they fell into step.

"It'll be back before noon."

Trey glanced up, wondering how she could know. Right now it looked as if the sky was clearing and sunny days were ahead.

They walked to the livery and found Brenda busy at the anvil. A hot fire burned brightly in the early morning air. A large dog of mixed ancestry lay on a pile of hay near the fire.

"That's Moses," Brenda said when she noticed Trey looking.

He nodded. "Good watchdog?"

"Nah. He loves strangers. Biggest coward in town but he looks mean."

And that he did. The dog lifted his head and bared long, uneven teeth. Trey took a couple of steps backward, not inclined to test the woman's sunny assessment.

The hot, sultry air of yesterday had faded and been replaced by a welcome breeze. Spanish moss swayed gently through the tall oaks.

Brenda led the stallion out of the stall and handed Trey the reins. He rubbed the animal's ears, his eyes mentally evaluating the horse's condition. They'd been together for the duration of the war, and he guessed Buck was more family than animal to him. Running his hands down the horse's sleek sides, he spoke quietly to his trusty companion. "You been eating your fill, big boy?"

The stallion snuffed, rolling his nose into Trey's palm. The two had been through many a battle and come back to fight another day. The horse was thin, but he'd fatten up once he got home.

Brenda returned momentarily, wagging the heavy saddle. "I'll saddle him for you."

Trey wasn't accustomed to a woman doing his work, even if she was big enough to skin a mule. He took the saddle from her and swung it up over the stallion's back, then cinched the leather straps tightly. By then Brenda was busy inspecting the animal's hooves. She paused at the left hindquarter, frowning.

"Did you know your horse has thrown a shoe?"

Trey walked around the horse to inspect the damage. Buck must have lost it shortly before Trey rode into town because the stallion had shown no indication of the problem earlier.

He stood back, hands on his hips, studying the problem. He couldn't ride on until the shoe was replaced.

"I can have a new one on him in nothing flat," Brenda offered. "No charge."

"All right," Trey conceded. A half-hour delay wasn't his first choice, but it wouldn't hurt much. Since the rain had let up, he could make better time now. "But I insist on paying you for your labor."

She shrugged and reached for the reins. "I'll check the other three and make sure they're on solid. All this mud is hard on shoes."

Trey looked down at his boots, caked with thick mud just walking the short distance from the house. She had a point.

"Brenda."

Trey glanced up. "Pardon?"

"Brenda. You can call me Brenda." She flashed an affable grin and he noticed that she had a missing tooth on the upper right side.

"All right. Brenda."

Grandma Speck took hold of his arm. "Well, now, looks like you got an extra hour on yore hands. I'll have Jane fill the wash-tub and you can have that hot bath, and Mira will shave you before you're on your way."

Trey opened his mouth to protest, but found he was being propelled down the street toward the undertaker's parlor. "Ma'am, I don't want to take a bath today—"

"Hogwash. You better grab the opportunity while you got it. You want to be clean when yore sisters hug you, don't you? And I can see that beard is itchin' you something powerful. Hurry along. We'll have you looking like new before you can say Jack Sprat."

Trey didn't know who or what a Jack Sprat was, but he knew one thing: the females in Sassy Gap were worse pests than his sisters.

"Mr. McAllister, please. If you will sit still this will get over with a lot sooner."

Trey twisted in the hard seat; the cape around his neck felt like a noose. He'd enjoyed the bath. The women had filled a tub with hot water and left him with a man-size bar of lye soap, clean towels, and thank goodness, his privacy.

Now the haircut—and who should be wielding the scissors but none other than the young Cajun girl with the crazy father.

"I should be halfway to Kansas by now," he groused.

"Kansas? I thought you told Dee you hailed from New Orleans. How much do you want taken off the top?"

He didn't correct her. "Not much." This was the second haircut in a month. He'd be bald if he wasn't careful.

She laughed—a clear, pleasant sound. In spite of her heavy French accent, she had a good command of English. Trey suspected she'd been schooled more than most young women.

She wagged her finger at him. "I see you are a tease." With that she drew a good three inches through the comb and snipped.

He winced.

"Such beautiful red hair," she murmured.

Trey hated it when people talked about his hair. Silence hung between them as Mira went about her work. He'd learned that she had a natural gift. She cut hair for everyone who came through the small town—everyone who wasn't scared to stay that long. He was afraid to glance at the mirror lying on the kitchen table. He liked his hair collar length, brushed over at the fore-head, and he had a hunch it would be a while before he saw that image again.

"What will Trey McAllister do when he reaches home?" she asked softly.

"Go back to living."

No more sleeping on the hard ground. No more eating dried meat and moldy bread. No more drinking bitter chicory coffee and listening to the sounds of friends dying at his side.

"Yes. I would imagine the last few years have been terrible."

Trey had thought about the future a lot lately. What did he plan to do? First he had to ensure his sisters would have a home. Now that the war was over and men were drifting back it probably wouldn't be long until some or maybe all of them got married. He could say one thing for his sisters: they were good-looking women. Great cooks, too. A man could consider himself lucky to win any one of the bunch.

As for him, likely he would settle in and start working the land. Maybe even give some serious thought to starting a family. Maybe.

Most men his age had made the decision early, but Trey had missed his opportunity six years ago. He concentrated on the quiet *snip-snip* and suddenly found himself wondering what Mira planned to do. Would she fight her father until her dying breath? Didn't seem like much of a future for a pretty young thing.

"What about you?"

The scissors paused. "*Mon cheri?*"

"What about you? Are you going to fight your father until you win?"

"I will never win," she admitted. She sat down, staring at the scissors. "But I will keep on fighting until either Jean-Marc or I can fight no longer."

"That doesn't sound sensible."

"No, *mon cheri*, it is not." She stood up and the blades on the scissors flew. "But what is life without freedom? Have you not just spent part of your life fighting, in part, for other people's freedom?"

"Slavery's different. And the war was about more than slavery. It was about differences of opinions between the government and states."

"Oh?" She paused again, lifting her dark brows.

Trey had never seen more beautiful eyes on any woman. Coal black, sparkling with life and headstrong determination. He'd wager that Portier had the same stubborn look.

Like father, like daughter.

"Why do you say this? When a person's freedom is taken away, what else can it be called other than slavery?"

Trey shifted, uncomfortable with her fierce defense. Actually, she was right. He had spent three years of his life fighting for exactly what she was fighting for, but somehow her spat with her father seemed insignificant when contrasted to the War between the States.

"Can't you find a way to make peace with your father without all this fuss? It seems to me that the other women are paying for your family dispute."

According to Grandma Speck, Sassy Gap lived in a continual state of siege, and the siege would not let up until Mira surrendered. Trey didn't know why that should bother him, but it did. Much more than he wanted it to.

"I do worry about that." The scissors paused. "But I cannot give in to Jean-Marc. If I do, my life will be over."

"You call him Jean-Marc. Why not Father? Or Papa?"

"Never! I will never acknowledge him as Papa." Her eyes burned brightly. "Never!"

Trey eyed the flying scissors nervously. He'd lived around women long enough to recognize theatrics; he had serious doubts that her life would be over, yet the woman was a stranger to him and he had no evidence of the true nature of the dispute. From what he knew it sounded like a family row, one best solved by the folks involved.

"You do not know Jean-Marc," she accused as though she had read his thoughts. "He is not a good man. People admire him because of his money and big house and plantation. Some even admire his ruthlessness and the power he has amassed. But they do not know him. I—" she stabbed a finger dramatically toward her chest—"only I know him, and that is why he is deter-mined to force me back under his control. It is also why I must fight him. He leaves me no choice."

Trey found himself starting to be drawn into the dispute regardless of his indifference. "Then why not leave? Move so far away that your father can never find you unless you want him to."

"I would not want him to, but Jean-Marc would find me no matter how far I ran." She shook her head. "So, I cannot run. I must stand and fight although it would be easier to run, and sometimes I long to do so. But it is impossible. You surely see this. He must be made to understand that I am no longer a child to be ordered around, but a woman who will not be silenced."

"Seems to me he'll be more likely to make trouble for you if you stay here."

She visibly stiffened. "I will stand and *fight*. Only cowards run."

Jean-Marc's words, no doubt. Still, Trey teetered on the edge of sympathy. Maybe the girl was right; maybe she had to fight for her independence. He'd known daughters whose lives were ruled by their fathers.

Even been engaged to one once.

If it hadn't been for Abel Wilson's iron hand, Trey would be a married man now with a child or two.

Bitterness burned the back of his throat.

The scissors paused a third time, and Mira's eyes grew distant with thought. "But if I was willing to leave—perhaps you would take me with you?"

Trey choked, and then cleared his throat to cover it. Take her with him? She couldn't be serious. A single woman and a single man traveling together? Grandma Speck had said Mira had been married briefly, but no matter. He couldn't take her anywhere. It just wasn't done.

"I couldn't do that."

She knelt to face him, eyes wide with expectation. "You said that I should put more distance between me and Jean-Marc."

"Your father. Call him your father!" Trey could see why the man would be annoyed.

"Never!"

Trey backed off. "Okay. I didn't mean that *I* wanted to get involved. This argument is between you and your father."

"But he has made it an argument between him and the women of the town."

Trey stood, ripping the cape off his neck. This conversation was going nowhere. "I wish I could help, but I can't. My advice

to you is to meet with your father and settle this matter once
and for all."

"Never," she stated.

He walked out of the kitchen, feeling heat from more than
the cookstove. He could feel her gaze following him through the
doorway. He'd tried to talk sense into a bullheaded father once
and met with no luck. There were some men who couldn't be
reasoned with, and he suspected he knew of two: Abel Wilson
and now Jean-Marc Portier. Yet he admired Mira for fighting.
Sharon had surrendered after the first shot.

Remorse filled the back of his throat when he remembered
how little his love had meant to Sharon Wilson.

But that water had gone over the dam a long time ago, and he
had learned a valuable lesson—you couldn't count on a female.
God had been good enough to let him learn that lesson and learn
it well. *"But thou, O Lord, art a shield for me; my glory, and the lifter
up of mine head."* The psalm should have meant that he'd stay and
help fight. But strangers? And females? He'd best ride on.

"Mr. McAllister!" Mira called. "I have not finished cutting
your hair!"

"Looks good enough," Trey called over his shoulder. He was
out of this town.

Dee and Vivian rounded the corner, wiping red, chapped hands
on their aprons. A rising wind snapped the pieces of freshly
laundered clothes hanging on the line.

"Is he leaving?" Viv called to Mira.

Mira paused in the kitchen doorway, simmering with frustration. "He is leaving."

"Oh, shucks." Dee crossed her arms. "I was hoping he'd stick around awhile."

"Mr. McAllister is not a man to stay anywhere for long," Mira observed.

Vivian gazed at the back of the tall, handsome man striding toward the livery. "But what a man." She sighed. "I caught him looking at me with that 'I'm a man and you're a woman' look."

Dee sniffed. "Your imagination is working overtime. I could tell he'd taken an extra close look at *me* and liked what he saw."

"Talk about imagination," Viv chided.

"Ladies, I can assure both of you that not one of us will see Mr. Trey McAllister again." Mira cast a glance in the redheaded stranger's direction. "He is not the sort of man to involve himself in other folks' troubles. Now go back to work. The sun will not shine after dark."

For a moment she had snatched at a straw, hoping he would help her, much the same way a drowning man snatches at a thrown rope. She'd hoped for his help in getting away, leaving Jean-Marc and her bitter memories behind, free from the knowledge that gnawed at her insides like a ravishing disease. She thought of her mother, the dark-haired Cajun beauty who had dreamed of happiness only to have those dreams crushed.

Mira sighed. Her leaving might benefit the women of Sassy Gap, or perhaps not. She knew Jean-Marc Portier as few others did. He never allowed anyone to cross him. He ruled with the absolute power of a tyrant, and no one could doubt his ability to control those around him. The women of Sassy Gap had defied him. He would never forget. He would never stop.

Dee's and Viv's faces fell.

"Well," Viv contended, "he did look special at me."

"Did not," Dee said.

Mira turned and softly closed the kitchen door.

CHAPTER 4

Settling his hat firmly, Trey swung into the saddle, hoping the twinge of conscience would ease before he hit the parish line. He felt bad about the women's plight but he couldn't get involved. He'd be crazy to get involved. Mirelle. Her father. The women's needs. They weren't his problems. There were problems enough waiting for him back home.

The sky was a dazzling blue, but dark clouds began to move in before he'd gone a mile. He studied the lowering sky grimly. He'd seen enough wet weather to last him a lifetime. He never would have thought it was possible, but he was getting downright lonesome for a Kansas drought.

He was also tired of oak trees with moss hanging from branches like strands of hair, and he was tired of mud. By the time he slogged three feet in this gumbo red clay, his feet felt like they weighed five pounds each. He felt sorry for Buck because of the way the clay was building up on his hooves. Every few miles he had to stop and clear the stallion's hooves of the muck.

By noon the heavens had opened up and rain came down like he was standing under a waterfall. Wind-driven sheets of needle-sharp drops pounded his back and shoulders and ran off the brim of his hat. Lightning crackled overhead and thunder roared like cannon fire. He felt like he was back on the battlefield.

He pulled up the stallion, staring grimly at the rain-swollen creek blocking his path. He had to cross that? Piles of brush and tangled vines swept past on the current, and he spotted a cottonmouth twined in the branches of a nearby tree. The snake's gaping mouth was as white as the cotton blossom for which it was named, and he mentally marked another reason for wishing he was home.

The stallion shied when he urged it into the roiling water. Trey didn't blame Buck. He didn't want to ride into that current either, but it was cross the creek or go back to Sassy Gap. He'd take his chances with the creek.

The water rose to Buck's belly and then to Trey's knees, filling his boots. Buck was swimming now, fighting against the current. Trey glanced upstream and saw a massive tree trunk bearing down on them. He knew the horse couldn't move any faster, so he jerked the reins sharply to the right, heading downstream. The stallion faltered, and for a minute Trey thought they were both going under. Then the horse lunged ahead, somehow gaining some footing. The tree swept past, riding as majestically in the turbulent water as one of the steamboats he'd seen on the Mississippi River.

Imminent danger past, Trey turned the horse's head toward the bank, mighty grateful when they reached solid land. For a few moments he had felt his very survival was in question. He knew the good Lord surely was with Trey McAllister, though he didn't know why.

Oh, he'd called on God often enough—every night, and most of the waking hours of the day. Bullets whining around a man provided a strong incentive to stay in touch. But there hadn't been time to sit and talk to God the way he used to do. Back home he'd sit on the creekbank holding a bamboo pole and waiting for a fish to bite. With the silence hovering around him, he would look up through the leafy tree branches overhead to the deep blue sky and think about his Maker.

At night he would sit on the porch steps studying the stars. He thought about the strong right hand that had hung them in the universe and was amazed at what a mighty God he worshiped. Sometimes he wondered if he'd ever regain that sort of innocent relationship he'd had with his Creator before knowing what it was like to kill someone you might have enjoyed as a friend under different circumstances. Just one more reason why he was eager to get back to Tyrone. He needed to get his foot back on the righteous path.

He rode on, Buck carefully picking a path through brush and mud. Trey's fickle mind dredged up a memory of black hair and snapping dark eyes. A charming French accent speaking words in a musical voice that echoed in his heart. Maybe it was because he hadn't been around women lately, but Mira Dupree wove her way through his thoughts like no woman had since Sharon.

Trey sighed heavily. Maybe he should have stayed to help her, but he immediately dismissed that foolish notion. He had a greater obligation to fill. Family came before the need of a casual acquaintance. Especially a *female* casual acquaintance.

He reached Mignon, Louisiana, at one o'clock in the afternoon. The street looked deserted. Sassy Gap had more buildings but Mignon looked a lot more prosperous. Men here moved from store to store and stopped in groups to visit. He wondered how many, like him, had stumbled across the women living in Sassy Gap and then rode away.

Mirelle stood erect, put her hands on her hips, and stretched her back. The rain clouds scuttling overhead meant that the brief period of sunshine was over. The clothing the women had so carefully washed this morning was only half dry. It would have to finish drying on the line rigged in the communal hall. She wondered if Trey would find shelter before the rain hit. Irritated at herself for worrying about yet another man who had come and then left, she went back to work.

Most of her anger was directed at Jean-Marc. She realized he had plenty of reasons to want her back under his thumb, but that didn't give him the right to mistreat the women of Sassy Gap. Their only crime was sheltering her. But to his twisted way of thinking that was reason enough. When they allowed her to stay instead of turning her out with no place to go except back to the man who held her in such contempt, they had aligned themselves against him. Jean-Marc would never forgive them for their kindness toward her.

Sassy Gap women were decent, God-fearing women who would never turn their backs on a fellow brother or sister in need, which didn't mean beans to a blaspheming, God-defying man like Jean-Marc. He lived by no other creed than his own. Nothing would be allowed to mock Jean-Marc Portier. He used everyone he met, taking what he needed, with loyalty and compassion toward none.

Mira shivered, knowing her father would win in this battle of wills simply because he had more ammunition. She could not fight him forever.

Mira moved indoors and stopped to pick up one of the charred boards from the floor of the funeral parlor. They had to get the room back in presentable order by late afternoon. Nan Wiley, granddaughter of the deceased, had promised to be here come rain or shine. Mira hated doing funerals in a downpour. The dirt turned to mud almost instantly and grew heavier with every shovelful as they filled the grave.

Dee approached, carrying an armload of charred lumber. She didn't seem her normal cheerful self this morning. "You think Trey will ever come back?"

Mirelle shook her head. No man ever had. "It is my fault. I should leave, move on so all this nonsense will stop."

"Now you stop thinking like that." Dee's smile transformed her rather plain features. "We're a family here, and you're a card-carrying, full-class member. We're not letting your hard-headed old goat of a papa run you off, so don't you even entertain the thought."

Mirelle flushed with pleasure. "I would miss all of you so if I left, but it seems like I bring nothing but trouble to you."

"Trouble is as trouble does." Dee glanced at the women scurrying around trying to restore the funeral parlor. "We've all had our share of trouble, and your leaving wouldn't change anything."

"I suppose not." Mirelle thought about the letters of condolence that each of the women had received from the Confederate government. Sassy Gap had given all it had to the cause. Eight good men had died, leaving their women to get along the best they could. She hated war, hated the way it destroyed lives. Like the private battle raging in her heart could destroy her? She feared it would.

Grandma Speck paused to look at them. "You girls all right?"

"Fine as hen's teeth," Dee said. "We've about got all the debris out of here, but it's a sorry-looking mess."

Grandma shook her head. "Sweep the floor and do what you can to make the room presentable."

"I'll get right on it," Dee said. "Viv and Jane will mop. Don't worry, Granny; we'll have it respectable before the family arrives."

"Wish we had a few flowers." Grandma Speck glanced toward the dais. "It looks so bare."

"Melody has that great big old fern." Dee gestured with the board she carried. "I'll pitch this on the lumber pile and then send her to fetch it."

"Helen has a spider plant, and I believe Jane still has that African violet she's been nursing through the winter," Mirelle said. "Bring those, too."

"It'll look real nice when we get through with it; don't you worry," Dee said.

She hurried off and Grandma Speck smiled. "Don't know what I'd do without you girls. I wouldn't be able to keep the parlor going without help."

"Well, you do have us, and we are more than grateful to you for all your good care." Mirelle patted the older woman on the shoulder. "Thank goodness the rain did not ruin the piano. Melody dried it off and rubbed it down with beeswax. It looks like new."

"That's a blessing. When you sing and play that piano it sounds like the angels gathered around the throne."

"Well, hardly that good." Mirelle laughed. "But I do my best."

Grandma Speck scurried off, giving directions on where to put the benches.

Mira thought of how lucky she was to have these women. They were like sisters, the family she'd always wanted. Now, because of Jean-Marc, she was bringing more hardship on them. She wondered what evil deed he would do next.

How far was Jean-Marc willing to go in order to bring her to heel? Mira was afraid his determination was to wipe them out if necessary.

Trey swung off the stallion in front of the livery stable and tied the horse to the hitching rail. Rain pounded on the tin roof. A lanky man chewing on a straw got up off a wooden stool when Trey entered the building. The man's overalls hung by one strap, and his shirt hadn't seen a washtub in a while. One cheek bulged with a chaw.

"Howdy, stranger."

"Like to bed down my horse. He's tired and needs a good feed."

"Been riding far?"

"From Sassy Gap."

Trey didn't miss the flare of interest in the man's faded blue eyes.

"Sassy Gap, hey? Everything all right over there?"

"Actually, they had a fire. Damaged one building, but we managed to save most of it."

"We?" The man stood back, eyeing him. "You helped the Sassy Gap women? That ain't wise, stranger."

Trey felt a faint stirring of anger. "Watching women fight a fire and not pitching in to help isn't my way."

"No, course not," the hostler said hurriedly. "Mine neither. I'd have done the same."

Why did Trey doubt that?

"I hear the men in this area are afraid to help the women." He watched the man's face. "Sounds downright cowardly to me."

The hostler flushed. "Well, I wouldn't rightly say afraid."

"What would you say?"

The man flashed a show of defiance. "I'd say they know they'd be fighting a losing battle. Jean-Marc Portier ain't going to quit until that girl of his comes home."

"Even if she doesn't want to?" Trey thought Mirelle should go home too, but it was her business whether she did or not.

"She's going to in the long run," the man predicted. "Can't hold out against Portier forever. Save them all a lot of trouble if she'd just give it up and do what he wants."

"So you think the women are fighting a losing battle?"

The man spat a stream of tobacco juice at a rat hole in the floor. "Yep. I think they are. But the girl is as bullheaded as her old man."

Trey clamped his mouth shut. If he said anything he knew

he would go too far. He agreed with what the fellow was saying, but he didn't like hearing it from someone else.

"Can you take care of my horse?"

"Sure thing. Bring him in and I'll bed him down."

Trey led the stallion inside and paid the account, then left the livery and wandered down the street. The rain had slacked to a light mist. Most of the people he met ignored the rain. Apparently they were used to the drizzly weather.

He stopped at the boardinghouse and rented a room, planning to treat himself to a night between dry sheets for a change. The front lobby didn't look much different than any of the others he'd been in. He wondered if having a fern in a wrought-iron stand and a brass spittoon were required hotel items. The room needed something different, like maybe one of those female statues wearing draperies and holding a lamp like he'd seen in New Orleans. He thought of Naomi's reaction to the idea. Well, maybe not.

The young man at the desk peered at him over gold-rimmed spectacles. "Been riding far?"

"Sassy Gap."

In this weather and considering the condition of the trail, he figured that was far enough.

"Sassy Gap?" The man grinned. "You been staying there?"

"Just passing through."

The young man nodded. "Most men pass through. Not a good place to stay if you value your life."

"Why's that?"

The stories were getting more interesting by the moment.

"Man named Jean-Marc Portier has a daughter living there. He'd be upset if any men took up residence in that town."

"This Portier? What's he afraid of? That someone would make off with his daughter?"

The man laughed. "He ain't afraid of nothing. He don't have to be. No one's going to take a shine to that woman unless they fancy suicide. All he wants is for her to come home."

"And if she doesn't?"

"Oh, she will. He'll see to that."

Trey stepped out of the boardinghouse a moment later and wandered down the street. Did everyone know about the women's problems in Sassy Gap? He felt bad for Mirelle and the others. Thoughts of black hair and snapping dark eyes flashed through his mind. He could have stayed and helped. His sisters would be anxious to see him, but he could send word. He'd been brought up to help folk in trouble. But more trouble could be avoided if Mirelle wasn't so stubborn. He set his jaw and walked on.

He couldn't worry about the women of Sassy Gap. There was the little matter of saving the family farm. The situation had to be serious for Betty Hargrove to write him. Si Hargrove's wife wasn't a flighty woman. She didn't make a habit of interfering in her neighbors' business.

Later that afternoon the mourners gathered in the funeral parlor. Mirelle sat at the piano and played softly, switching from one familiar hymn to another. At the moment she was playing "Precious Memories," one of her favorites. She absently hummed along, running the words through her mind. *Precious memories, how they linger.*

How indeed. She remembered her mother, so lovely, so tragic, and dead at such a young age. *Not much older than I am now,* Mira thought. Her fingers moved automatically over the ivory keys as she thought about her own short-lived marriage to Paul, the young man who had been brave enough to fall in love with Jean-Marc Portier's daughter and steal her away. She sighed. She had done Paul an unpardonable injustice, marrying him to escape Jean-Marc's tyranny. Now Paul was dead and she hoped he had never suspected that she had never cared for him the way he cared for her.

Her thoughts now turned to Trey and guilt swept over her. What was it about this man? He was so unlike Paul, strong and decisive where her husband had been easily swayed. She had always wished that Paul had been a stronger man. Trey. Trey was different. He'd touched her life briefly, but powerfully—

One of the mourners sneezed, and she forced her attention back to the task at hand.

Nan Wiley, Jake Barrows's granddaughter, sat in the front row, perspiring uncomfortably in a black sateen dress with a high neckline and unfashionably tight sleeves. Mirelle thought maybe the dress had been packed away, waiting for a funeral. A faint whiff of mothballs trailed Nan.

Nan's brothers—Slade, Seth, and Toby—were here. Mirelle had a slight acquaintance with Slade. He was the most decent one of the boys, which wasn't saying much considering Seth and Toby had lived on the fringe of trouble all their lives. Nan and Slade had held the family together. Mirelle thought Nan had done most of the holding. From what she had heard, Nan Wiley was a good woman who'd had a hard life.

It was time for her to sing now, and Mirelle let her voice soar into the first notes of "Amazing Grace."

The song spoke to her in a more powerful way every time she sang it. She had been that lost wretch once and had been saved by the most amazing grace of her Lord. She saw Nan wipe away a tear.

Grandma Speck stood up to read the obituary. "Jake Barrows departed this world—"

A gut-wrenching sob startled her. Mirelle stared in surprise at Seth Barrows.

"Grandpa!" he bawled.

Nan rested a hand on his shoulder, comforting him.

Mirelle caught Jane's expression and bit back a grin. She was staring at Seth, eyes wide, as if she were horrified by the outburst. Jane whipped out a handkerchief and blew her nose into it. Tears streamed down the girl's cheeks, and Mira shook her head in disbelief. Jane was attracted to the worthless Barrows.

Mirelle's amusement faded. This could be bad. Jane believed in love at first sight, but Seth Barrows wasn't a decent man.

Grandma Speck caught Jane's eye and shook her head.

Mirelle breathed a sigh of relief. Grandma would handle the infatuation. Jane tended to cave in to emotion. Grandma Speck was well aware of Seth's weaknesses and she would make sure Jane knew "never the twain would meet."

Grandma carefully spread open her Bible. "We are gathered here to say good-bye to Jake." She fixed Seth with a gimlet eye. His watery eyes blinked but he remained silent.

"Jake was a good man. He believed in God and he tried to

pass that belief along to his family. It wasn't his fault it hasn't taken yet."

Seth and Toby squirmed.

"The good Lord has prepared a place for people like Jake. It's called heaven. Some people think everyone is going to heaven, but some folks are gonna be surprised. Only those who have claimed Jesus as their Savior and call Him Lord are bound for that shining white city in the sky."

Seth hung his head. Toby seemed to have developed a strong interest in a cut on his left forefinger. Nan leaned forward and gave them both a stern look, inclining her head toward the speaker.

Grandmother talked for thirty minutes, then sat down. Mirelle sang "In the Sweet By and By" before the mourners filed past to view the remains.

Dee and Viv then closed the casket. The women carried the pine box out to the waiting wagon Nan had provided and led the procession to the cemetery.

Mirelle walked beside Jane and gripped her hand.

Jane sniffled. "You suppose Grandma Speck don't plan on letting me see Seth."

"I would say that you are correct."

Jane was quiet for a minute. "He's not as good-looking as Trey, is he?"

"No, he is not."

Mirelle thought of curly red hair and blue eyes that lit up like stars when he smiled. There was not a man in this parish— or the next—that could compare with Trey McAllister's looks or character, but he'd walked away like all the others. So why did she care? Why did she keep thinking about him?

A jagged spear of lightning split the sky, and the rain poured down again.

Trey stopped by the café for supper. The room was full—mostly men. He sat down at an empty table and glanced at the menu written in white chalk on a blackboard. *Smothered venison steak, mashed potatoes and gravy, grits, dried apple pie, and coffee: 25 cents.*

Sounded good to him. All except the grits. He'd never taken to the Southern dish and didn't try to pretend. He preferred his meal ground finer and made into hoecakes. Or corn bread served hot and dripping with freshly churned butter.

His food arrived and he had to admit it was good. Maybe not as good as the meal the women cooked in Sassy Gap, but close. He'd not likely lose any weight in Louisiana.

A man approached his table. "Anyone sitting here?"

"No. Have a seat."

Trey's glance skimmed the newcomer. Tall, lanky, dark hair and eyes. Looked to be about thirty. Cajun, he'd guess.

The man held out his hand. "Daniel Lewis. I'm the pastor of the community church here in Mignon."

"Trey McAllister." A preacher. Well, from what he'd seen this town probably needed one.

The two sat in the comfortable silence of men who didn't have much to say and didn't feel called on to say it. Daniel tried the venison steak too. He cut a bite, speared it with his fork, and looked at Trey. "I don't remember seeing you before. Are you new in town?"

"Just rode in from Sassy Gap."

Trey waited for the usual response.

Daniel Lewis surprised him. "Ah. Sassy Gap. Grandma Speck and the women are well, I trust?"

"As well as they can be. They had a fire, you know."

Daniel put down his fork. "What burned?"

"Part of the funeral parlor."

"Oh, my. They depend on that business for their income. I hope it wasn't damaged beyond repair."

Trey recalled the charred roof, the smoke-damaged walls, and felt a twinge of guilt. "It's in pretty bad shape, but it can be repaired."

Daniel shook his head. "By those poor women?"

Trey nodded. "Understand no men will help them out."

"They're afraid of Mirelle's father."

"That's what I've been told. Hear he's pretty hard-nosed."

"An apt description. Jean-Marc is a driven man. He won't rest until he breaks his daughter's will."

"And when he does?"

Daniel shrugged. "He will have destroyed her identity."

Trey had a hunch the preacher was right. It made him uncomfortable to think about eight women struggling to hang on in spite of all the odds. Before he could voice a response, he was interrupted by the voice of a man at the next table.

"This time tomorrow it'll all be over in Sassy Gap."

Trey stopped eating, straining to hear the conversation. He noticed Daniel's interest was caught as well.

A short, rotund man spoke up. "How so? You going to burn them out?"

"We tried that but some saddle tramp helped them put out the fire."

Daniel glanced at Trey, grim faced.

Trey turned slightly to identify the man who was bragging about finishing off Sassy Gap. He'd never seen him before.

"What you going to do this time, Curt?"

The short man leaned forward, his eyes glistening. He licked his lips. The little buzzard was hanging on to every word, not caring who got hurt as long as he could enjoy the gossip.

Trey's hands curled into fists as he fought the urge to give this sorry example of humanity a lesson he wouldn't forget.

"We got us a surefire idea this time," Curt bragged. "Ain't no way it can fail. Jean-Marc's going to have to hand over that bonus he's promised."

"What? What are you going to do?" The short man was practically salivating.

Curt laughed. "We're gonna poison the spring where they get their drinking water. What do ya think about that?"

The short man shook his head in amazement. "Don't that beat all. That'll do the trick."

Trey sucked in his breath. What if one of the women drank the water? What if they gave it to little Audrey? Or to Mirelle? He started to shove back his chair but Daniel's hand clamped his arm to the table.

Trey stared at him and Daniel shot him a pain-filled glance. "You can't fight them all," he said softly.

Trey got a grip on his temper. "We have to do something," he hissed back.

Daniel shook his head. "It's wrong. What they're going to do is wrong, but we can't stop it."

"Who says we can't?"

Trey knew his voice was raw with anger but it made him mad to see men torturing women. It wasn't right. How could he overlook plain meanness and not answer to the Lord?

Daniel sighed. "There isn't a thing we can do. Half the men in this town work for Jean-Marc Portier. We'd never get out of town. They know my sympathies, and they follow me everywhere I go. Do you think I'd sit here and do nothing if I could stop them? Anything we do will just make it harder for Mirelle and the women."

Trey picked up his coffee cup and absently drank from it. Daniel was right. This wasn't his fight. He'd better ride on in the morning the way he'd planned, but the idea burned him.

"This goes beyond a father wanting his daughter to come home. You heard that braggart. If anyone drinks that poisoned water they could die. What kind of man would do that?"

They had some hard cases back in Kansas, but even the worst of them wouldn't pull anything like this. Call it the code of the West or whatever—men who lived on the prairie didn't fight women.

The pain in Daniel's eyes deepened. "Jean-Marc is a hard, determined man who will have his way at all costs. Anyone who crosses him ends up moving somewhere healthier—if he lives that long."

A quiet man watched from the corner, taking no part in the general hilarity.

Trey indicated him. "Who's that?"

Daniel swiveled around to look, then turned back. "Tom Addison."

Trey watched the man out of the corner of his eye. Tall, well built with stern features, Tom watched the others with a contemptuous expression in his frosty blue eyes.

"Tom owned a plantation just south of here," Daniel said. "Had many slaves. Yankees burned it into the ground. He came home from the conflict with nothing but a bitter hatred for the North and contempt for everyone who profited from the war."

Trey cut another bite of steak and chewed thoughtfully. "This Jean-Marc, did he lose his plantation?"

Daniel shook his head. "If anything, he grew more prosperous. There are rumors he switched sides whenever it suited him, but no one will come right out and say so."

Trey glanced toward Tom Addison, then looked back at his plate. "What about him?"

Daniel sighed. "Tom's a rigid, stern man, but he's fair. If he knew for sure Jean-Marc changed his allegiance to the Union to save his plantation, he'd burn the house down around Portier's ears. But he won't do anything without proof, and if anyone knows anything, they're not talking."

Trey polished off the rest of his steak before pointing out the question that still bothered him. "That doesn't explain why Mira's father wants to destroy Sassy Gap."

Daniel frowned. "There's a reason, all right. Something that goes deeper than bringing Mira home on a leash, but I can't find out what. I've been snooping around, but I haven't learned anything."

"You want to be careful," Trey said quietly.

If the preacher picked a fight, standing alone against every man in town, he'd be as helpless as a baby calf in a Kansas blizzard.

Daniel looked affronted. "Are you saying I should put my own safety or personal preferences ahead of doing what's right? Look around you. Every man in this room is either working for Jean-Marc or afraid to cross him! If I don't help the women, who will? If I can find out Portier's next move maybe I can call in help."

"What kind of help?"

Daniel indicated Tom Addison. "If I can prove to Tom that Jean-Marc turned traitor during the war, Mira's father will be too busy saving his empire to worry about a shabby little town like Sassy Gap."

"And if Jean-Marc finds out you're the one who betrayed him?"

Daniel shrugged. "It's a chance I have to take. How can I face the God I serve if I run away from those in need?"

Trey left the café wondering the same thing. How could he face God with Sassy Gap on his conscience?

Though his bed was comfortable enough, sleep eluded him. He tossed and turned. Maybe it was because he was used to sleeping on the ground, but he had a hunch it was the thought of Mirelle drinking poisoned water.

He stared into the darkness, torn between the women and his sisters. "Lord, I don't know what to do. I realize they need help, but why me? I can't neglect my kin to help someone I barely know. That wouldn't be right either. If You can show me a way out of this, I'd sure appreciate it."

The following morning he was awake before dawn, eager to be free of Mignon, Louisiana, and the rumors. Rumors he refused to think about. He was going home, where men didn't pick fights with helpless women.

Thunder shook the room. Didn't it ever do anything in Louisiana except rain?

Telling himself he owed it to his family to keep going west, Trey rode for two hours in pouring rain. But what he'd heard at the café and what Daniel had said kept running through his mind, along with the Scripture "Inasmuch as ye have done it unto one of the least of these my brethren, ye have done it unto me." Guilt nagged at him. What difference would a couple of days make?

Before noon Trey turned around and headed back east.

Back to Sassy Gap.

He'd send a wire to the local bank in Tyrone. He'd known Jack Trooper, the banker, all of his life. Maybe Jack could help him out for a few weeks where the farm was concerned.

He'd try to talk Mirelle into reconciling with her father before someone got killed. If not, then he could ride away with a clear conscience, be done with Sassy Gap and its problems once and for all.

He'd do the best he could and leave the results up to God.

CHAPTER 5

With a horrified gasp, Mira stepped back from the water's edge. Trout floated on top of the pool that was fed by an underground spring, their bloated bodies bobbing in the swift current. A crow landed on the bank, stopped, cocked its head to one side, and then flew away without drinking. Even the birds sensed that the water was tainted.

Mira brought a hand to cover her mouth and fought back tears. *Jean-Marc.*

Visual proof of his insane obsession lay like a coiled rattler in front of her.

How could he have done this?

How could he be so cruel?

She had prayed and believed good would win out, trusting God would hear her petition, but still Jean-Marc prospered while wreaking his vengeance upon the innocent women of Sassy Gap. Why would God allow such a tyrant to live? How much longer could this game continue?

Until you concede, an inner voice reminded her.

Concede? Never! Eternity would come and pass before she would yield. She had escaped him once. He would be more watchful this time. The stakes were higher now and she could never go back.

But this . . .

She bowed her head, letting the tears flow. "Oh, Lord, I am so tired of fighting this battle alone."

You are not alone. The words rippled through her mind, as soft as a spring breeze.

She apologized immediately. God had been true. He'd kept her safe thus far. She took a deep breath in an effort to calm her racing pulse. No, she was not alone. God, her constant companion, had given her the strength to endure all she had suffered at the hands of Jean-Marc Portier.

Jean-Marc had vowed never to let her go. His rage had been frightening when he heard of her marriage to Paul. He refused to recognize her status as a widow or to speak of her as Mira Dupree. He still spoke of her as "my daughter, Mira Portier," ignoring that she was a grown woman. She and Paul had briefly lived in Sassy Gap, and Jean-Marc had kept his thumb on them the whole time.

A slow, burning anger began in the pit of her stomach, growing in volume until it erupted like a scalding fountain. She could be passive no longer. Jean-Marc Portier wanted a fight. Well, then, she would take the battle to his very doorstep.

She whirled, overcome with anger as she carried her fishing pole back to town. A day of reckoning had arrived. Jean-Marc had forced this confrontation. *Let us see how he enjoys hearing a few truths.*

Brenda glanced up from the anvil when Mira burst into the livery shed.

"I'm taking Pris for the morning."

"Hey—wait a minute—"

"Don't let anyone go to the spring!"

"What—?"

Before the blacksmith could finish the question, Mira grabbed the mare's bridle and, refusing a saddle, swung aboard. She galloped out of town, aware of Brenda wiping her hands on her apron as Mira rode away.

Riding hard, her anger boiling, Mira covered the ten miles to Belmonde, the Portier plantation. She was in no mood to compromise in any fashion when she galloped up the narrow lane of the stately plantation.

She was furious.

And covered in mud.

She swung off her horse and greeted Macon, the white-haired servant who stepped forward to take the reins of the tired horse. The black man flashed a warm smile, openly delighted to see her. Mira's feet swiftly covered the ground, boots clicking on the boards of the long, narrow porch. Before going into the house, Mira stared around at what she'd once taken for granted. She was repulsed by the opulence around her. Opulence her mother's money had paid for. Jean-Marc, the son of a poor planter, had married up, as the neighbors put it. Oh, she had heard gossip, words stored in her heart as she tried to understand the secrets hidden behind the gracious facade Jean-Marc and Linette Portier had presented to their part of the world.

Beds of brilliantly colored flowers lined each pathway. Acres and acres of lush grounds, stables, outbuilding, slaves quarters. Jean-Marc's slaves had chosen to remain with him after the war ended, partially due to the fear of the unknown. And Mira had to admit that he could treat them with great compassion, even while being cold to her.

The house and surrounding grounds were beautiful, but to Mira they seemed infused with evil. The women of Sassy Gap existed like paupers while Portier and his thugs lived like kings. Porticos towered above her as she strode to the double glass doors of her enemy's private sanctuary. She'd show no formality today. She would not permit Macon to announce her arrival. Today Jean-Marc would face her wrath disarmed and at a disadvantage.

Stepping quickly through the open doorway and striding to an anteroom, she found her adversary sitting at his desk, which had been carved by her great-grandpapa from the trunk of a plantation oak. Everything about Jean-Marc was large: his home, his den, Jean-Marc himself. Towering inches above the average man, the Frenchman's stature intimidated even the bravest. He had black eyes and wore his hair in a long queue that hung below his collar. Women swooned over the wealthy and power-ful patriarch, but Mira wasn't impressed. She saw beyond the facade. She knew the real man.

Rising to her full five-foot stature, she met his startled gaze and said in a flat, uncompromising tone, "How dare you."

"Mira?" Jean-Marc pushed back to rise, and a small fist planted in the middle of his chest caught him off balance.

"Do not bother to get up. This is not a social call."

A wry grin appeared at the corners of his mouth, and the mere hint of his arrogance infuriated her. Poking her forefinger on his brocade jacket to emphasize each word, Mira said, "You can burn our buildings. You can shoot out all the town's windows and uproot the hitching posts. You can even poison our water supply, but you will *never*—do you understand me?—*never*, break my spirit!"

Jean-Marc pushed his chair back but didn't attempt to stand again. "My dear Mira—"

"I am not your 'dear' anything!" She stepped back, swiping a stray lock of hair off her forehead. "You will send Macon to Sassy Gap with fresh water. Immediately."

Jean-Marc laughed. "And, pray tell, why should I do that?"

"Don't play innocent with me. You had your—your despicable hired help poison the spring."

A look of complete innocence formed on his face. "Someone poisoned your water supply? Why, wouldn't that mean you have no water to drink or fresh fish to eat? The scoundrels. I will set my men to work to immediately find and punish the culprits."

Mira's upper lip curled with contempt. "Please. Spare me this nauseating display of hypocrisy."

His hand came up to cover his heart as though her words cut deeply. "Daughter, you do your father a disservice—"

She cut him off. "You are not my father! Do you think I'm a complete fool?"

He half rose from his chair, his features stoic. "You know?"

"Of course I know. I've always known."

"Who told you? I'll have the hide off anyone who dared to talk!"

"*You* told me. I heard the names you called my mother. I saw the way you treated her. But I am not like her and I am not afraid of you." She paused for breath. "Leave me alone," she said softly. "You will not break me. You will not change me, you will not bend me, and you cannot frighten me like you did Mama."

Pride warred with resentment on his features. "You will not speak of your mama in that fashion."

"Why, Jean-Marc?" She tilted her head. "Are you afraid she will rise up from the grave and tell the world what a bully you are? how you struck her at will and treated her like chattel? Are you afraid someone will learn how you hit her, knocked her off balance so she fell down the stairs? afraid she would bear witness that you killed her?" Mira laughed. "Who would believe it of Jean-Marc Portier? Oh. Wait." Her eyes narrowed. "Perchance everyone would believe it. No?"

Jean-Marc rose, standing threateningly over her. "Have you no shame, Mirelle? The Good Book says 'honor thy father and mother.' Why would you drag your mother's good name through the dirt?"

Mira's lips curled back against her teeth in a snarl. "You care nothing about her name. You only care that no one knows a woman betrayed the great Jean-Marc Portier. You used her, just as the man who sired me used her."

A dark flush of anger stained his cheeks. "You want to know about your father? Then listen well. He came from west Texas, a cattleman looking for a new strain of stock. He saw her and he wanted her and she chose him over *me*." He sounded as if even now betrayal was fresh, a deep wound.

"But she married you." Mira forced out the words.

"She had no choice. Marry me or face the scandal of having a child out of wedlock."

"You never loved her." Mira was as certain of that as she was of the next breath she would take.

"Ah, but I loved this magnificent plantation she had inherited from her father." He waved his hand, encompassing the room. "Well worth the inconvenience of raising someone else's brat, wouldn't you say?"

"My father went away. Did he know about me?" She had to hear the truth even if the answer came from someone who hated her for what she was not.

Jean-Marc laughed, and Mira knew the sound would haunt her forever. "He never left. She would have gone with him, and I couldn't allow that. No, my innocent, the swamp holds its secrets."

Mira grasped the back of a chair to keep from falling to her knees, staring in horror at the sneering face of the man she had despised for so long. "You killed him."

"No, of course not. Why should I dirty my hands on the likes of him?"

"I see," she said slowly. "You paid someone else to do your dirty work, just as you pay someone else to drive us out of Sassy Gap. How contemptible you are. You have to pay others to fight women for you."

For a moment she thought he would strike her; then his lips drew back in a vicious, mocking parody of a smile. "Doesn't the God you worship say in His Word that you must forgive? Do you have forgiveness in your heart for me?"

She knew he was only taunting her about her beliefs. He wasn't interested in her forgiveness, didn't think he needed it. Mira lifted her chin. "You bring shame on yourself to speak of the Good Book. Only those who believe on it should claim its promises and commands."

"The Good Book commands forgiveness."

Forgive the man who had destroyed both of her parents? Even God wouldn't expect that of her; would He?

How could she forgive the evil this man had done?

She whirled and stepped out onto the veranda, pausing to catch her breath in the mild breeze.

Jean-Marc stood in the doorway behind Mira. He supported himself against the frame and stared at her. "You cannot run far enough or fast enough to escape me. You belong to *me*, and what belongs to me I rule."

She bit her lower lip, refusing to face him. "Your blood does not run through my veins. I never knew the man who gave me life, but I will make you pay for what you have done. No matter how long it takes or how much it demands from me, I will bring you to justice."

His jaw firmed. "As far as the world knows, you are my daughter. No one ever knew differently. Should you attempt to do anything it will be your word against mine. Which of us do think anyone will believe? A wayward child or a heartbroken father?"

Silence swelled between them. From the moment Mira had entered the world, she'd been at odds with this man. Never once had they shared the close, loving relationship of father and daughter. Mama used to say that Jean-Marc, deep down, loved her with all his might, but she knew that wasn't true. Mira had never seen him show even the slightest hint of affection to anyone. Mama said he had wanted a son, but God had not granted his wish.

Still, Jean-Marc was not a man who could be ignored.

Mira drew a deep breath and started walking across

the veranda, hoping to get away from Jean-Marc before she cried.

His voice came from behind her, brushed with a mocking laughter. "Oh, Daughter? You do remember that your dear papa's forty-fifth birthday celebration is approaching? Macon will be sending a party invitation in a few weeks. I believe the staff is planning something quite grand for the occasion. You will be there."

Mira kept walking, ignoring the taunt. If she came, she would bring a dish.

Fish.

Jean-Marc sat at his desk, staring at nothing. Mira was even more of a threat than he had realized. He had suspected she knew he'd hit Linette, causing the fall that had killed her. That was one of the reasons he wanted Mirelle where he could control who she saw or talked to.

It hadn't occurred to him that she knew he wasn't her father. Obviously she'd been sneaking around, listening when he'd argued with Linette. Mira had always been a sly brat, poking her nose in where she had no business. Linette had doted on her. The only time she'd defied him was when he wanted to send Mira away to school.

That and the fact that she had never signed a deed leaving him the plantation. Her will left this house and all of the grounds to her next of kin. He had managed to convince the court and the judge he had appointed to that post to grant the title to him. But times had changed. The Yankees and their carpetbaggers had arrived. He couldn't count on his claim standing up in court if Mira decided to challenge him.

He got up from the old desk and yanked on a tapestry bellpull.

A few moments later Macon entered the library. "You rang, sir?"

"Send one of the hands into Mignon and tell Curt Wiggins I want to see him right away."

"Yes sir, Master Jean-Marc. I'll see to it."

Jean-Marc watched him leave. Macon had a good thing going here. No reason for him to leave, same with all of the former slaves. He treated them well, paid them a pittance, and they rewarded him by staying and turning out good work. He'd been an excellent businessman where the plantation was concerned . . . even Linette had found no fault. He was under no delusions where Macon stood, though; he and Lillybelle, the cook, had been Linette's servants, and any loyalty they held had gone to Mira.

Linette. She'd been a beautiful woman, even more beautiful than Mira. He'd planned to marry her from the moment they met. Montrose, his father's plantation, had been the equal of Belmonde before his own father had sapped its resources through gambling and hard living. With creditors closing in on Montrose, Jean-Marc had seen Linette and Belmonde as his best chance for survival. A chance that was almost destroyed by a good-looking, fast-talking Texan, but no one had bested Jean-Marc Portier yet. The Texan moldered away at the bottom of Big Swamp, and Linette was buried in the family cemetery.

He had not known about the coming baby when they married, but it wouldn't have mattered. He needed the plantation. He'd made sure Linette understood no one must know Jean-Marc Portier had been manipulated into marrying a woman who carried another man's seed. Linette had known she would pay a harsh penalty if she yielded to temptation and gossiped with her friends. He had discouraged visits from her old friends. Now Mira knew.

He clenched his hand, crumpling the bill for six soft linen shirts he'd picked up from the stack of papers littering his desk. Another weapon she held over him. He'd treated this small community as his own little fiefdom. Wouldn't they all like to gossip about the man who controlled their lives. Laugh at him for being gullible. That must never happen. No one laughed at Jean-Marc Portier.

Jean-Marc had finished his bookkeeping chore when he heard the knock on the door and Macon going to answer.

Seconds later Curt Wiggins slouched into the room and approached the desk. He sat down uninvited and crossed his legs. "You wanted to see me?"

Jean-Marc carefully hid his distaste for the man, resenting that he had to rely on such scum. Big, running to fat, and badly in need of a bath, his bushy black beard smeared with the stains of tobacco juice, Wiggins was the sort who would sell his own grandmother down the river for a silver dollar and a jug of white lightning.

Jean-Marc hated doing business with men of this caliber, but no one else would take on the job of running the women out of Sassy Gap. He could bully men who lived here into not interrupting the harassment, but not even he could make them wage war against women. And he needed the land the Gap sat on.

He tapped the well-manicured nails of his left hand against the desktop. "I hear you poisoned the water at Sassy Gap."

Wiggins grinned. "Now who told you that?"

"My daughter. She was extremely upset." As far as the world knew, Mira *was* his daughter and he would see they continued to think so.

"That so, now?" Wiggins laughed. "Guess they'll be moving out then. She comin' home?"

Jean-Marc shook his head. "The women are a stubborn lot. They will not move yet. It will take time. Something we don't have an abundance of. We must not delay our next step."

Curt Wiggins smacked one hand against the chair arm, frustration creeping into his tone. "You telling me they're planning on staying there with the spring poisoned and all those dead fish floating belly-up and starting to stink? That ain't sensible."

Jean-Marc yielded a wry smile. He had to get along with the man. "I've never known women to be overly burdened with common sense."

"Ain't it the truth?" Wiggins slapped his thigh, good humor restored. "But then, their brain ain't what we're interested in."

"Apparently not," Jean-Marc said drily. He'd have to air the room after this specimen of the unwashed masses left. "We must discuss our next move."

Wiggins leaned forward. "I got some ideas on that."

"No physical harm is to come to the women," Jean-Marc warned. "We do not want to go so far that we anger the people who live in this parish."

"Those yellowbellies?" Wiggins scoffed. "They ain't goin' to do anything."

"I hear that preacher, Daniel Lewis, is friendly with the Sassy Gap women. He could cause trouble."

"I can take care of him," Wiggins boasted. "Just say the word."

"You are not to touch him. There are many who call themselves Christians here who would rise up in arms if we harmed a preacher. No, we must make living in Sassy Gap so unpleasant the women have no choice except to leave."

"I can handle that," Wiggins promised. "You just relax and leave it to me."

Jean-Marc eyed him dispassionately. Why did he have to work with fools? He knew the answer. Intelligent men would have nothing to do with his schemes. "You have not been overly successful so far."

Wiggins flushed. "Just the breaks of the game. We'd have burned that funeral parlor to the ground if that saddle tramp from Kansas hadn't shown up to help them put out the fire."

"A regular white knight," Jean-Marc agreed. Another cowboy interfering in his life. Well, this one could be disposed of too, if it came to that. "The fact that you chose to set the fire in the middle of a violent rainstorm didn't have anything to do with it, of course."

Wiggins jaw set in a belligerent line. "You calling me stupid maybe?"

Jean-Marc stiffened. If he didn't need this yokel he would shoot him on the spot. "I am not calling you anything, but from now on I will make the plans. Now this is what I want you to do. . . ."

"Sakes alive!" Grandma Speck reached for the reins and Mira slid off the horse. "You had me worried half sick. Didn't know if you'd get back in time for Getster's burial or not."

"I am sorry that I concerned you, Grandma, but I had something that would not wait." Mira absently arranged her hair. She could not tell anyone what had taken place between her and the man the community believed to be her father. Even she could not absorb the evil deeds Jean-Marc had dismissed so casually. How could she expect anyone else to believe them?

"You know about the spring?" Grandma asked.

Color crept up Mira's cheeks. "I am so sorry."

"Ain't your fault. He won't best us; we'll get our water from someplace else."

The two women proceeded into the mortuary, where mourners had already started to gather.

"I am sorry you had to prepare Mr. Getster alone."

Some folks favored wakes where the family would sit up all night with the deceased, but the Getsters wanted a public burial.

"No bother. Isn't like it's the first time. But I was worried about you, little gal." The old woman eyed Mira curiously. "Brenda said you burst into the livery earlier and shot off on Pris like a scalded cat. Said you didn't say where you were going."

Mira removed her riding gloves. "I paid Jean-Marc a visit."

"Oh, my." Grandma's jaw went slack.

By now the two women had entered the hushed room. For

the time being the subject was closed, but Mira knew it was far from over. Grandma would question why she had ridden the ten miles on the day they had a service. What answer could she give? Not the truth. It would seem like a betrayal to the mother who had loved her. But how could she bring Jean-Marc to justice for two murders without baring her mother's sin for all to see?

Mira was filled with guilt. She was all the help Grandma had when it came to burying folks. The other women were squeamish and usually did little more than stand at the door and hand out slips of paper with the deceased man's name and family written on it. Sometimes they'd help carry a loved one to the grave. Dee usually oversaw such occasions, but Mira noticed that she was missing this morning.

Both women walked to the dais, where Mira slid onto the piano stool. The old upright piano had been donated last winter by a grieving widow. Before that the music was unaccompanied and often amounted to little more than first verse of "When the Roll Is Called up Yonder." The unexpected gift, along with Mirelle's talent, made the services more pleasant for the grieving family.

With her fingers resting lightly on the keys, Mira waited for Grandma's signal, which came promptly. With uplifted palms, the older lady brought the assemblage to their feet. Mira hit the first note of "Amazing Grace" and the music swelled. Herman Getster's services had begun.

Grandma Speck kept the message short but meaningful. She spoke of the man's family, his service to community and God, and the fact that the Widow Getster had donated three Bibles in memory of her late husband's name.

Outside the mortuary dark rain clouds moved in again as the next storm began.

Mira winced when Grandma closed the service in unison with a loud boom. Rain splattered on the singed roof. Color crept into her cheeks. Singed roof. Broken windows. It was a wonder anyone cared to do business with them, or allowed her to stay. The reason for the damage was no secret.

The front door opened, and Brenda, Vivian, and Dee carried in large buckets. While the deceased's family paid their last respects to a loving husband, father, and grandfather, the women quietly set to positioning the vessels under the gaping holes in the burned roof.

Mira discreetly wiped a drop of moisture off her forehead and quickly closed the sheet music before it got drenched.

Trey McAllister's handsome face popped into her mind, and she felt a stab of disappointment mixed with resentment. He was the first man to ride through town who had lingered overnight. Mira sensed that here was a man who would not be afraid to face Jean-Marc if he chose to help.

Which he had not. Instead he had ridden away without a backward glance or seemingly a care for the women's predicament.

Still, she knew deep in her heart that should he have chosen to help, he would have been a formidable force.

The click of the pine box shutting drew her back to the present. Enough wishful thinking. There were practical matters to be seen to.

Carrying her Bible under her arm, Grandma led the procession to the front door. Several men were in attendance today, but a couple of them were openly anxious to make a hasty retreat. Emmett Sloan was one. Mira resented the young farmer. He had called on her once, before Jean-Marc's men had paid him a pointed visit. He'd never come courting again.

Coward, she silently accused when she lifted her skirt and brushed past the blue-eyed, blond-headed farmer. Sympathy shone in his eyes, but she needed sympathy like Jean-Marc needed another bull. She needed action, someone with the fortitude to put a stop to her tormentor's tyrannical behavior.

She coldly eyed Emmett and took her place at the head of the line inside the door. Rain hammered down. Umbrellas appeared liked butterflies on a July afternoon.

Grandma approached, frowning. "I've asked Brenda, Viv, and Dee to help."

"And their response?"

"Well, they weren't happy but they said they would." Giving a brief nod, she walked back into the funeral parlor and Mira followed.

The women were waiting beside the dais with long faces. On occasions when the deceased was light and the box thin, Jane, Grandma Speck, and Mira carried the remains to the cemetery, which sat some fifty yards behind the parlor. Mr. Getster was a hefty sort, weighing well over two hundred pounds. This necessitated more womanpower.

With a succinct nod, Grandma took her place at the front right. Mira stepped up on the left. Viv, Brenda, and Dee manned the back of the box.

"Ready, ladies?"

The women nodded.

Hefting their burden the five began the slow and arduous journey to Herman's final resting place.

Carrying a pine box did not allow for the luxury of hauling an umbrella. Rain poured over their heads, blinding the five women when they exited the parlor. Swaying under the heavy weight, they turned due south and laboriously plowed through the puddles, drenching them to the skin. Mira could hear Viv's and Dee's breath coming in short, uneven gasps. The mourning procession followed behind, Widow Getster wiping tears.

Mira's anger simmered. There were at least five stout men in the crowd, and not one had stepped up to help, knowing that if they did Jean-Marc's men would hear and retaliate.

Biting her lower lip, Mira bent into the driving rain, her face set with grim determination. The ground was swamplike—water and sticky mud. Mud clung to her shoes, legs, and dress hem. Dee slipped, lost her grip, and went to her knees. Staggering, Brenda caught the middle of the box and held on while Viv attempted to redistribute the weight.

Dee struggled to her feet and once more took her place. The women's soaked dresses clung to them, adding weight to their already too-heavy burden. Their shoes might well be ruined.

Anger at Jean-Marc hummed through Mira's taut body.

Viv went down next. Even Mira slipped once in the gradual ascent up the small, slippery incline. The men in the crowd hung back, their heads low and gazes on the ground. When one of the pallbearers would lose footing, a wife would lean over to protest to her husband but she would be swiftly silenced with a harsh look.

As far as Mira was concerned, the men in this area were a bunch of lily-livered cowards. Filled with disgust, she took another hitch with her hands and made an attempt to carry more than her load.

Grandma noticed her effort. "There are five of us. We're all in this together, child. Relax."

Finally, the grave came in sight. The five women carefully set the pine box beside the marked gravesite. Grandma Speck stepped to the head of the casket, and Mira held an umbrella over the old woman for protection. Grandma said the last she was going to say about Herman Getster and offered a short prayer. Digging and closing the grave would have to wait until the ground hardened. Meanwhile, the box would be wrapped in canvas for protection.

The mourners dispersed quickly, hurrying to waiting buggies and home to get out of the wet. An elderly man—Mira was not certain who—paused to slip a coin in Grandma Speck's hand before he made his getaway.

Money, Mira thought. Men thought money could buy anything, including respect. Well, he was wrong. She had no respect for any man who would stand by and refuse to help them.

"That man?" she asked under her breath. "What is his name?"

"Old man Stoops. Lives 'bout fifteen miles from here. Buried his wife a few years back."

"Why would he not help? Does he not know money is useless to us? We need a man's protection. We need a roof over the parlor, new windows and fresh meat and—"

"Stoops knows all that," Grandma said drily.

Mira knew they had discussed the subject a hundred times; she also knew who was responsible for their continuing grief. She. Mira Dupree. If she would leave—give up—the misery would cease.

In the distance, Mira saw a rider, possibly a late mourner. The big stallion grew closer and her heart sprang to her throat.

Grandma Speck paused on the end of the porch and watched the rider approach. "Well saints alive—isn't that the McAllister man?"

Viv and Dee broke into wide grins.

"See," Viv said. "I told you he fancied me. He's come back!"

"You!" Dee laughed and brought her hands up quickly to scrub mud off her cheekbones. "It's me he's back to see."

The rider approached, rain beating down on his hat and shoulders. The horse slowed, and suddenly Mira was looking up at the handsome redheaded stranger, wishing with all her might that maybe, just maybe, he had come back because of her.

"Ladies." He tipped his hat and rain ran off the brim.

Dee tittered. "Mr. McAllister."

Viv edged Dee aside with her hip. "So glad to see you."

"Thought you were long gone," Grandma observed. "Forget something?"

"Yes, ma'am."

"Oh?" Grandma turned to shoot an inquiring look at the others. Each woman shook her head, indicating that none had noticed anything left behind.

Grandma turned back. "What'd you forget?"

Trey shifted in the saddle. "My manners, ma'am." He took a hammer out of his saddlebag. Turning back, his eyes found Mira's. "Soon as the rain slacks up, I'll get started on that roof."

CHAPTER 6

Morning came with the promise of a clear day, but a gray line of clouds in the west indicated the reprieve was only temporary.

Trey, working feverishly to get a section of the roof finished before another storm hit, felt he was racing Mother Nature. He kept checking over his shoulder to see if she was gaining on him. A gust of wind battered the tree branches as he nailed down shingles on the steeply pitched roof. The hammer blows were quick and powerful, like a bevy of woodpeckers.

Brenda, tall and well muscled, hauled up stacks of shingles after Viv and Dee tied the rope around them. Trey watched in appreciation when she hoisted the shingles to her shoulders and carried them to him, striding confidently over the high, pitched roof.

"You're not afraid of heights?" he asked.

She grinned. "Don't reckon there's much danger of the wind blowing *me* over."

"Bet you're good at dancing," he teased. "Real light on your feet."

She shrugged. "When I get the chance. But not many men want a woman who can whip them arm wrestling. Had me a man, but he died before we could wed."

"Could be the men around here don't know what they're missing."

"And not likely to find out. No man is going to cross Jean-Marc Portier."

Trey nailed a shingle in place and reached for another. "I'm here."

"You wouldn't be if it wasn't for Mira."

He stopped hammering and stared at her.

She shrugged. "I've seen the way you watch her."

He didn't like to admit it, but he had come back because of the pretty dark-haired girl. Not only because what was happening in Sassy Gap was unfair, but because Mira was the innocent cause of it and felt so guilty about it all. He knew she felt trapped by the whole situation.

He didn't know how he could explain his delay to his sisters. Naomi in particular would be hard-pressed to understand how the need in Louisiana could be as bad as the need in Kansas. He felt uneasy about trying to make her understand how long black hair, dark eyes, and a beguiling accent could lure him away from family duty. But there it was.

He grinned at Brenda. "That obvious, am I?"

"Not unless a body is looking." Brenda stared past him at the western horizon. "I'm not like the others. I know you wouldn't be interested in someone like me. Not when you could have your choice."

Trey hefted his hammer and selected another nail. "Don't sell yourself short, Brenda. Any man would be lucky to have a good woman like you."

"But not you." It wasn't a question, and he didn't insult her with insincere words.

"Nope, not me."

She grinned. "At least I'm not like Dee and Viv. I've got enough sense to know if a man's interested or not."

"Dee and Viv are good women too." Trey accepted a shingle, shifted it into place, and nailed it down. A mite forward, but considering the lack of male companionship in Sassy Gap, he could understand their behavior.

"That they are," Brenda agreed. She pointed to the darkening horizon. "Better hurry with that last row. It's going to rain like pouring water out of a boot in mighty short order."

Trey glanced at the darkening sky and figured she was right. He hurried to finish the roof. A bright flare of lightning followed by a boom of thunder sent him back down the ladder. He'd learned about lightning on the battlefield, seen it strike men and horses. A wise man took cover when nature went on the warpath.

The women were gathered in the community room. A fire blazed on the hearth, and the smell of vegetable soup blended with the fragrance of fresh-baked corn bread.

Audrey came running when he entered the back door after putting up the ladder. "Trey, Trey!"

He caught her in his arms and swung her high in the air while she squealed with delight. "Hey, Punkin. What have you been doing?"

She laughed down at him. "Playing."

"Playing with what?"

She struggled in his arms. "House. Down, Trey. Put me down."

He lowered her until her feet touched the floor. "Okay. You're down. Now what?"

"C'mon." She grabbed his hand, pulling him over to the far corner of the room.

He watched as she caught up a homemade ball fashioned by winding rags around a rock and felt a stab of anger. A child like Audrey needed toys. Store-bought toys.

She ducked her chin and rolled her eyes up at him. A natural flirt. Were women born knowing how to catch a man's attention? Little Audrey would have every boy in town hanging around her when she got older, and it would take more than Portier to keep them away.

"Play catch with Audrey," she ordered.

"Okay, we'll play catch."

She threw the ball to him and he caught it. He leaned forward, grinning at her. "Here it comes. Catch it now."

She held her arms outstretched, hands together. He tossed the ball into her hands and she clutched it to her chest. "I caught it, Mama! Look, Mama! I caught it."

Melody's lips curved in a slow, sweet smile. He grinned down at her, thinking she'd make some man a perfect wife: good-natured, pretty, friendly, and always soft-spoken. And she had a charmer like Audrey for a daughter to sweeten the deal. A man would be a fool not to consider a combination like that. But then some men were born fools, bypassing a treasure for fanciful thinking.

Mirelle was putting plates on the table. She caught Trey's

glance and smiled. Warmth started in his chest and spread upward. She had that effect on him, but as far as he could tell the feeling was far from mutual. Mira was friendly, but that was all. He sighed and threw the ball for Audrey again. Women were fickle creatures, and while he'd come back to help right a wrong and had done it for Mira, that didn't mean he intended to stay longer than to help them get a few things done.

Fred and Lois, Grandma Speck's cats, dozed by the fire. Fred, a big black-and-white tomcat, and Lois, a three-colored calico, had free run of the room. Grandma Speck loved those cats more than she loved life. They kept her company. She said she never got lonely with them around. Trey didn't know how she could be lonely with seven other women and Audrey underfoot most of the time.

Jane called the women to lunch and Trey joined them. Melody washed a protesting Audrey's hands and face and led her to the table.

"I want to sit by Trey," the little girl demanded.

Laughing gently, somehow pleased by the demand, he pulled out a chair and helped her into it.

Mira sat on the other side of Audrey, and she reached over and patted the child's arm. "Be quiet now. Grandma Speck's going to ask the blessing."

Audrey immediately put her hands together and bowed her head, closing her eyes.

Trey met Mira's gaze. Her smile did things to him.

Grandma Speck cleared her throat and Trey bowed his head. Grandma didn't brook any interference when she talked to the Lord.

Audrey demanded Mira's attention, and she cut a piece of corn bread and handed it to the child. "Drink your milk, too."

The little girl grabbed the glass in both hands and drank deeply. Mira glanced around the table, looking at the women who were like sisters to her. Until she'd moved to Sassy Gap she hadn't known many people or had a lot of friends. When she was growing up Jean-Marc hadn't allowed her to socialize with their neighbors. She was expected to be above their common behavior. She'd found a love and warmth here she hadn't known since her mother's death.

Trey was talking to Dee, who had bested Vivian in the daily contest to see which one would sit by him. Viv glowered at them from three seats away. Mira caught her frown and smiled at her, noticing her discomfiture.

Viv grinned back and devoted her attention to her supper.

Mira sighed. Vivian and Dee were close friends. She would hate to see their friendship broken because of jealousy over a man who didn't care for either of them that way. While Trey was polite to both women, she did not think he was romantically inclined toward either. She did not completely understand why he had come back to help since he didn't seem attracted to any of the women in Sassy Gap. But he had been raised a gentleman. Anyone could see that.

She watched as he finished eating and left the table. Dee and Vivian's eyes followed him to the doorway, but it was their night to do the dishes. Mira hoped they would not take their frustration out on the china and glassware. She waited until the others were immersed in their evening chores before slipping out of the building and wandering toward the parlor.

Trey sat on the parlor porch in one of the rocking chairs Grandma Speck kept there for the mourners, watching as Mira crossed the street, picking her way carefully around mud puddles. The storm had blown over for the time being, and a watery moon peeked from behind gilt-edged clouds. Pale moonlight brushed her hair and dress with silver; she was as pretty a woman as he'd ever met. No doubt about that. His heart skipped a beat. He'd miss her when he finally left Sassy Gap.

But he had to leave.

And soon.

She hesitantly climbed the steps and he spoke softly, not wanting to startle her.

"I'm over here."

She gasped, and one hand flew to her throat.

"Sorry. I didn't mean to frighten you."

"You did not. I mean, I was not expecting you to be here."

"You weren't looking for me?" he teased. The thought that she might brought him pleasure, and he had to wonder why. Mira wasn't a woman to slip around visiting men at night, and he wasn't fool enough to think she had romance in mind now, either. The thought brought a subtle regret.

"Actually, I *was* looking for you. I wanted to talk to you." He could hear a defensive note in her voice.

"All right. I'm listening."

She perched on the edge of another rocker, and he noticed she didn't relax. She must have something important on her mind.

"I know you think I should go back to Jean-Marc," she began.

"Seems the sensible thing to do."

"Well, I cannot," she flared. "It would not be sensible."

"If you say so," he soothed, but curiosity overcame him. "Just for sake of conversation, why not?"

"You do not know him. He is cruel and unfeeling. Jean-Marc lives only for himself and what he wants."

Trey leaned forward, hoping to make her see the advantage for everyone involved. "Mira, look at the way you live here. Have you ever thought that he wants something better for you?" It had to hurt her father to see his daughter living in poverty. Why did she have to be so stubborn?

"We had something better until he set out to destroy us." Bitterness ran through her words like a scarlet ribbon. "His men set fire to this building. Do you think he would care?"

"I'd think he would."

Any father would. Trey didn't understand the bitter battles between Jean-Marc Portier and Mira Dupree, but it did seem to him that a lot of things could be ironed out if the two of them sat down and talked about it. Communication usually solved a problem if given a chance.

"Well, he would not have." She held out her hands. "He poisoned the spring. Oh, he did not do the dirty work himself.

He has too much money and power to slip around in the night poisoning water and killing fish. He would hire that done. And he would threaten anyone who would help us."

Trey was silent, feeling his way through the conversation. He didn't know firsthand about the relationship between father and daughter. Maybe because he'd lost his own parents so young he just assumed that others would want what he'd missed out on. Maybe things were different in Louisiana.

Mira went on, her voice breaking as she recounted her troubled childhood. "He physically abused my mother. She wasn't strong and couldn't stand up to him. He hit her more than once."

Trey's jaw clenched at the thought. He guessed some men would hit a woman, but he couldn't understand how they could. "Did he ever hit you?"

"No. He never abused me physically, only verbally." She sounded startled at the vehemence with which she uttered the words. Trey was a little startled himself. "There are things I cannot talk about, but I hope you will believe me when I tell you there is not nor can there ever be any father-daughter love between us."

He heard her chair squeak when she shifted positions. "I did a terrible thing once. A young man I knew asked me to marry him. I did not love him, but it was a chance to get away from Jean-Marc. So I ran away with Paul. We moved here, and then he was ordered into the war. He was killed and I remained in Sassy Gap. I could go back home, as you suggest, but I would be going back to a prison. I would not be allowed to escape again."

A stab of jealousy surprised Trey by its intensity. "Your father approved this marriage?"

"No, of course not. I pray Paul never knew how I used him," she said softly.

Trey was quiet for a moment, thinking about his answer. "I don't believe it would have mattered that much. If he really loved you, he was probably blind to your real motive." Hope springs eternal in the human heart, and this Paul had probably thought himself the luckiest man alive to have Mira Portier as a wife. Any man would.

Including himself? The idea startled him. Since Sharon's betrayal he hadn't allowed himself to think seriously about another woman. Until now. Was the young Cajun woman more of a threat to his bachelor status than he had realized?

Mira heard the sincerity behind Trey's words, and a subtle sense of relief crept through her. He was only trying to be nice, but she had fought so hard for so long that it took only a few kind words to overwhelm her.

"Thank you," she whispered.

He cleared his throat. "You getting chilly?"

She got to her feet. "A bit. Yes."

She turned toward the door, but somehow he was standing beside her. She hadn't heard him walk across the old porch, a sign of how much she'd let her guard down. She was always alert, keeping an eye out for Jean-Marc's henchmen. Not that she thought Trey McAllister worked for her enemy, but there was something about him that broke down her carefully erected barriers. That alone was dangerous.

"Mira?"

She turned toward him, right into his warm and strong arms. She leaned against him, breathing deeply of the clean scent of lye soap and fresh air. "Yes?"

His voice was low and husky. "You need to find a way to forgive your father."

She stiffened.

"You have to forgive him if you want God to forgive you," he insisted. "It's the only way you can go on with your life."

Mira pushed away from him, shocked. "Forgive him?"

"And it seems to me you're carrying a lot of guilt about Paul."

She pushed against him. "You're wrong. And . . . if I were, it is none of your concern." How could she have been so foolish, expecting him to understand?

His arms dropped away.

"Then forgive your father. Something's eating away at you. You have to find the cause and get rid of it. As long as you carry a load of bitterness in your heart, you won't find peace. You have to forgive him for your own peace of mind."

She stepped away, pushing her hair into place. "It is late."

Trey did not realize what he was asking. Even if she told him the truth, all the vile and wicked things Jean-Marc had done, would he believe her or would he think it female hysterics? The battle between Mira and the man posing as her father was her own private burden. She could not expect Trey McAllister to share it.

Mira nodded. "Mr. McAllister."

"Mrs. Dupree."

Mira heard the sudden coolness in his voice. She stepped inside, fighting tears. He did not—could not—understand.

He was a man.

The door closed behind Mira. Trey stared up at the sky, searching for an answer. She had rejected his advice but he knew he was right. Forgiving her father wouldn't help Jean-Marc, since he hadn't asked for her forgiveness and apparently didn't want it. But forgiving him would help Mira put the past behind her. She couldn't find peace as long as she carried so much hatred for her father.

His sister Naomi's voice came to him. *"Submit yourself therefore to God. Resist the devil, and he will flee from you."* Trey knew James 4:7 by heart. He'd heard his sister repeat it often enough.

He faced the funeral parlor behind him. Although there wasn't a dead body sharing his space, he couldn't bring himself to sleep there another night. He went to the stable instead.

Trey finished breakfast and stepped outside to find Grandma Speck sitting on the back stoop, enjoying the morning sun with her cats.

He sat down beside her. "Looks like it's going to be a nice day."

"Beautiful, but it won't last."

"Probably not." He grinned. "I had a talk with Mira last night."

"So she said."

She'd told Grandma Speck?

"Did she tell you I think she ought to go home?"

"Yes. She also said she'd told you what Jean-Marc is like. Why would you want her to go back?"

"I think she ought to forgive him and go on."

Well, maybe he thought she'd exaggerated some, the way his sisters did sometimes. He guessed maybe some other man might be taken in, but he'd lived around women too long not to know how they liked to dramatize things.

"I'd think you'd feel the same way, a religious lady like yourself."

She nodded. "I do, as far as it goes. But forgiveness isn't as easy as you seem to think. Sometimes it takes a while to reach the place where you're ready to forgive. And it's hard to forgive someone who keeps hurting you."

"I know that," Trey protested.

She sounded like she didn't think he'd done any forgiving. Well, he could tell her about carrying a load of anger and the healing that came from forgiveness. He was an expert on the subject. His sisters had made him so mad at times that he'd been ready to hog-tie and muzzle the next one that came at him, but time had cooled his resentment. Funny. Now he vaguely understood that they'd had his interests in mind all along.

Lois jumped up on Grandma's lap and stretched out full-length.

The old lady rested her hand on the cat's back. "Does God forgive an unrepentant sinner?"

He shook his head. "No. We have to repent and ask for forgiveness."

"Then what makes you think God expects Mira to forgive an unrepentant sinner? Are we supposed to be more forgiving than God?"

"You're trying to confuse me. What about the rest of you? Wouldn't you be better off if Mira went home?"

Lois jumped down and went to investigate a black bug crawling in the grass.

Grandma shook her head. "Not really. Guess you don't understand. We're family here. No one wants her to go back to that man. It wouldn't be in her best interests."

"The rest of you could leave, go to Kansas with me." His sisters would take the women under their wings in a heartbeat.

"Much obliged, but we'll never leave Sassy Gap. It's all we have."

Trey got up, stretching. "Your choice. The offer holds if you want to think about it."

Grandma Speck smiled up at him. "Seems to me you're awfully concerned about something you don't think is your problem."

She was right. It wasn't his problem.

Mira came outside and sat down on the stoop beside Grandma. She watched Trey's retreating back.

"What is bothering him?"

The older woman patted her hand. "Don't you go worrying about him. He's a good man. He's never met your daddy so he doesn't understand. No one could until they meet up with the pure, unadulterated orneriness of Jean-Marc."

Mira sighed, wishing she could tell this good woman the truth. But what would Grandma Speck think of her mother? She could never betray the woman who had given life to her. Jean-Marc didn't know it, but his secret was safe with her.

"I never wanted it to be like this. All my life I have longed for a father. I have never had one."

She thought of the man from Texas who had never returned to his home in the West, and a longing filled her heart for the father she'd never known. Would their relationship have been different? loving? She thought maybe so. Hoped so.

"You're wrong, child." Grandma Speck picked up Fred and stroked his fur. "You've got a heavenly Father who knows your every worry and care. You're not as alone as you think you are."

"I know." Mira impulsively hugged the older woman. "I have you and the others, too. It is only that—"

Grandma nodded. "Nothing takes the place of our own family. But while we might want them, they don't always want us."

Mira stifled a sigh. Grandma didn't understand; no one did. Except God.

Trey wandered down to the spring. It wasn't a pleasant sight. The dead trout were starting to smell. Nothing moved in the brushy thickets. Even scavengers rejected the poisoned prey. He knelt, gazing into the murky water. He didn't understand these people, and he was starting to feel suffocated with nothing but women around. He missed his old unit. Everything had changed in the past few weeks, so much that he felt unbalanced. Add Mira and the problems the women had—

He didn't want to stay, but didn't feel right leaving.

He thought about riding into Mignon to talk to Daniel but decided against it. What he ought to do was ride out to the Portier place and talk to Mira's father. This Jean-Marc must be a reasonable man when approached in the right manner.

Now that he thought about it, Trey believed he'd hit on a good plan of action. He strode back to the stable and saddled up. Brenda, who was nothing if not thorough, had told him in detail one afternoon where the Portier plantation was.

He took his time, riding slowly, going over in his mind how he'd approach the man. Fortunately it appeared they might finally get one full day without rain. It felt good to have the sun on his back again. But Louisiana gave him a closed-in feeling: too many trees, too much rain and humidity, too many people.

Brenda had said the plantation was ten miles from Sassy Gap. He decided he'd gone about that far when he spied a lane turning off to the right. A double line of majestic oaks lined the narrow road. Wrought-iron gates topped with a crest stood open, inviting visitors to enter. Trey eyed the opulent mansion from the road with some shock. Mira had lived here? Why would she prefer the ramshackle buildings of Sassy Gap to this?

The narrow lane led to a circle drive, which brought him out to one of those big houses with pillars he'd seen all over the

South, most of them burned-out shells. Somehow this one had survived intact. Steep stairs led to a wide veranda. The lawn looked like a battalion of slaves must work every day to produce grass as soft and plush as green velvet.

He pulled up his horse and leaned forward, crossing his arms on the saddle horn, feeling like a fish on dry land. What would it be like to live in a place like this? You could put his family's house in one wing and still have room to hold a square dance. He shook his head, wondering again why Mira would choose Grandma Speck and a funeral home over this mansion.

He walked his horse down to the front of the house and tied him to a low branch of a magnolia tree. When he reached the steps leading up to the front door he drew a deep breath. For the first time he felt a ripple of uncertainty. Mira might be stubborn, but she was smart. Maybe she had enough reason to turn her back on all of this.

He climbed the steps and reached for the front-door knocker.

A black gentleman opened before his second knock. "Yes, sir?"

"Jean-Marc Portier, if he's home."

"Whom shall I say is calling, sir?"

"Trey McAllister."

The man looked doubtful, so Trey added, "From Sassy Gap."

"Ah. Will you wait in here, sir?"

He led the way into a parlor that was fancier than any Trey had ever seen. Chairs and love seats upholstered in red velvet were scattered around the room. Lamps with red and pink roses painted on the double globes sat on carved tables of dark wood.

A painting of a man in a dark broadcloth coat and snowy white cravat hung over the white marble mantel.

Trey stepped closer and stared up at the stern face and direct eyes. Was this Mira's father? If so, she must take after her mother. There was little warmth in the hard but attractive face.

The butler cleared his throat, and Trey turned around to look at him.

"Mr. Portier will see you now."

Trey followed him into what he took to be a library or an office, but he had no time to look around. His attention was fixed on the man behind the desk, the man in the painting. Jean-Marc had the dark hair and eyes of most Cajuns. He also looked like a man who gave no quarter in any fight. Trey had a hunch Mira would never face a tougher opponent.

Portier's eyes held a touch of contempt. "You wish to see me?"

"I know your daughter."

"I see. And your mission here is?"

"The women at Sassy Gap are hurting. I understand that you want Mira to come home. I know the two of you don't get along, and I thought maybe if you got together and talked about it you could work out the problems between you."

That was before he had seen this arrogant, hard-faced man. Any working out would be done on Jean-Marc's terms.

Well-sculpted lips curved into a sneer. "There is only one solution. My daughter must give up this madness and come home."

"She won't do that."

Trey was surprised by a flicker of something close to hatred appearing in Jean-Marc's eyes.

After a moment the man answered. "No, she won't."

"Then why won't you go talk to her? Ask her nicely to come back, rather than trying to force her to do what you want."

Trey had a feeling he was wasting his breath. Asking nicely wasn't on this man's agenda. He was beginning to see what Mira was up against, and why her anger ran so deep.

"Why should I?"

"Because you'll lose her if you don't."

Jean-Marc's gaze moved around the room, his expression unreadable. He picked up a letter opener and examined the monogrammed handle. "Perhaps you mean well, but this is between my daughter and me. If she comes back and is properly obedient, then I will forgive her. If she insists on staying in Sassy Gap, then I will destroy them all."

His voice had a cold, matter-of-fact tone that caused the hair to stand up on the back of Trey's neck. "That's your final answer?"

"Mira knows my terms. She would do well to abide by them. This continued refusal to surrender will only bring disaster on her and her friends."

Trey was incredulous. "That seems unreasonable. I'm trying to negotiate a peace between you."

If the man desired a truce now was the time to bend. Trey held Jean-Marc's hard gaze.

"If you want to help, tell the women to abandon Sassy Gap. As long as they remain there, the battle will continue." Jean-Marc opened a book lying on his desk and started reading.

After a moment of silence, Trey left the room and the butler showed him out.

He rode away thinking that Mira's father was all she had

said and then some. If the milk of human kindness flowed through Jean-Marc Portier's veins, it had clabbered. Trey had run into some hard cases in his day, but Mira's father was the coldest, hardest, most arrogant man he'd ever had the misfortune to meet. Mira and the women of Sassy Gap were fighting a losing battle. He guessed that included him, since he'd thrown in his lot with them and he didn't plan to walk away now. He had a different perspective of what they were up against now, and he couldn't fault Mira for not wanting to go back to Jean-Marc. He wouldn't let her go back to that tyrant. Now it was his fight too.

CHAPTER 7

The old adage "When things can't get any worse they do" crossed Trey's mind Friday morning. He'd cut roof shingles yesterday until he was so sore he could barely move. He rolled out of his bedroll to the sound of a commotion—women's voices raised in outrage. What was the problem now?

In the last week things had reached the point where he hated to get up in the morning and face what new trouble had befallen them during the night. One thing he could say for Jean-Marc Portier: he never pulled the same trick twice. The man's imagination apparently had no limit.

Trey dressed and pulled on his boots, wincing when the women inched up the volume. "Sounds like a gaggle of geese," he muttered.

He found the reason for their distress when he walked to the barn. There wasn't a cow or horse to be seen. His gaze took in the henhouse, and only then did he notice the silence.

There were no animals anywhere.

Even the cats that hung around the barn were missing.

By the time he got to the kitchen Brenda and Jane had Grandma Speck cornered on the stoop, talking to the elderly woman in low soothing tones. The older woman seemed to have folded in on herself, for the first time looking frail and ill.

Mira looked up when Trey approached.

"Where's the livestock?"

"Gone."

"Gone?"

"Gone." She lifted her palms and repeated, "Gone."

"Buck too?"

"Buck too."

His horse! They'd taken Buck? Trey frowned. "What happened to them?"

Mira's gaze rose to the heavens as if seeking help. "Well now, *who* could have done such a nasty deed?"

Trey shifted his stance and studied the ground. "How could two cows, three horses, a henhouse full of sitters, and nine cats be gone? I slept in the stable!"

"Then you must sleep like a rock." Grandma sniffed. "And it's eleven cats, not nine." She sniffed. "The jackanapes even took Fred and Lois."

In Trey's limited time with Grandma, that was as close as she had ever come to swearing. Fred and Lois were family; the two cats never left Grandma's side. No wonder she looked like she'd taken a body blow. Fred and Lois were all she had left.

As though Grandma read his thoughts, she explained, "Fred wanted out during the night, and Lois naturally went with him. I fell back to sleep, figuring the two would scratch on the screen when they were ready to come in. When I awoke this morning I realized they hadn't come back. I spent the better part of two hours searching the woods and stream, but they're nowhere to be found."

That accounted for her appearance. Trey didn't want to think of a woman Grandma Speck's age stumbling through the woods calling for her friends. It wasn't right. He'd make that cold-hearted buzzard of a Frenchman pay for this if it was the last thing he did on this earth.

"It is Jean-Marc," Mira said. "He was not happy to try to burn us out, to poison our water supply; now he has taken away our milk, butter, and eggs."

Trey kept silent about his visit to Jean-Marc. No doubt it had egged Portier on.

Melody protectively pulled Audrey to her side. "They took our cow. What will she do for milk? A child needs fresh milk."

"Do not worry." Mira reached over and patted the worried mother's arm. "We can buy milk for now."

"From who? No one will sell us milk!"

Audrey's eyes sparkled with tears. "Trey, they took Grandma's cats."

"I know, Punkin, but we'll get them back."

"You will? For sure?"

"For sure."

His heart slowed at the seriousness of her expression. She was too young to suffer through the hardships forced on this town by an arrogant man determined to have his own way.

"Mr. Peepers too?"

Her pet banty rooster? He'd forgotten about the feisty little bantam chicken that Audrey had taught to take grains of corn from her hand.

"Mr. Peepers too."

And if that French blackguard had hurt any animal he'd answer to Trey. Personally.

"The man ought to be horsewhipped!" Grandma Speck's ire rose. "No fish, no eggs, no butter, no milk. He's trying to starve us out now. There's not an ounce of compassion in that man's dark soul."

Mira whirled and walked away.

Trey turned and followed the distraught girl. He had to do something to give her hope and ease her stricken expression. "I'll walk to Mignon and see if anyone's seen the animals."

"Ha," Mira said. "Show me a man, woman, or child who would dare give you any hint about those animals or sell you a replacement."

"Then I'll walk until I find someone who will. I want my horse back, and I want the man responsible for stealing him!" He felt as strongly about Buck as Grandma did about her cats . . . or little Audrey about her pet chicken.

"No! Jean-Marc would only turn his wrath on you for help-ing."

"Look, Mira, he can't keep this up. Audrey needs milk. The women need bread and meat. Without those hens you won't have eggs and you can't do any baking."

He glanced at the empty livery, missing the familiar sight of Buck nickering for attention. This time Portier had gone too far!

"I know." She burst into tears. "Do you not think I know it? I pray about this every day and night, but God does not listen. Other than give in to Jean-Marc, what must I do?"

He drew her close and held her until her emotion was spent. She rested her head on his chest, sniffing as the emotional storm subsided. She felt good in his arms, like she had a right to be there.

"Oh, Trey, I'm going to have to give in to him. I cannot bear to see the others suffer anymore. Little Audrey should not pay for my sins."

He couldn't let her do it. "There has to be a way to stop the man. We just haven't found it."

"There is not," she stated with resignation in her voice. "He will never let me go. Never."

"He did once." Trey didn't like to think about her husband even though she'd confessed that she had married him only to escape Jean-Marc's domination. "Mira, this goes beyond all that's sensible. Either the man is insane or he has some other reason besides forcing you to give in. What's going on?"

Mira dried her eyes and stepped back. "I cannot tell you that."

"You *have* to tell me. I'm fighting in the dark here. Whatever the reason, it can't be that bad."

"It is." She turned her face away. "It will cause you to think ill of me."

"Never." He tilted her chin up so she had to look into his eyes. "Listen, Mira. I think you're one brave lady; nothing can ever change that."

He felt her shudder. "It is not my secret."

The words were spoken so low he could barely hear them.

"Then whose secret is it?"

She was silent and he gave her a little shake.

"Come on, Mira. Don't hold out on me. Anything you tell me will be held in confidence. I'd never betray you."

"I know." She sniffled. "Oh, Trey, it is so sad."

"Life can be hard sometimes."

He waited for her to go on.

Finally she sighed. "Jean-Marc is not my father."

"He's not?"

Anything Trey had ever thought of saying went straight out of his mind.

She stepped back and averted her face. "You are repulsed by this, no?"

"No." Trey looked down at her, taking in the downcast eyes, the humiliated expression, and his heart lurched when he realized how hard this was for her. "Then what is this all about?"

She drew a deep breath, wincing as if the effort hurt. "My parents were not married."

He shook his head. "I don't care about that, Mira. It doesn't have anything to do with you. None of this is your fault." She lifted her gaze to his, and he could see a flicker of hope in their depths. "So what is the real reason he wants you back?" he asked softly.

Anger blazed in her eyes. "Jean-Marc *murdered* my parents."

For the second time Trey felt the air driven from him. He shook his head, trying to clear his thoughts. "You're sure about this?"

From her expression he had the sense that she was about to erupt. "All right, I guess you are, but you're hitting me awfully hard with these revelations."

"It was at your insistence I *hit* you, as you say."

"Does anyone else know this?"

She shook her head. "Just me. He wants me under his control so I cannot talk about it."

Or he wanted to shut her up permanently.

Trey's blood ran cold. "He keeps the men away from Sassy Gap so no one will marry you and take you away," he guessed.

Mira dabbed at the corners of her eyes with her handkerchief. "Not much chance of that. Paul is dead, and no man will ever come close to me with Jean-Marc's tyranny hanging over him."

A smile creased the corners of Trey's mouth. "I'm a man. I'm standing right here, fairly close."

She glanced up, color flooding her cheeks. "It—it is not the same. You are not here because of me."

"Well, I'm sure not here because of Grandma Speck."

They looked at each other and then burst into strained laughter.

He hadn't realized he was going to voice his thoughts. Now that he had, he didn't know exactly how he hoped she would react. He didn't need her thinking that he was here for her out of any personal interest. He wasn't. But Jean-Marc had taken Buck and Buck was family. Trey realized he was bordering on fighting mad. Audrey was a baby. A man couldn't stand by and allow a baby to be mistreated. Without eggs and milk and fresh meat the child would suffer, and Trey wasn't going to let that happen.

"There must be a way to fight him," he suggested.

Mira raised hopeless eyes. "How?" Her tone was flat, and for the first time Trey heard defeat in her voice.

How? That was something he needed to think about. But it could be done. No man was invincible.

"You call a meeting this evening. Tell every woman to be there."

"But why?"

"Don't argue, just call the meeting. Meanwhile, help the women look after Grandma. She's white as a sheet."

"Fred and Lois are almost as close to her as we are."

Trey was aware of the woman's deep affection for the animals. Jean-Marc knew where to hit and make it hurt.

He walked away and Mira called after him, "Where are you going?"

"To think," he said.

He had roughly six hours to come up with a plan that would pit eight women and one man against the most powerful man in the community and all the resources he had to carry out his evil deeds.

Six months wouldn't be long enough.

Jean-Marc sat by the fire in the library, staring into the flames and nursing a glass of his favorite red wine. The house creaked in the wind, even one as well built as Belmonde. Last night's mission had gone off well. Every animal owned by the women of Sassy Gap had been taken. Curt Wiggins had claimed McAllister's black stallion for his own.

His lips curled in a sneer. Wiggins was probably safe enough. Even if McAllister could manage to walk to Mignon, he seemed too well mannered to take on a dirty fighter of Wiggins' caliber. True, the Kansan had been in the war, but he had survived without a scratch, which said he had been incredibly lucky or extremely cautious.

He frowned. Of course, stealing McAllister's horse meant he was stranded in Sassy Gap with no transportation, which could be a problem. The man had already made a nuisance of himself by putting out the fire at the funeral parlor. He had even had the temerity to come here, seeking to negotiate a peace between him and Mira. This McAllister was an interfering busybody. It would be far better to send him on his way. Wiggins would have to return the stallion.

The last thing he needed was McAllister hanging around. If the fool stayed he'd have to get rid of him.

Permanently.

That evening, the women met in the funeral parlor. Rose-colored lamps threw a ghostly glow across the room. Outside rain was starting to fall.

Trey stepped up on the dais and removed his hat. They were all waiting to hear what he had to say. Precious little, if he had to admit it. He'd racked his brain all afternoon. Prayed until he was about prayed out, and the only idea he'd hit on seemed almost too foolish to speak out loud. He ran a hand through his hair in frustration and was rewarded by overhearing a conversation between Dee and Vivian, who were seated in front of him and didn't bother to lower their voices.

He watched Viv elbow Dee. "*Ummm ummm ummm.* Just look at that man."

"I see. I see." Dee grinned.

Trey felt the blood rush to his face.

Viv lowered her voice, but not low enough. "Has he called on you yet?"

Dee's features remained aloof. "What makes you ask?"

"Just wondering. You seem to think he has designs on you."

"No more than you think he has for you." She straightened a pleat at her waist. "Has he called on you?"

"Dear me." Viv kept her eyes on the dais, while Trey tried to avoid looking at either of them. "Aren't we nosy tonight?"

Dee turned to face her. "Well, has he?"

Viv lifted a shoulder. "That's for me to know and you to find out. A lady never tells her business."

Dee looked away. "He hasn't."

"You don't know that!"

He hadn't, Trey could tell them both. And he didn't intend to.

"He hasn't," Viv conceded.

Mira slid into a seat beside Dee and the conversation ceased. Brenda led Grandma Speck into the parlor and seated the still-red-eyed woman on the front pew. Fred and Lois had been with Grandma for thirteen years; their sudden disappearance was shocking and inexcusable. Trey knew no one wanted to think that Jean-Marc would have destroyed the animals, but not a one doubted his perseverance.

Brenda pecked on the podium, trying to silence the gathering. "Ladies. Shut up! Mr. McAllister has something to say."

The women quieted.

Brenda might not be the last word in tactfulness, but you had to admit she got results. Trey cleared his throat. "Good evening."

Several echoed the greeting. They trained their gaze on the stranger they hoped would be their savior.

"I asked Mira to call the meeting tonight to see if we can come up with a way to put an end to this dispute once and for all."

Grandma Speck stared at the crumpled hanky in her fist.

"I don't think I have to point out that you have a big problem," he began.

Heads nodded. Trey was saddened when he looked at their expectant expressions. They seemed to think he could work some sort of miracle, and miracles were something he was fresh out of. All afternoon he'd wrestled with the question: how could you defend a town with no resources against a man who had everything? He'd come up with pitifully few answers.

Jane spoke up. "Are you saying that you're willing to help us?"

A murmur went up. Mira shifted in her seat, eyes focused on him. If it wasn't for her he would be long gone by now. Instead, he was holed up in a town with eight helpless females. The hour was fast approaching when he would either have to fish or cut bait. He knew he'd fish.

At the moment his instincts told him to ride on and let the women come to the inevitable conclusion that either Mira would return to Jean-Marc's protection or they would have to abandon Sassy Gap and move so far away that Mira's father could never find them. Portier knew that right now he had easy prey. That's what angered Trey. The women were virtually helpless because they had no money and no viable way to flee. They needed men to help them fight, and Trey was the only man around.

But he couldn't stay forever. Time was running out for him in Tyrone, Kansas, too. He'd received a wire from Jack saying he'd paid the taxes but the girls needed him to plant late crops and mend fences if he hoped to raise the money to get the farm out of hock. Trey looked at Mira's expectant face and knew he couldn't leave her behind. Not unless he did something to change her circumstances. Although he didn't want to, he would have to go up against Jean-Marc and his bullies. Considering the way he was outnumbered and outgunned the decision seemed insane. A verse flickered through his mind: *"If God be for us, who can be against us?"* He surely hoped God was weighing in on his side.

Addressing Jane's question, Trey shook his head. "I'm only one man; even if I should agree to help I can't do much against Jean-Marc's crowd. He has at least a dozen men and the will to carry his fight to the bitter end."

Brenda nodded. "Which should be approaching soon. The animals are gone. We have no fresh water or eggs or butter. We don't even have glass in our windows."

"We can live without eggs and butter, and we can tack animal hides across the windows." Grandma Speck lifted her red-rimmed eyes. "We can get our water from other sources until the pool clears, but we can't allow evil to succeed. Jean-Marc has to understand that he cannot force his will on others."

"But the Good Book says that we should live peaceably, that vengeance is His." This came from Dee.

"The Good Book also says an eye for an eye," Viv argued. "Look how God dealt with evil in the Old Testament. Time after time when He'd had enough He destroyed whole cities, includ-

ing the women and children. Surely God doesn't approve of
Jean-Marc's cruelty."

"But we are not God." Mira's soft accent filtered through
raised voices. The room silenced. Eyes focused on the young
French girl, the source of the trouble.

"We are not God," she repeated, "and the only logical way to
end this war is for me to return to Jean-Marc's home."

"Never," Grandma Speck declared. "As long as I draw breath
I will not allow you to be under that man's thumb."

Other voices lifted in protest

Brenda offered her thoughts. "If you left, Mira, then we
would be forced to go our own ways. Without you to help,
Grandma would have to close the parlor and without it we
would have no funds."

"Others could help Grandma—"

Dee broke in. "You know that isn't true. We've talked about
it and no one other than you can—or will—do all that needs to
be done to those bodies before a funeral. The washing, the
combing of hair, dressing the body. We can pass out service
cards and even help carry remains to their final resting place,
but I, for one, cannot do what you and Grandma do. I'd swoon.
Honestly."

The women wagged their heads in agreement.

"You can't leave, Mira. There has to be a way to best your
father."

Hopeful looks turned back to Trey, who had stood silently
by and listened to the exchange.

"There are only two solutions that I can see: One, you move
the town so far away that Jean-Marc won't be able to find you.
Two, Mira goes home."

Even he hated the second alternative. It was as if he and Sassy Gap were throwing Mira to the wolves, but he had to give her a choice. Then he'd consider what he could do to save her.

Brenda crossed her arms. "How could we even *think* of moving? The horses are gone; we have nothing to pull the buckboards and barely enough money to feed ourselves. Nobody for a hundred miles around is willing to sell us squat. Without the hens and milk cow, we'd have nothing to eat except the fresh game we'd manage to kill, and the summer vegetables we've raised, which wouldn't last long.

"Besides that, where would we go? We'd have to travel hundreds of miles to escape Jean-Marc's power."

"I'm willing to take you to Kansas with me."

Heads pivoted back toward Trey.

"My sisters would take you under their wing."

"I will go home." Mira's abrupt announcement stilled the women's voices.

"No!" Viv cried. "Then Jean-Marc has won, and your life would be over. He would arrange a loveless marriage, and you would be caught in his trap forever."

Mira's dark eyes clouded. "I know."

Trey spoke again. "Or we can stand and fight."

Arrange a marriage? Where had that come from? Something else she hadn't told him? He hated to think what kind of man Portier would choose for the young woman he hated.

"We?" Viv asked.

"You," Trey corrected. "I'll help but I want you to learn to defend yourselves." His gaze met Mira's. "For starters, we post guards at each end of the street. When anyone approaches the guard can sound the alarm."

"Then what? How do we fight back? We have no guns, except yours, and even if we had more we're women. We can't fight men."

Trey considered what she said, hoping for inspiration. "How many tomatoes do you have?"

The women exchanged puzzled looks.

"The early vines are still producing," Jane said. "The late ones are just starting to bloom."

"There's your weapons. How about apples?"

"There's a grove in back of the livery," someone said.

Trey nodded. "Tomorrow morning, we'll strip every vine and tree branch. How many baskets do you have?"

"Plenty," Jane volunteered. "And if we run out we'll use buckets."

The women were starting to get excited, babbling among themselves.

"Jean-Marc will likely target the orchard next. With the water gone, the fish dead, the stock missing, he'll hit the last of your food supply. We'll be ready this time."

The boast sounded foolish even to him. How could he hope to defeat a mob with a bunch of women throwing apples and tomatoes?

God, this won't work.

Yet one plus God is a majority.

Trey swallowed. He didn't know where the words came from, but he'd go with them. It wasn't as if he had a choice.

Melody stood up. "We have a couple of bushels of turnips in the root cellar."

"And there's that row of walnut trees on the north end of town."

A grin spread across Trey's features. "A turnip can leave quite a goose knot on a man's head. How's your aim, ladies?"

Most shook their heads negatively.

"Tomorrow morning, sunup, I'll teach you how to throw. Now don't tell me that some of you haven't hurled a rolling pin or something similar at a man, some time or another."

Laughter broke out and the mounting tension eased.

"But, Mr. McAllister?"

The room quieted.

"Yes, Jane?"

"This will only temporarily delay anything Jean-Marc tries. We need a permanent solution."

Women's voices rose, agitated now.

Trey motioned for silence, his features sobering. "Jane's right; tomatoes, turnips, and apples are temporary fixes. But they're the best we can do for the time being."

Grandma Speck slowly got up, leaning on her cane. "We might not beat Jean-Marc's men, but we can hurt 'em," she said. "If I find out who took Fred and Lois I'll whop 'em up the side of the head until they see stars."

Others nodded.

Viv reached out to take Mira's hand. "No more talk of leaving. We're in this together. We'll fight with whatever means we have, and if that doesn't stop your father then we'll find other ways."

Mira squeezed Viv's fingers. "Thank you." Tears brimmed her eyes.

Someone suggested they draw to see who would stand guard tonight. Nobody trusted Jean-Marc to wait long to finish off Sassy Gap. Names were thrown in a hat and each woman drew a piece of paper. Someone had already decided that when Melody's turn came up the others would look after Audrey. Since the women all slept in the community hall no one would notice the extra work.

The luck of the draw put Brenda and Jane on the first watch.

Trey put on his rain slicker. "I'll bring the turnips up from the cellar. It's not likely anyone will do anything tonight because of the weather. If they show up tomorrow we'll be waiting."

"I can't hit the broad side of a barn," Jane informed him.

"Well, I can, and I'll stand watch with you ladies tonight."

So it was decided. Sassy Gap would fight back with turnips, tomatoes, hedge apples, and cooking apples.

"Mighty poor choice of weapons," Trey muttered to himself as he left the parlor. "But it's all we've got right now." He stopped to look up at the sky. "Lord, if You've got a spare miracle no one else needs, I'd appreciate it if You'd send one our way."

"I won't do it."

Jean-Marc whirled from where he stood staring into the fireplace. "What did you say?"

Curt Wiggins blanched, but he held his ground. "I won't give that stallion back. He's the best piece of horseflesh I've ever owned, and I've earned him doing your dirty work."

Jean-Marc approached and placed both hands on the desk, palms down. "You will do as I say."

"No, sir. Not to go against you, but I've taken a liking to that stallion and I ain't giving him up."

It took a tremendous effort, but Jean-Marc held his temper in check. Once he got that recalcitrant woman under his roof where he could contain her, he would never have to put up with scum like Curt Wiggins again.

"It is a good horse," he agreed, fighting to control his voice. "But I have better in my stable."

"But they ain't doing me no good; are they now?" Wiggins' voice was reasonable. "They belong to you. This one belongs to me. Big difference there."

"I only meant that I would recompense you for the stallion."

"What does *recompense* mean?"

"It means you give the stallion back to Mr. McAllister and I'll give you one of my horses in return."

"Now why would you do that?" Wiggins squinted suspiciously up at him. "Don't make sense to me."

Jean-Marc sighed, silently begging for patience. "I want Mr. McAllister to be able to ride out of town," he explained. "As long as he is there to help, the women will stay in Sassy Gap."

"I got a better idea. I'll just shoot him and we'll both keep our horses."

"You'll do no such thing." Jean-Marc glowered at him. "I make the decisions and you'll do this my way."

"Talk is, you didn't used to be so squeamish," Wiggins taunted. "I've heard tales of people who crossed you and were never heard from again."

Jean-Marc froze. What kind of tales? He'd been discreet in ridding himself of his enemies, or so he had believed. That was the problem with hiring thugs to do the work. You couldn't trust them. He let his voice take on the quality of cold steel, knowing the only way to control men like Curt Wiggins was through fear.

"Would you like to repeat that gossip to my face?"

Wiggins sat very still, his eyes flicking toward the door. He wet his lips and a tic appeared in one cheek. "Now, there ain't no call to get riled. I was just joshing."

"No, you weren't 'joshing.' You were trying to push me into doing what you wished. Listen to me very carefully. I give the orders. You obey the orders. You never question what I say and you never defy me. Is that clear?"

Wiggins shifted his gaze away from Jean-Marc. "There ain't no call for this. I never said I wouldn't give the horse back. If that's what you want then that's the way it will be."

"You are right, Mr. Wiggins. It will be the way I want. If you can't follow orders I will find someone who can."

And I won't need you.

He didn't speak the words aloud, but he didn't have to. Wiggins got the message all right. You could see it in the way he seemed to shrink in his chair. Jean-Marc almost smiled at the man's fear.

"How do you want me to go about giving the horse back?" Wiggins' voice trembled the slightest bit.

"I will tell you exactly what I want done."

After Jean-Marc gave explicit instructions, he dismissed the man. Wiggins appeared relieved to be allowed to leave. After-ward, Jean-Marc sat alone, savoring a final glass of wine. Curt

Wiggins had been a useful tool. Unfortunately he knew too much. Eventually he would have to be eliminated.

The sun was rising when Trey stood before the ragged ranks of his "army." What had he been thinking? How could this ragtag bunch of women stand off against Jean-Marc's hired guns? He'd picked out a target, but teaching a bunch of women to throw? Accurately? The task made fighting the Rebs seem like child's play.

"All right now. We're going to try to hit the trunk of that oak tree."

"Are we using apples or turnips to practice?" Melody asked.

Trey frowned. *Does it matter?* "Neither," he decided. "No use wasting ammunition. We'll use rocks."

The women scattered, picking up apple- and turnip-sized rocks until they had an adequate pile.

"Now I want you to step up to this line one at a time and throw as hard as you can at that tree trunk."

Dee stepped up first, squinted, firmed her lips, drew back her arm, and let fly. She missed the tree by a country mile.

Trey shut his eyes and gave an inward groan. This was going to be even worse than he had anticipated.

Vivian had a better arm. She only missed by three feet.

Melody's rock fell short of the tree. Way short. Ten feet short.

He rolled his eyes. *Lord, why did You let me ride into this mess?* These women couldn't defend a stick!

Brenda stepped up to the line, picked up a rock, drew back, and nonchalantly let fly. The rock hit the tree and ricocheted like a speeding bullet.

Trey perked up. Now that was more like it.

Three hours later the women's aim had improved considerably. They were hitting the tree two times out of three. Dee had worked out a system. If she aimed a few feet to the left she hit it every time. All she had to do was remember not to throw directly at the object she wanted to hit.

Vivian clipped the edge of the trunk and Dee clapped her hands. "How about *that*? Shoot, we're just plain good."

Trey sighed. Well, David killed a giant with a stone. Maybe with God's help these women could hold off a band of renegades with apples and turnips. Grandma Speck would be praying for them.

He took off his hat and wiped the sweat from his forehead. Prayer was about the only loaded weapon in their arsenal.

CHAPTER 8

Tomatoes and turnips. Trey would have given his last dollar for a steak but they'd eaten vegetables (and ammunition) now for three days. What they didn't set aside for defensive purposes, they ate. He was going to have to do something about this situation. He didn't want to take time away from repairing the parlor, and he wanted to stay close in case Jean-Marc's men staged a daylight raid, but he needed to go hunting.

Grandma Speck barely touched her food this evening. Trey studied the elderly woman who was wasting away before his eyes. Losing Fred and Lois was killing her as surely as if Jean-Marc had murdered her with his bare hands.

Some might say it was foolish to get so attached to animals, but when you've lost everything and have seen your husband killed in front of you by a band of marauding raiders, animals who loved you without asking anything in return could hold a tender place in your heart.

Melody sat on his right with Audrey on his left. Like they were a family. He felt cornered. He liked Melody; who wouldn't?

She was a lovely woman but she wasn't for him. He didn't know how to tell her that. Lately, she'd taken to bringing his lunch into the parlor every day and then staying to eat with him.

Audrey tugged on his sleeve, her eyes dancing. "Trey, Trey?"

"What, Punkin?"

"I found a lizard today."

"Well, how about that. What color was it?"

"Blue." Her eyes sparkled. "And it lost its tail."

"I expect it'll grow another. What happened to it?"

"It ran under a rock." She spread her hands at shoulder level. "And it's all gone."

"All gone, hey? Well, I expect that's for the best."

If Jean-Marc had men watching the women of Sassy Gap, he had to know there was a young child here. What kind of heathen could wage war against a child? A mighty determined one.

Melody planted her hand on his arm, claiming his attention. "Trey, dear. See that Audrey eats her greens, please."

Trey recoiled. *Dear?* Both Viv and Dee looked like they'd bitten into sour pickles. He fought an urge to gently correct Melody, denying the endearment. But that would only embarrass her, so he let it pass.

His gaze found Mira sitting beside Grandma Speck, urging her to eat a bite more. He didn't have to worry about her calling him *dear*. She'd not had much to do with him lately.

Audrey slanted a rebellious look up at him.

He nodded at her. "Eat your greens."

Her chin raised a fraction. "Don't want to."

"Don't blame me. Your ma just passed the order on down."

"I don't like greens."

Melody nudged him. "Make her eat them. She can't do what she wants."

He'd had enough. "I'm not getting into this battle. She's your daughter. You make her eat them."

He caught the smirk Dee gave Viv and the way Melody's lips tightened and her cheeks flushed. If he didn't get out of this town he was headed for big trouble. He pushed away from the table and rose.

"I'll go hunting tomorrow. It's time we had some fresh meat."

He heard Audrey's wail as he shut the door behind him. "Come back, Trey. I'll eat greens."

Mira stood as the door closed behind Trey. She hadn't missed the exchange between him and Melody, nor the silent messages Dee and Viv sent each other with smirks, raised eyebrows, and facial gestures. Trey was a disturbing influence in Sassy Gap but it wasn't his fault. When you put eight single women together with one man competition couldn't be far away.

She turned back to Grandma. "Eat a few bites more. The food will give you strength."

"I can't." The older woman shook her head. "I know you're trying to help, but seems like the fire's gone out of me. Guess I shouldn't place so much importance on a couple of animals, but I can't help it."

Mira took her hand. "Please, *ma chèrie*. Fred and Lois were special cats. Of course you miss them."

Grandma Speck wiped her eyes. "I never thought I'd say it, but I'm tired. Almost too tired to go on, and I don't have the passion to fight anymore. I'm ready for the good Lord to take me home."

"Do not speak that way." Mira couldn't help the shiver of fear that rippled up her spine. "We could not make it without you. Do you not know that you are our guiding light?"

"No, child, I'm not. That position belongs to the Almighty. He guides us and He lights our way."

"Ah, but you are our earthly inspiration."

Grandma Speck sighed. "Every one of us is gonna reach the end of the road someday. I've got to mine, and I'm ready. I want to go home. Silas is up there waiting for me." Her face shone with anticipation. "And there are others who have already gone on. I'm going to see them."

Mira blinked back tears. She did not like it when Grandma spoke like this.

The elderly woman reached out and touched her arm. "There, child. I'll hush up. But when you reach my years, you'll realize there are worse things than death."

"Like what, Grandma?"

"Loneliness. Or living without the Lord. That's the worst mistake a person can make. A lot of people don't have anything to look forward to, but I have eternity."

Mira nodded. "As do I and I am grateful."

She wondered about Jean-Marc. Nothing in his life pointed to a faith in God.

Forgive him. Trey's words came back to echo through her mind. No. She pushed the thought away. She could never forgive Jean-Marc Portier even though she knew the Lord Almighty commanded it.

She envied Grandma Speck's undying faith. After her first outburst she hadn't said one word against Jean-Marc. Surely she had not forgiven the man who stole her dear pets. Mira realized she needed to know the truth.

She reached out and covered Grandma's cold, frail hand with her own. "Tell me; I must know. Have you forgiven Jean-Marc for taking Fred and Lois?"

The older woman blinked and stared at her as if pulling her thoughts back from a distance. "What? Do what?"

"Have you forgiven—?" She could not go on.

A sad but peaceful expression flickered over Grandma Speck's face. "Forgiven him? Of course I have. I had no choice."

"No choice?" Mira choked on the words. "Look at all he has done to you: set fire to your business, stolen your pets—"

"Oh yes, and I'll not say it was easy, but with God's help, all things are possible."

"But Jean-Marc never asked your forgiveness. Why are you required to forgive him when he never says he is sorry?"

Grandma sat quietly, looking thoughtful. Mira tried to respect her silence. Finally Grandma sighed. "The Bible does teach God does not forgive an unrepentant sinner."

"So why would God expect us to do something He won't do?"

"Child, remember our Savior hanging on that cross? He'd been abused, spit upon, and now He was dying. He looked down on those people who were laughing and talking like His crucifixion was a party, and do you remember what He said?"

Mira almost whispered the words. "'Father, forgive them; for they know not what they do.'"

Grandma nodded. "Who asked His forgiveness?"

Trey wandered toward the shed. He didn't particularly like sleeping in a stable, but if it was good enough for the baby Jesus it was good enough for him. And it was a whole lot better than a half-burned funeral parlor, where Grandma Speck and Mira were liable to bring in a dead body any time. During the war, he'd slept anywhere he could, but if he ever got home he was going to sleep on fresh sheets in a real bed every night for the rest of his life.

He didn't rightly know who would wash those sheets, but in a pinch he could probably handle it.

He stopped to check the creek. Ordinarily he'd be taking water to Buck, but Jean-Marc had put an end to that. He would walk to Mignon and ask about the stallion. He couldn't help but believe that Buck was around somewhere close. His resolve hardened to get his four-legged companion back.

The creek, naturally fast-flowing water, was starting to heal itself, although it would take some time for the fish to come back to the pond. He'd helped the women rig rain barrels to catch runoff from the roof, and the way it had been raining, they had plenty of drinking and cooking water.

Trey climbed to the hayloft, spread his bedroll on a pile of soft hay, then stretched out, staring into the darkness. Stars visible through a window made heaven seem close tonight. He felt closer to God when he could look at the sky and see the glories of the Master's hand.

Tonight it was difficult to appreciate God's handiwork. He was in a mess. He never should have come back to Sassy Gap. Even if he repaired the fire damage and replaced all the animals, what was to stop Jean-Marc from sending his hired monkeys back to destroy everything again?

He'd been brought up to respect others and their property as well. Wanton destruction to get your own way seemed cowardly to him. So did hiring someone to do your fighting for you. That might be the way men acted in Louisiana, but not in Kansas.

And then there was Melody. He was starting to feel trapped. She seemed to be taking a lot for granted. He saw her as one of eight women, nothing else, but he had a strong hunch she was entertaining hope for something more.

His thoughts turned to Mira. He wanted to take her away from Sassy Gap, but he knew that wasn't the answer. Jean-Marc, unless convinced to do otherwise, would hunt her down. She couldn't run fast enough or far enough to escape that hard, bitter man. Besides, it was too late for her to run. The battle had gone on for too long. For Jean-Marc it was more than a matter of saving face. He couldn't afford to let her go.

Mira had the ammunition that could destroy Portier if she ever chose to use it. So far she had decided to protect her mother's memory, but everyone had a breaking point. He had a feeling Mira was approaching hers.

He sighed. Every instinct told him to leave, but it was too late for him, too. He tried to deny it, but he couldn't. He had to deal with the truth. He was emotionally involved with both Mira and Audrey. He couldn't abandon them to Jean-Marc's ruthless manipulation.

They'd taken Buck.

Now they'd stepped on his ugly side.

Mira sat by the fireplace, staring into the flames. Grandma was growing weaker every day. The situation here was worsening instead of getting better. The women would be better off if she surrendered. She could let Jean-Marc win the battle for now. But she knew it wasn't that simple. Once she gave in she would never have the courage to fight again.

Melody sat down in the cane-bottomed rocker across from her. "Audrey is so fond of Trey."

"I can see that."

Mira didn't want to talk about Trey. At least not with Melody. She'd seen the way the two of them ate dinner together every day.

Melody smiled. "He's going hunting tomorrow. We'll have fresh meat."

Mira nodded. "It will be nice to have something besides vegetables to eat." And it would. So why did she have a strong urge to strike this lovely woman, to wipe that possessive look off Melody's face?

Brenda joined them, leaning against the rock wall of the fireplace. "I heard Trey say he's going hunting. I think I'll go with him."

Melody's expression hardened. "He doesn't need any help. I'll bet Trey's an excellent shot."

"I'm a good shot too," Brenda said. "With both of us hunting we could bring home more meat."

Melody cleared her throat. "I believe you have someone coming to have their horses shod tomorrow. You'll be busy."

Brenda's eyes narrowed. "How do you know? No one's mentioned it to me."

"I was here when Grandma set up the appointment. It slipped my mind until this moment." Melody smiled. "I don't guess you'll be able to go hunting with Trey."

Mira got to her feet. "I think I will go to bed."

She walked away but not before she heard Melody say, "Poor Mira. I don't think Trey's interested in her at all, do you?"

No, Mira confirmed silently, *he is not interested. And I do not want him to be.*

Rain fell again the next morning. Still Trey shot and field dressed a doe after dawn. He packed the fresh meat back to town, thinking how much he missed Buck. He'd never realized how many things he needed a horse for until he found himself without one. He missed the other animals too. Having lived on the prairie all of his life, he'd grown up depending on livestock for his livelihood.

The women were more excited over the fresh venison than they would have been over a bag of money. It brought home to

Trey how important the basics were. Folks could live without luxuries, but the women of Sassy Gap were getting short on the basic requirements for living. He wondered how much longer they could hold out.

He looked at the sky, searching for a break in the clouds. He was so sick of wet weather. Everything he touched felt damp. Rooms smelled musty; clothing felt clammy. After breakfast the rain slackened, and he decided to go down by the creek to look for wood. Jane could use some to bake those wonderful biscuits in the cookstove oven.

Brenda called out a greeting when he passed the black-smith shop. He waved at her and trudged on. Business had picked up there recently—a good sign. Trey had a hunch most of the men patronizing the smithy were Jean-Marc's spies. He didn't trust them, but their money spent as well as the next man's.

He dragged up wood, planning to carry it to the community building later, where he'd use an ax to cut it into stove-length pieces. A footstep in the loose gravel brought him spinning around. Mira was walking up the creekbank toward him. "What are you doing out here?"

Her shoulders lifted in an expressive shrug. "I needed to get away for a while. Too many women together for too long is . . . most annoying."

He grinned. "It can get irritating sometimes."

"You do not seem to find Melody irritating?"

"You jealous?"

He liked to see the flush spring to her cheeks.

"Of course I am *not* jealous. Do not be so certain of yourself. I would not have you as a precious gift."

He laughed and started to protest, but an object floating in the river caught his eye. He paused, staring at the thing.

"What's that?"

"What?" She swung around to see were he was pointing. "Oh, my! It is a casket!"

"The one you covered with canvas?"

"Mr. Getster!" she exclaimed.

"Jean-Marc's men must have brought it down here and put it into the creek."

She ran toward the edge of the swollen stream, slipping and sliding in the mud.

Trey followed on her heels. *No way can we catch that thing.* Obviously they were going to try, though.

Mira glanced over her shoulder. "We have to get it! Grandma Speck will be beside herself. If anyone hears about this it will ruin her sterling reputation!"

Lord, I do not want to do this. "Who in their right mind would blame Grandma? With all this rain nobody could dig a grave."

"Oh, many will blame her! It would be one more thing for Jean-Marc to use against us." She scrambled after the bobbing casket.

Well, if they had to, they had to. Trey ran along the creek bank, following the casket as it bounced along on the surface of the high water. He could hear Mira scrambling over the gravel bed.

Fortunately, the casket caught on the branches of a fallen tree. Here the water ran swift but was so muddy Trey couldn't see how deep it was. The only thing he knew for certain was that he didn't want to wade out into it. This bayou country was thick with snakes and gators. He'd heard men talk around army campfires, and he knew enough about gators to know he didn't want to meet up with one.

Mira didn't hesitate to plunge out into the waist-deep water and make her way toward the stalled casket.

Trey watched, hands on his hips. Why hadn't he just ridden on through Sassy Gap that day?

He had no choice. He couldn't let a woman make him look like a coward. Stepping gingerly, he waded out beside her. They reached the casket at the same time, and he pulled Mr. Getster loose from the branches. He'd float the box around the obstruction and push it to shore.

A chunk of driftwood hit him in the back, startling him so much he let go of the casket. It bobbed on down the creek, riding the swift current.

"We're losing it!" he yelled.

Trey lunged forward, actually getting his fingers on the smooth pine before his feet went out from under him and he went down with a splash that sent waves slapping against the shoreline.

He struggled to his feet, spitting muddy water. The things he went through for this woman!

The casket bounced along before coming to ground at the end of a mudflat.

Trey grabbed Mira's hand, and they started wading across the thick, gooey mud. Just to help her keep her balance, he told himself. The fact that her hand felt soft and fragile in his had no bearing on his sudden quickened heartbeat.

"Whoops!" One foot slid out from under him, bringing him down to his knees. More cold, wet mud squished over the top of his boot.

Mira pulled him to his feet. "Come on. Stop dawdling. We have to get it before it floats away again."

Dawdling? She called this dawdling? He drew a deep breath.

"Ahhh!" Mira's scream echoed off the opposite bluff when she lost her footing and sat in the sticky mud.

Trey reached down to help her up. "Dawdling, Mrs. Dupree? We have *work* to do."

She glared at him. The sparks from her eyes were enough to ignite a bonfire.

He reached the casket and paused, trying to figure how to get it back to shore. "Can you carry one end of this thing? The mud's too sticky for us to drag it."

"I will try."

She set her jaw, looking determined enough to manhandle the pinewood box by herself if need be. He had to hand it to her; the woman had grit. Trey took the front end, letting her walk forward while he backed his way toward solid ground.

"No. Wait! Hold on!" His feet slid in opposite directions and he tried to regain his balance.

"*Mon cheri*—do watch where you are stepping!"

Mira slipped and turned loose of the casket.

Trey hit the mud, twisting to one side. He heard the casket smack the ground and prayed the lid would stay shut. He was in no frame of mind to deal with Getster face-to-face.

He had been concentrating so hard on catching the box and getting it out of the water that he'd lost sight of what it held. There was a dead body wrapped in that pine box. His childhood imprisonment with Grandpa McAllister flashed through his mind.

He hauled himself to his feet. "You can take it from here, can't you?"

Mira glared at him. "Me?"

Trey shrugged. "Sure. You look pretty capable."

She pulled herself up, bracing her hands on the lid of the casket. "You are amusing me. Ha ha. You are *not* funny."

"Ha ha," he mocked and leaned over to give her nose a playful tweak. "Let's get this thing to shore."

They fell two more times before reaching a rocky shingle that joined the mudflat. Trey collapsed, exhausted, on the gravel. He prayed no other caskets had been set free.

Mira collapsed near him. Trey shot her a look that he felt should have singed the thorns off a cactus. She began to giggle.

"What?" he demanded.

"You are covered with so much mud all I can see are the whites of your eyes."

He grinned. That sounded like the old command "Don't shoot until you see the whites of their eyes."

"You should talk."

Her hands shot up to cover her cheeks. "Why?"

"You look like a mud maiden."

"I know I have a little mud on me but—"

He interrupted her with a hoot of laughter. "A little? I'd say you're packing enough mud to fill the cracks between the logs in Brenda's smithy."

She stared at him, her eyes wide in the mud mask of her face. He guessed they both looked funny. She snickered, and he threw back his head and laughed. It felt good. He hadn't done that much since the war started. Mira joined him in a good belly laugh.

He brushed the drying mud out of her eyebrows before

indicating the casket now resting on the gravel. "Look what we can do when we work together."

She sobered. "Can we work together?"

"Sure we can. We did just now."

"And you are willing to help me?" she asked.

"What do you think?"

She cocked her head prettily. "I am afraid to think."

He hesitated, aware that she was baiting him. "Just don't carry your thoughts too far," he warned.

They walked side by side on their way back to town in search of a handcart to haul the casket to the cemetery. Mira sneaked a look up at Trey. He was covered with mud from head to toe, but she knew exactly what he looked like under the disguise. Her fingers curled with the urge to reach out and touch him.

Don't carry your thoughts too far.

She would admit only to herself that she wanted more than being friends, than his "help." Much more. But a woman in her situation, with an enemy like Jean-Marc, had no right to involve anyone in her problems. She couldn't endanger Trey's life by dragging him any further into her affairs.

His temporary help. It was all she could hope for.

Trey pushed open the door to the community room, and they stepped inside. Jane dropped the saucepan she was holding, the utensil clattering to the floor.

"What happened to you!"

Trey explained, "We came to get the cart to haul Getster back to the cemetery."

"We let Jean-Marc's men violate a burial." Jane groped for a chair and sat down, her face troubled. "That's a bad sign. We'll be punished somehow. Trouble will come as sure as daylight follows dark."

Brenda shook her head. "That's foolish talk. How could we know they would go that far?"

Uncertainty crossed Jane's face. "You mark my words. Trouble will arrive before morning."

Dee picked up a potato and a paring knife. "We've already got trouble. But I can tell you one thing, I'm not about to touch that casket."

"Me neither." For the first time since Trey had entered their lives, Vivian and Dee agreed on something.

Brenda put down the shoe she had been mending.

"I'll help. I'm not afraid of a casket." Her glance raked the other three women. "Not like some I could name."

When they reached the stable Brenda and Mira waited while Trey unloaded the cart. Brenda squinted at the sky. "Looks like the weather's clearing."

"Praise the Lord!" Mira brushed ineffectively at the mud on her dress. "I have had enough mud and rain to last me a lifetime."

Trey helped the women climb into the cart and they sat down in the bed together, bracing against the rough jolting as he pulled them to the creek. With three working they got the casket onto solid ground and then into the cart. When they reached the cemetery they lowered the casket back onto the ground. Trey staked the casket to the ground with rope.

"There. That should hold it. Jean-Marc's men won't have time to tamper with Getster without someone noticing."

At least he hoped not. They'd have to cut the heavy rope and that would take time; time they didn't have.

Before dawn, Trey slipped away from town, hoping for a little privacy. Melody had shadowed his every move until he had to get out of sight for a while. She was a pretty woman, a fine woman, and he'd be the last to deny it, but sometimes a man needed breathing space. From hints the other women kept dropping, he knew they believed he had a serious interest in the young mother.

Trey cringed. He'd held his own in the war, and there wasn't a man on the face of this earth he was afraid to meet in a fair fight. He was handy with his fists and even handier with guns, but here he was sneaking out of town, afraid to be alone with a young woman he could lift with one hand. It wasn't that he was scared of marriage, but a man liked to have a hand in the picking. Melody doing all the chasing sort of took the fun out of it.

If it had been Mira, now, he wouldn't mind being chased. He remembered the way they'd scrambled through the mud, maneuvering the casket out of the creek. A grin tugged at his lips. She was a woman who would stand beside her man. A fighter, but feminine, soft and sweet—

He stopped, staring in disbelief through a gap in the brush

lining the creekbanks. There, tied to a low limb in plain sight, stood Buck. Trey resisted the urge to shout. Buck was back! He froze in position, letting his gaze search the clearing, noting for the first time the utter silence. Not a bird calling. He crept closer, muting his footfalls. Buck hadn't tied himself to that tree. So you could bet someone was hiding, waiting for Trey McAllister to walk into a trap.

Well, that wasn't going to happen.

His gaze searched the surrounding brush, looking for someone or something out of place. Nothing. Ten minutes passed. A squirrel chattered off to his right. A mockingbird came in for a landing, but swerved away at the last minute. Something had disturbed the squirrel and startled the bird. He mentally marked the spot before slipping away, working through the brush as silently as the Kaw Indians he had trailed back home.

He trod lightly, careful not to step on a fragile twig or loose rock. For once he was grateful for the rain rustling through the leaves overhead, masking any sound he might make. Trey worked down the creekbank until he could wade across unseen. Safe on the other side, he crept through the screening of brush until he could see a broad back, a drooping, rain-soaked hat brim, a rifle held at the ready.

Trey took a position behind the crouched figure. "Looking for someone?" he asked genially.

The man spun around, looking startled at the sight of the pistol pointed at his chest. "Uh. . . I was . . . huntin'. That's it, huntin'."

Trey eyed him silently, letting him sweat. "That your horse?"

"No . . . no, but I noticed him. Nice bit of horseflesh, if I do say so."

"You the rotten, lily-livered swine that stole him?" For the first time Trey let a flicker of anger shine through his words.

"Who, me? Why, no, I wouldn't do a thing like that. I'm no horse thief."

"Because if you did, let me tell you what we do with horse thieves where I come from. We hang 'em."

The man blanched. "What were you sneaking up behind me for?" he blustered. "What you want?"

"The truth. I know who you are, because I overheard you bragging about planning to poison the water supply at Sassy Gap."

The man shook his head. "No *sir*. You didn't hear me say no such thing. You got me all wrong, friend."

"I'm not your friend. Your name is Curt Wiggins and you work for Jean-Marc Portier and you stole the animals from the women at Sassy Gap on his order. Now you've brought my horse back, and I want to know why."

The man wilted. "All right, I'll talk. My life ain't worth much anyway. I'm a walking dead man."

"Why's that?"

"Because I crossed Portier. I took the animals, but I had help."

"From Portier?"

A sneer crossed Curt's face. "You won't catch him doing anything to get his lily-white hands dirty. He hires people like me looking for an honest day's wage to do his dirty work for him."

"I wouldn't call what you did particularly honest. How did you cross Jean-Marc?"

"He told me to bring the horse back so you'd ride out of town and I said no."

"And—?"

"Nobody says no to Portier. So I brought the horse back, and I know that he'll kill me when I've done what he wants. I could see it in his eyes." He motioned to Buck. "I got mad when you helped put out the fire. Made me look bad to Portier. He blamed me because it didn't burn. I was aiming to shoot you and take the horse and make a run for it."

Trey shook his head in disbelief. "You planned to kill me because I got in your way? How are you different from Jean-Marc?"

"How?" Curt stared at Trey, his expression incredulous. "Can't you see? You're still *alive*. I didn't get the job done. Jean-Marc Portier don't fail. You're alive. I won't be. It's that simple."

Trey sighed. The man's logic was beyond his understanding. "What did you do with the other animals?"

"Well, there's where I crossed him again. I was supposed to shoot them, but I couldn't do it. Shooting a man, now, well, it's lead-shot sure that man's done something real bad somewhere. Probably deserved to be shot. But an animal, it ain't hurt no one. It's just plain wrong to kill an animal unless you got a need."

Trey listened to Wiggins, bemused. Something was wrong with this thug's thought process. He lifted the pistol from where he had absent-mindedly lowered it during the past dialogue. "You're going to take me to them."

"Now why would I do that?" Curt asked reasonably. "There ain't nothing in it for me."

"That's where you're wrong," Trey said. "Because if you don't I'm going to shoot you. Not enough to kill you, just enough to hurt."

Curt stared at him. "You mean that, don't you?"

Trey nodded.

"Tell you what," Curt said. "I'll make you a deal. I'll show you where the animals are if you'll turn me loose after we get them back here."

Trey thought it over. He didn't want to kill the man. He was against shooting someone made in the image of God unless it was absolutely necessary, and he did want to get the women's animals back. He didn't see how he could manage it without help.

"If I turn you loose you'll go straight back to Jean-Marc."

Curt shook his head. "You're dead wrong on that, friend. That's the one place I can't go. I'm heading west as fast as I can ride. Hear a man can make him a fortune out there."

Trey figured all Curt would make was trouble, but as long as he was making it far from Sassy Gap that was good enough.

"You got a horse?"

"Got him tied back in the brush a ways," Curt said. "Tell you what, I'll just hop on behind and you can give me a lift."

"Why don't you think again? I'm not stupid enough to turn my back on you. Hand me your rifle and start walking."

Curt shrugged. "Whatever you say."

Wiggins led the way to where his horse was tied out of sight. Trey followed, mounted on Buck. It felt good to be astride a horse again. A man wasn't complete without his horse.

As soon as Curt was in the saddle they followed a winding path through the woods. After a bit they came out to a small clearing and a rough pen where the cows and horses were confined.

Trey watched as Curt opened the gate and drove them out. "What were you planning to do with them when you left?

Curt shrugged. "I'd have turned them loose. They'd have made it all right—plenty of grass and water."

Trey cast a look at the darkening sky. Plenty of water? Curt had called that right. They'd had more rain in the past few weeks than Kansas got in a year.

Curt swung into the saddle. "If it's all right with you, I'd just as soon get these critters back where they belong. I've got some serious riding to do."

"Wait a minute," Trey objected. "There were some chickens and a bunch of cats."

"Well, yeah, I guess there were," Curt agreed. "I turned them loose. Never had any luck with chickens. I'm a cow-and-horse man myself, and those cats scratched and carried on something awful till I let 'em go."

"Where?"

"Where what?" Curt asked.

Trey sighed. "Where did you turn the cats loose?"

"Oh. Well back in the brush a ways. I figured they'd either find their way back home or a fox would git 'em. Not much loss if one did."

Trey thought of Grandma Speck grieving her heart out for those two cats and wanted to knock this worthless piece of humanity out of the saddle.

"Tell me," he said. "Those tricks pulled on the women. Were those your ideas or Jean-Marc's?"

"Most of them were mine," Curt bragged. "All except stealing the animals. Portier thought of that."

"Didn't bother you going up against a bunch of women?"

Curt leaned his arms on the saddle horn. "No, can't say it did. It was a job; that's all."

They had reached the creek now, and the animals, sensing home, plunged across and trotted up the path toward Sassy Gap.

"You going to let me go now?" Curt asked. Trey didn't answer and he protested, "That was part of the deal. I thought you were a man of your word."

"Are you?" Trey asked.

"No, don't guess I am," Curt admitted. "You can trust me on one thing though: I want to be a long way from here before Portier finds me gone."

"All right," Trey handed him his rifle. "You'll need this. Get going and don't look back. I'll be watching."

"Friend, you got my word on it."

Trey figured that was about as much good as a boat in a sandstorm.

The outlaw reined his horse to leave, and then twisted around in the saddle. "I'll give you one good piece of advice. If you go up against Jean-Marc Portier—and you will if you hang around Sassy Gap—don't show any fear. He takes it as a sign of weakness."

"I'll remember that," Trey said. He watched until Curt was out of sight. Then he followed the animals to Sassy Gap.

CHAPTER 9

Elation filled the town when the animals were safely back in the barn. All but the cats. Grandma viewed the stock, then turned and walked away, her grief still evident.

In the communal kitchen the next morning, Trey tossed Audrey up in the air, then pretended to drop her. The child squealed with delight. The game had become a daily ritual, one they each looked forward to. Mira realized it was part of the strong devotion Trey was developing for the little cherub. Audrey, for her part, dogged his footsteps, demanding his attention.

"Again!" she exclaimed.

"Again? Okay, here we go!" He threw her up, caught her, and then pretended to let her drop into the dirt.

Mira listened to the playful antics while she hung wash, wondering how long it would take Trey to recognize his feelings for Melody. From the moment he had come back, she had watched the attraction bloom. Melody took Trey's dinner to him every day. The three would go off to eat their noon meal together, sitting beneath an oak. Mira watched the small family group with envy festering in her heart.

But she wasn't the only one who longed for Trey McAllister's attention. Dee and Viv trailed him around like lovesick pups. Mira thought their outright obsession was silly, but perfectly understandable.

The women of Sassy Gap had all agreed that they would stick together. They didn't need men. But that agreement flew right out the window every time a male rode through town. And now this man had stopped. And captured their hearts.

Mira turned to watch the three, drawn by the sounds of laugher. Trey had swung the little girl up to his shoulders, where she now rode, arms clasped around his neck, while he walked around the parlor inspecting his work. Bundles of new shingles caught the sun. The work would take weeks, and Mira found herself hoping that Trey planned to stay around that long. He seemed more and more anxious to leave, speaking of the need to go home, and she knew his sisters' plight weighed on his mind. One day he would leave, and she wondered if he would take Melody and Audrey with him. The thought disturbed her, and she tried to push it away by pretending indifference, but in her heart Mira knew she would miss the red-haired, blue-eyed man whose friendship had become so important to her.

Evening had come and gone three times since they'd fished the coffin out of the creek and Jane's prediction that something awful would happen hadn't. So far they'd only had one night raid that resulted in men fleeing with goose eggs on their heads. Actually, Jean-Marc had been unusually quiet lately. Mira guessed Wiggins' betrayal had silenced him for a while. She turned back to the wash when she spotted Melody walking her way with a purposeful stride.

Mira paused, holding a wet shirt in her hands as Melody walked up.

"Can you do me a favor?"

Mira lifted a brow. "But of course."

"A man sent word this morning that he thought he had spotted Fred and Lois a few miles from here. Grandma got so excited that she almost had a fainting spell. So I agreed to ride over and see if I can find them."

Mira nodded. "It would be a real blessing if it turns out to be true."

"Yes, it would." Melody's eyes focused on Trey and Audrey. The two were still roughhousing. "I was wondering—I take Trey his dinner. Would it be possible for you to check on the cats for me?"

Mira felt herself stiffen. Ordinarily she'd do anything to help, but this morning she resented Melody's assumption that no one else, other than Viv and Dee, found Trey interesting. Melody hogged too much of Trey's time; others should have an opportunity to enjoy his company.

"Have you forgotten that there's a service this afternoon?"

Melody snapped her thumb and forefinger. "I had forgotten."

"Mrs. Potts."

"I remember." The young mother stood, mouth pursed in thought.

"Why don't you ask Jane or Helen to go?"

"They're finishing up the last of the canning this morning."

Mira recalled seeing the basket full of late beans on the

table. She pinned a petticoat to the line and deliberately kept her tone indifferent. "I could take lunch to Mr. McAllister."

"Yes—" Mira could see the wheels turning in Melody's head. *Competition*, she was thinking.

The nonsense of it all immediately hit Mira. Of course she didn't have the slightest designs on Trey, though she did enjoy their conversations. They had agreed to work together, and she had no intention of breaking that agreement. But she would enjoy his company, and it wouldn't hurt Melody to share this once.

The afternoon they'd rescued Getster's casket had been a special memory to dwell on when she was alone, when Trey was gone.

Melody appeared to do battle with the idea of someone else eating dinner with Trey. It took a moment for her to finally relinquish the right.

"If I hurry, I can be back before dinner."

Mira nodded. "It shouldn't take long to ride a few miles." She didn't mention the possible hours it would take to search out the leads if no one actually had Fred and Lois in their immediate possession. That was Melody's problem, not hers.

"I'll hurry." Melody spun on her heel and hiked back to the house, her mind obviously preoccupied with making a quick journey.

Grinning, Mira pinned the last of the wash to the line. Then she picked up the basket and began humming softly under her breath. What a glorious day.

Unexpectedly glorious!

Thank you, Melody.

Trey nailed down a shingle and then paused to drink from the water jug. He swiped a forearm over his brow and stared up at the sun, thankful it wasn't late August. He could work longer when the heat wasn't so insufferable. He'd heard the summers here were even hotter and more humid than in Kansas. He planned to be gone long before then.

"Mr. McAllister?"

When he recognized Mira's voice, he crawled to the edge of the parlor roof and peered down. Usually Melody was the one to come check on him.

"Up here!"

The young French girl stood below him, holding a large woven basket. He glanced back at the sky and wondered if it was noon already. Either she was early or the sun was off.

"I have brought your lunch!"

He gathered his tools and laid them in a pile before shimmying down the ladder. His boots touched the ground, and he turned to grin at her. "Where's Melody and Audrey?"

Mira brushed passed him, walking toward the spreading oak. "Someone sent word that they thought they had seen Fred and Lois a few miles from here. Melody went to check."

"Oh." His gaze roamed the empty street. "Where's the little elf?"

"She was playing when I left." Mira paused to spread a blanket over a patch of grass under the shade of the large, mossy oak. "You know how the women fuss over her when Melody isn't around."

Trey took off his hat, wiping the sweatband with a cloth. "She's a cute little thing."

"I hope you do not mind I came early. It is wash day, you know."

"How early?"

"An hour and a half." She switched subjects. "I notice that you seem taken with children."

Mira set plates and cups out and then removed a dish of turnips from the basket.

Trey sat down on the blanket and rested his back against the tree trunk.

"I am sorry there is no meat. We finished the last of the venison."

He smiled, thinking a plate of fried chicken would taste good. Chicken and dumplings. A thick steak. Fried quail—and gravy.

Mira dished up turnips, added a slice of bread, and handed him the plate.

"Aren't you going to eat?"

"I am not hungry."

He studied her small frame and decided she probably ate like a bird. She was what his sisters would call a hummingbird—small and delicate.

He took a bite of turnips. "What about you?" When she lifted an inquiring brow he clarified. "Do you like children?"

"Oh yes." She smiled. "I adore children."

"But none were born during your marriage?"

She shook her head, her eyes dark now. "None. It was a short marriage, but even had it been longer I would not have had any children."

Trey grinned. "Don't rightly know how you can say a thing like that. Children have a way of showing up unexpectedly sometimes."

"Mine will be expected," she stated.

He took another bite, meeting her gaze. "You sound pretty sure of yourself."

Settling back, she primly adjusted her dress around her knees. "I will not have a child for Jean-Marc to torment."

Trey got it and he guessed he couldn't blame her, considering what her life must have been like. She ducked her head, not looking at him. Her fingers pulled idly at grass stems. He eyed her, momentarily disconcerted. She looked so delicate, so vulnerable. A dark fury rose up inside him as he thought of Jean-Marc's harassment of this innocent woman, but he immediately tamped it down. Anger was a luxury he couldn't afford. A man could get careless when he lost his temper . . . or lost his head over a woman.

Mira looked up, her gaze catching his. A soft flush tinted her cheeks wild-rose pink. "I suppose you think I am terrible."

"I don't think that. I think you're very brave."

A lot of females would be having a bad case of the vapors if they had to put up with one-tenth of what Mira Dupree faced every day.

"Seems a shame, though." He shoveled another forkful of turnips into his mouth. "Lovely young woman like you. From what I've seen, you'd make a good mama."

She shrugged. "I love children—and someday, when Jean-Marc is gone, I will have lots of babies."

"Yeah? What if you go before Jean-Marc?"

The idea appeared foreign to her. "That cannot be—I am very young."

"I've seen men die younger than you. Doesn't seem wise to plan your future around someone else's death."

Her back stiffened and he saw that he'd struck a nerve.

"I will take my chances."

Trey finished off the bread, his eyes searching the area of the community building. "You think Audrey will come outside to play?"

"I think it will be her nap time soon."

He handed his empty plate to her. "What makes you tick, Mrs. Dupree—other than fighting Jean-Marc Portier?"

"Tick?" She seemed unfamiliar with the phrase.

"Happy. What makes you want to get up in the morning and keep going."

She sat back, her eyes distant now. He wondered if she'd ever thought about happiness. Her first marriage had not been founded on love. Then the endless fight with the man the world believed to be her father. She was young. She couldn't have experienced much happiness in her short time here on earth. So what kept the lovely Mira going?

"I do not think of such things," she said softly. "There is no time." She turned to face him. "And you? What makes you do this 'tick' thing?"

"Ah." He lay back, tipping the brim of his hat over his eyes. "The thought of going home, fixing up the home place, going to church again on Sunday mornings. Waking up to the sound of nature instead of the crack of rifles. The scent of flowers instead of the stench of death."

"You have fought long?"

"Long enough."

"And the sisters who are waiting for you. You are anxious to be with them?"

Yeah, he was anxious. He fought guilt every time he thought of home. He should be there saving the family homestead, not lingering in Sassy Gap. Trey felt torn between duties. On the one hand he had the sisters who had raised him and depended on him. On the other there was this dark-haired Cajun. One look from Mira and he forgot everything except how much she needed him. How wise was he?

"I would think you would be in a hurry to go home. The war is over and you have been gone for so long."

He grinned. "Trying to get rid of me?"

He would be in a bigger hurry if he hadn't gotten a third wire from Jack. Seemed like Sam Coulter and Toby Dakes had been helping out around the farm. Crops were planted and fences mended and it sounded like, if Ellie and Sue Ann weren't real careful, there'd be a double wedding before long.

Mira blushed. "You know that is not so. We have appreciated your help, more than we can say."

He plucked a grass stem and chewed it, thinking of how pretty she looked. "I miss them. It will be good to be home and with family again."

"Family." She shook her head. "My family is the women of Sassy Gap."

He tilted the brim of his hat slightly until he was looking directly at her. "You don't plan to remarry someday?"

She lifted one thin shoulder. "I cannot say. I did not love my husband, and I found the role of wife most distressful."

His voice softened. "Only because you didn't love your husband. Love changes everything."

She murmured a word in French. "Love is not for me."

"Ah, love is for anyone who seeks it." He pulled the brim lower. "And kids. Who wouldn't want a houseful of kids running around? Then when you're old and decrepit, they'll be there, fussing over you."

She smiled. "I thought you hated fussy women."

"Who said I'd have girls? I'm thinking four or five boys."

"Oh, so many!"

He grinned. "I suppose you want daughters."

"Oui." She picked at a thread at her waist. "The way you go on about Audrey I would think you would want this also."

"Ah, the little imp. Yes, I could take four or five little Audreys running around."

"Your family is growing rapidly, sir."

They lapsed into silence and his mind wandered. As stubborn as she could be, he admitted to himself that Mira was a charmer. Pushy, sometimes, but he didn't mind. And he didn't want to see her return to that tyrant's domineering ways. But neither did he want to get into a battle that he couldn't win. Much as he was drawn to Mira, he couldn't see any future for them. Portier was resourceful and stubborn. He and the women could hold him off just so long; and he could help them only so long.

Meanwhile, Trey realized he would have to guard his growing feelings for this woman. Hang around for a while longer to satisfy his conscience that the women were reasonably trained and armed—if potatoes, turnips, and tomatoes were a threat to anything other than the dinner table—and then move on. He could teach them to shoot, even buy them some rifles. But if their marksmanship was anything like their rock-throwing ability, they'd most likely shoot each other.

"Are you always this quiet?"

Mira's voice stirred him. "Hmm?"

"Are you this quiet when you are with Melody?"

The corners of his mouth lifted in a smile. Was that jealousy he heard in her voice? Mira?

The idea that she found him desirable pleased him, though he knew it shouldn't. Even if he were to give in to the way he felt about this woman nothing could ever come of the attraction. Portier would see Trey in his grave before he'd allow him to take Mira out of his reach.

"Now why would you mention Melody?"

The question took her by surprise. He noted the bright red that suddenly infused her cheeks.

"Well. I . . . the two of you sit together every day."

"Hmm . . . we do?" He grinned. "You noticed that?"

The teasing seemed to get under her skin, and he enjoyed the game even more.

"I did not notice. . . . I mean . . . it is not exactly a secret how you feel about Audrey." She worried the loose string at her waist.

"Now there's a little gal I could give my heart to," he conceded. "Let's see." He rolled his eyes and pretended to mentally calculate. "I'm twenty-four and she's three. By the time she's marrying age I'll be looking at forty. Old enough to be her father. But if she isn't picky, and if she doesn't mind leading her husband around on a cane, I think we might have a future."

Mira did not rise to the taunt. "Ah, but Audrey's mother is a different matter. She's twenty-two, very pretty and smart, a widow in need of a father for Audrey."

Trey slowly eased the brim of the hat up until his eyes met her. "Your point?"

"Surely you know you have many admirers in Sassy Gap."

"You don't say. And you're one of them?"

She still refused to bite. "I do say. Dee and Viv argue over you all the time, and Melody—well, she was very hesitant to let me bring your lunch today."

"You *don't say,*" he emphasized.

She nodded. "I do say. You have made quite a splash with the women."

He rose onto one elbow and whispered. "You don't suppose that's because I'm the only man in town."

She seemed to ponder the suggestion and then dismissed it. "No."

"No?"

"No. You are quite appealing."

Now *his* cheeks felt warm. Forward? He'd never thought of Mira being forward. So what was going on here? He turned slightly to look at her. "Are you flirting with me?"

She picked at the raveling thread. "You are in sad shape if you do not know when a woman is flirting with you."

Trey rolled to a sitting position and shook his head. He reached into his pocket and took out a knife. The blade flipped open, and he leaned over and cut the loose thread, dropping the cut end in Mira's lap. A suspicion formed in the back of his mind. This behavior was so unlike Mira that he knew she must be up to something. All that talk about family . . .

"Could it be that you're flirting with me in order to convince me to take you away from here?" he asked.

Dark eyes, innocent with sincerity, met his. "What an awful thing to suggest. Do you think it odd that I find you handsome and strong and—"

"More than capable of being made a fool of?" He reached over and brushed the tip of her elfin nose. "Just because I eat turnips doesn't mean I just rode into town on a wagonload of them."

She knocked his hand away in a flash of irritation. "I do not see why you won't help me! You know the trouble would stop if I left, and it's impossible for me to leave without your assistance."

"My dear Mrs. Dupree, the trouble would only intensify if I were to take you home with me."

"I do not want you to take me *home* with you. Simply take me somewhere far enough away that Jean-Marc cannot find me."

"And that would be?"

"Well—what is between here and Kansas?"

"Not enough." He reached for a second piece of bread and took a bite. "Distance isn't going to solve your problem; that ogre will find you if you run to the ends of the earth."

She shook her head. "You talk as if you have met Jean-Marc. Yes, he is evil, but if I am gone and he has to endlessly search for me—"

"He will find you."

"You do not know Jean-Marc!"

"I've met him."

She gasped.

He hadn't meant to let that slip, but she might as well know. Their one brief conversation had only reinforced what Trey knew. Jean-Marc would never give up when it came to ruling Mira.

"You have spoken with him?"

"I rode over and had a talk with him. He's everything you said: determined, mean-spirited, obsessed."

She inched closer, her eyes catching and holding his. "You spoke to Jean-Marc about me?"

Trey shifted uneasily. The sudden spark in her eyes—all soft and feminine—meant trouble.

"I wasn't talking to him about you in particular; I was talking to him about the town and what he was doing to it."

Her smile turned warm as spring honey. "You talked to Jean-Marc about me."

"About *all* of you," he corrected.

"He is most terrible; is he not?"

"What he's doing is terrible," Trey conceded. "Don't think I'm condoning his actions, but you know as well as I do that he has no intention of letting you get away from him. He'd send his cutthroats after you."

She didn't answer and he plowed on. "You know, Mira, he must have loved your mother. Surely he had some affection for you when you were very young."

He enjoyed Audrey so much it seemed impossible to believe anyone could hate a child, particularly one as cute as Mira must have been. After all, the man had to live with the knowledge he'd killed his wife. That had to hurt.

"Love." She spat the word distastefully. "He cannot *love* and do the things he does."

"When a man hurts he'll do most anything."

Trey hadn't forgotten the bitterness he'd felt over Sharon's betrayal. The pain was still strong, but it was her face that he'd seen in battle, spurring him on to vent his rage and frustration against the enemy.

In a way she'd saved his life. If it wasn't for his anger he might be dead today, though anger could never be quenched without the good Lord's help. He couldn't count the nights he'd spent on his knees, praying for a forgiving heart. Forgiveness had been slow in coming, but it had come. This was why he knew Mira had to forgive Jean-Marc. She couldn't begin to heal as long as she carried so much hatred in her heart.

Now Sharon was just another woman, and he'd learned to stay clear of women. Fair exchange.

Trouble was, Mira was right. He loved Audrey, and he sure wanted kids of his own someday. Only that required a woman's involvement, and he hadn't quite figured out how to get around that hurdle.

It was one thing in his life that his sisters couldn't do for him.

Praise the Lord.

They glanced up to see Melody running toward them. A wide smile creased her beet red cheeks.

"Hello!" she called.

Mira got up and began to gather the dishes. Trey still lazed at the base of the tree.

"Did you find Fred and Lois?" Mira asked.

Melody shook her head and slipped to the ground. She panted. Sweat rolled off her temples. "There's been several sightings of stray cats, but I couldn't find nary a one."

"You're back early," Trey observed.

"It didn't take me long to realize that Fred and Lois could be anywhere."

"Or nowhere at all," Mira murmured.

Trey heard the troubling remark. "I told you Curt said he turned them loose. You think he lied and they destroyed the cats?"

Wordlessly Mira nodded.

Melody's smile faded. "Grandma must never know what you suspect."

"Of course I will not tell her. She has not eaten a meal in days and barely takes a little broth before retiring. She is grieving herself to death."

Melody looked at Trey. "Did you eat early today?" She sent Mira a resentful look, then slipped her arm through Trey's. "No matter. I'll walk you back to work and bring you a glass of water."

Trey turned to look over his shoulder at Mira when the two walked off. "Thanks for dinner."

He'd enjoyed this time with her. He wished he could do more to help. Even though he'd met Jean-Marc and knew the man to be arrogant and abusive, even though he knew all the ways he had harassed Sassy Gap, it was hard to believe they couldn't work out a truce if they sat down and talked about their differences.

Mira didn't look his way. "Sorry there was no meat."

"I'll kill another doe. There'll be fresh venison by tomorrow night."

"Thank you."

Mira didn't need meat; what she needed was a way out, but for the time being he was fresh out of answers for that problem.

Even for a pretty French girl with eyes as sad as the opening chapters of Job.

Jean-Marc greeted his guest, although he wasn't looking forward to the coming interview. Perhaps he could put the annoyance off until after dinner. Give him more time to come up with a plausible excuse. From the look of Richard Holman III, owner of the Union Pacific Railroad, he wouldn't be in the mood to listen to excuses, plausible or otherwise. A tough man clearly not in awe of Jean-Marc Portier, his very bearing seemed to say, "You're a big man in your little corner; I'm a big man in the world." The fact that it was true did little to smooth Jean-Marc's ruffled pride. He wasn't accustomed to being held accountable to anyone.

Richard Holman accepted a chair and a fine Havana cigar. He struck a light and held it to the stogie, inhaled, and blew out a cloud of fragrant smoke. "Well, Portier? I expected to have good news from you by now regarding Sassy Gap."

Portier? Jean-Marc swallowed his indignation. "News will be forthcoming shortly. Be patient."

"I have been patient. But there comes a time for results."

Macon interrupted them to announce dinner, and Jean-Marc struggled to hide his relief. Not a moment too soon. They sat down to braised duckling with wild rice, delicate mushrooms stuffed with ham, potato soufflé, and boiled mixed vegetables.

Holman smiled in appreciation. "You set a good table."

"I always have," Jean-Marc replied. "It's my belief you can tell the quality of a man by the quality of his food."

The meal passed pleasantly enough, but as soon as Macon served after-dinner coffee and left them alone, Richard Holman returned to the subject of Sassy Gap.

"We're getting tired of waiting. Time is passing and we need answers. When will the town be vacant?"

"Soon. I assure you that negotiations are under way. The women are even now getting ready to move to a new location."

Holman stirred his coffee. He slanted a look at Jean-Marc from under bushy dark eyebrows. "Who owns that land?"

"The land will belong to me."

"But it is not yours at the present? Perhaps we should talk directly to the citizens of Sassy Gap."

Jean-Marc leaned forward in his chair. "Believe me, that is not necessary or wise. You will have the land."

"Soon." Holman set his cup on the table. It wasn't a question; it was a demand.

Jean-Marc nodded. "Soon."

After Richard Holman left, Jean-Marc called for Macon. "Send for my men. Immediately."

Thirty minutes later, the men trailed in, their apprehension showing in their dark scowls. Jean-Marc waived a negligent hand toward the chairs Macon had instructed the house servants to arrange. "Make yourselves comfortable, gentlemen. We have some things to discuss."

He waited until the last straggler found a place to rest before going to sit down behind his desk. For a few minutes he was content to let the silence stretch out, building suspense. One man shuffled his feet and another muffled a cough. Tension showed in their faces.

Jean-Marc tapped the desk with a silver letter opener shaped like a lion, savoring the similarity. He, Jean-Marc Portier, was a lion among men, forced by necessity to deal with the corrupt of the world.

"I wish to know one thing. Why are the women still at Sassy Gap?"

The lead thug, Hi Yates, cleared his throat. "We've wondered the same thing. Seems like they're awfully stubborn or someone's slipping them a little on the side to stay."

Jean-Marc eyed him coldly. "To whom would you be referring?"

"Look at it this way. We've done everything we were supposed to do and still they're hangin' on. We took their fish, their milk and eggs, and they're still there, laughin' at us. Don't seem like everything is on the up-and-up."

"Has it occurred to you that the saddle tramp has something to do with it? He's capable of hunting I suppose. After all, he was in the war."

"We can take care of him," Yates said. "You say the word and no more saddle tramp, whatever his name is."

"His name's Trey McAllister," one of the men spoke up. "He's from Tyrone, Kansas."

"Then why is he still here?" Jean-Marc's voice was silky soft.

The man looked like he wished he'd kept quiet. "He sent a wire the other day. Maybe he's planning on clearing out."

"I suppose it would be too much to hope for that you would remember the message."

The man licked his lips and swallowed. "Sure. It said, 'Home soon.'"

Jean-Marc accepted the words, but they left a bitter taste in his mouth. Apparently the man had something to do. In Sassy Gap? Something concerning Mira? He had seen the other women, and while a couple of them looked well enough in a common sort of way, they couldn't compare with Mira Dupree. He had no illusions as to what kept Trey McAllister in Sassy Gap. That liaison could never be permitted. Mira could not be allowed to drift so far away that she would feel safe to talk about what she knew.

Things were different after the war. Judges and officials Jean-Marc had once controlled were out of office now, replaced by people appointed by the Yankees, people who didn't know Jean-Marc Portier. Not yet anyway. It took time to build connections. They would, in time, learn he was the man to see if they wanted everything to run smoothly. In the meantime there was the problem of Mira and Trey McAllister. Mira, through her stubbornness, and McAllister, through a misguided attempt to help, were all that stood between him and the town of Sassy Gap.

He realized the men were waiting for him to say something. He pulled his thoughts together. "Has anyone seen Curt Wiggins lately?"

Jean-Marc still had a score to settle with that man.

Hi spoke up. "Gone."

"Gone where?"

Hi shrugged. "How would I know? I'm just one of the hired hands. I figured you'd know, seeing as how you and Curt were so thick."

Jean-Marc's eyes narrowed. "Meaning what?"

"Nothing in particular. Just that he got his orders directly from you. We got ours from him. Seemed reasonable to think you'd sent him somewhere."

"I sent him nowhere." Jean-Marc thought for a minute. "Find him and bring him to me."

"Find him?" Hi shook his head. "I was scouting around Sassy Gap this morning, and McAllister's got his horse back. I figure Wiggins hightailed it out of the country."

Jean-Marc gripped the letter opener so tightly that his knuckles bloomed white. He'd ordered Wiggins to return the stallion, but the man had obviously betrayed him.

"And that ain't all. The females got their livestock back. Horses and cows too."

"I told him to shoot those animals."

How *dare* a nothing like Curt Wiggins defy an order from Jean-Marc Portier!

"I don't know what you told him to do, but he kept them in a pen out in the woods. Curt was funny that way. He didn't mind shooting a man. Always said no doubt he had it coming. But he balked at killing animals unless it was for food. Claimed it was a waste of time."

Portier threw the letter opener across the room, shattering a crystal vase filled with roses. Water and crimson petals exploded, showering those nearby.

No one moved. It seemed as if they barely breathed.

Good. Let them see his fury. Perhaps they would think before they double-crossed him. He yanked the bellpull.

Macon arrived almost immediately. Probably lurking outside the door seeing what he could hear. You couldn't keep a secret from the servants. The thought gave Jean-Marc pause. He glanced at the butler. "Clean this up."

"Yes, sir. I'll summon one of the maids."

Uppity fool. Show him who is boss around here. "I told *you* to clean it up. Get it done."

"Yes, sir, Master Jean-Marc. Right away."

Macon gathered up glass shards and crushed flowers while the others watched in silence.

Jean-Marc let the lesson sink in. They were no better than the former slaves who served in his house. They took orders from him and they obeyed those orders. Failure to do so would result in severe penalties. He let his gaze wander around the room, looking at each man in turn.

"Where did Curt go?"

Hi Yates shook his head. "No one saw him leave. He was there one day, eating breakfast in the café, and then we never saw him again."

Jean-Marc mulled this over in his thoughts. McAllister had his stallion, the women of Sassy Gap had their animals, and Curt was gone. The man didn't have a compassionate bone in his body, so obviously he hadn't given the animals back because of a guilty conscience. Therefore someone had forced Curt to tell where the animals were. The question was, who? He'd met McAllister—definitely not the type to make a hard case like Curt Wiggins do anything.

Unless he was wrong about the man. That notion was too

ridiculous to entertain. Jean-Marc knew he was a sound judge of character. Seldom did he read a man wrong, and he hadn't been wrong about Trey McAllister. The man was the cautious, peace-loving kind. Probably one of those Christians who went around spreading sweetness and light.

Still, Curt had left the stallion behind.

He put the thought aside to be considered later. "I want those women out of Sassy Gap."

"Would be a lot easier if you'd let us go in and load them up and move them out," Hi said. "I could have wagons there by daylight. Have them out by noon, quit playing these games."

Jean-Marc pursed his lips, strongly tempted but discarding the idea with great reluctance. "No. That would cause more problems than we need."

"I don't see how," Hi said. "They're just a bunch of women; no one cares what happens to them."

"There's where you're wrong," Jean-Marc said. "A lot of people around here don't like the way we're treating them."

"Who cares what they think? They can't do anything about it."

Jean-Marc explained patiently. "Have you ever seen an uprising? I have, long ago, and it wasn't pretty."

Slaves had rioted at a plantation east of New Orleans. He'd been with the group who arrived at the burned-out shell of a house. He'd seen what they'd done to the owner of the plantation—and to his wife and daughters. The people here wouldn't do anything like that, of course, but they could rise up and cause him plenty of trouble and bring the authorities down on him. He didn't dare risk it.

"I still say we can do it," Yates said stubbornly.

Jean-Marc slapped the desktop. "Listen to me. I don't pay you to think, I don't pay you to argue with me, and I don't pay you to tell me what to do. Neither do I pay you to take off on your own and do anything I don't know about. If you can't take orders from me, then get out. Now."

No one moved, although a couple looked uncomfortable and Jean-Marc made a silent note of their names. He glanced at Macon, who had brought a broom and was busy sweeping up the slivers of glass. "Leave that. Go back to the kitchen. I'll lock up."

"Yes, sir." Macon quietly left the room.

"I take it you don't trust the butler," Hi said.

"I don't trust anyone. Now here's what we're going to do, and I want it done *exactly* the way I say."

Later, after he had locked the door behind the men, Jean-Marc climbed the stairs to his bedchamber. The upstairs maid had turned down the bedding, and a carafe of water stood handy. He sat deep in thought. Macon had come with the house. He'd been young then, and a house servant. Linette had groomed him to be a butler. In spite of her shortcomings, his wife had run a gracious, competent home. She had been trained from childhood to be the chatelaine of a fine house, and she had filled her role well.

He thought of Linette: beautiful, willful. Once he'd broken her spirit she had been malleable . . . until she had found the pocket watch that had belonged to her lover. He'd made a mistake keeping it.

Over the years he'd taken a good deal of satisfaction from holding the fine gold watch in his hand and reading the inscription. *To Benjamin from his loving wife, Linette.* The harlot had married her cowboy, but they hadn't been able to cheat Jean-Marc out of his rightful place as the master of Belmonde.

He had carried that watch to a dinner after Linette had been particularly difficult, enjoying the feeling of power it had given him. Although he'd been careful, she must have seen it . . . and recognized it. He'd come into his dressing room to find her with the watch in her hand. When he tried to take it from her, she had run from the room. He caught her at the head of the stairs, and in the ensuing scuffle she had fallen, thereby solving all of his problems.

He'd played the grieving widower, never marrying again, using her money to build his empire. Now Mira threatened everything he had created for himself. Under no circumstances must she be allowed to bring him down.

CHAPTER 10

Trey was helping Brenda in the blacksmith shop when he heard Dee calling. She rushed inside to confront them, holding one hand to her chest and gasping for breath. "Mira needs you."

His heart dropped to his boots. "What's wrong now?"

"Some lowdown varmint turned a skunk loose in the funeral parlor."

Oh no! *No.* Say he didn't have to tangle with a skunk. He'd battled enough of those marauders around the henhouse back in Kansas. Nothing smelled as bad as a polecat. He realized both women were looking at him as if they expected him to ride up on a white horse. Being the only man in a town full of women brought heavy responsibility.

He carefully replaced the tongs he'd been using to remove red-hot horseshoes from the coals. This was the worst yet. Fighting a whole battalion of Johnny Rebs would be easier than taking on a skunk.

"Anything we can do?" Brenda asked.

"No. I can handle it."

He couldn't ask a bunch of women to do his fighting for him, much as he'd like to. Trey walked out the door and strode down the street to the funeral parlor, feeling like he was going to meet a firing squad.

Mira met him on the porch. "Oh, Trey, whatever will we do? We have a funeral tomorrow."

"Just stay out of the way. I'll get rid of it."

All the same, he'd bet that would be the most fragrant funeral known to mankind, and he'd be barred from attending.

He stepped inside and paused by the door, letting his eyes search the room. No skunk. Could be a false alarm, although a subtle scent that had nothing to do with flowers hung in the air. Trey tiptoed toward the back door. Maybe if he left an exit the skunk would leave on its own.

Sunshine streamed through the wide-open door as Trey advanced into the room. Now, if he were a skunk, where would he hide? Maybe behind the small lectern Grandma Speck used. He strode confidently in that direction. Opening the back door had made the room lighter and gave him a sense of being in control. After all, he was smarter than a skunk.

He peered behind the dais. Nothing. A quick glance behind Mira's piano revealed that space to be empty too. He turned and came face-to-face with a small black-and-white animal marching toward him with precise steps, as if said animal had something on its mind. Trey backed away, wishing he had thought to bring his gun.

The skunk advanced relentlessly.

"Shoo! Get on out. This is no place for you."

He waved his arms with no results. This was one very determined skunk. Trey whirled to escape and stumbled over a chair.

"Whoo-hah!"

His arms flailed the air before he toppled over, falling flat on the floor. He pushed himself up on his elbows in time to see the skunk turn around and raise its tail. A noxious cloud filled the air. Trey gasped for breath. He was dying! He pulled himself up to his hands and knees, watching as the skunk, having made its point, walked with an air of dignity toward the back door and left the parlor.

The women aired the room the best they could, mopping with hot water and lye soap. Trey retired to the stable with a tin washtub and five quarts of canned tomato juice, hoping to dilute the odor enough to make it bearable. As he sat in his vegetarian bath he reflected bitterly that even Audrey had refused to come near him. Grandma Speck had roused enough to suggest he take his meals outside for a while. Trey shook his head at this desertion.

A man didn't know lonesome until he'd met a skunk.

Mira swept the floor of the community room, wondering what would happen next. No doubt it would be something dreadful. She was sure Jean-Marc stayed awake at night inventing new ways to torment the women of Sassy Gap. The parlor was finally starting to air, although she could still detect a pungent scent.

A commotion from outside sent her running to the door with Jane right behind her. A herd of stray hogs was rooting in the garden. Brenda ran back and forth, trying to drive them out, but no one could drive a hog anywhere it didn't want to go. It wasn't in their nature.

Mira rushed down the steps, waving her arms and yelling at the headstrong porkers.

The other women heard Brenda shouting and came running to help. Dee plunged past the row of snap beans, chasing a black-and-white sow romping across the bean patch, trampling the young vines to a pulp. The hog squealed and headed toward the far end of the garden, where Brenda, with Vivian and Jane's help, crowded a white sow and three piglets through a gap in the fence.

"Get out of here, you slab of bacon!" Dee swung a stick and whacked the sow across its portly rump.

Mira chased a red shoat, trying to head him off before he hit the corn rows. Dee raced to help but stumbled over a loose stone and turned her ankle. Game to the end, she hobbled down the row yelling threats at the marauding swine.

Melody chased a scrawny boar into the strip of honeysuckle that bordered the fence line. She tripped over a vine and sprawled headfirst in a muddy low place next to the potato patch. Mira stopped to help her up, squelching an unruly desire to laugh at Melody's muck-splattered dress and face. Mud crowned her hair.

Melody swiped at her skirt, smearing the grime and making it worse. "Oh, look at me. My last clean dress!"

Mira patted the young woman's shoulder, being careful to avoid the worst of the mud. "Wash out the dress and hang it in the kitchen," she advised. "The heat from the fireplace will dry it."

"But what will I do until then?" Melody wailed. "I can't sit around in my petticoat until my dress dries."

Mira thought for a minute. "I think I've got something that will fit you. As soon as we fix that hole in the fence so the pigs can't get back in, I'll see what I can do."

"Oh, Mira, you're a sweetheart." Melody reached out as though she was going to hug her, then stepped back. "Sorry, I wasn't thinking. You probably don't want to hug me."

"Not right now," Mira said and laughed. "I'll wait until you are not wearing a couple of pounds of mud."

Brenda herded the last sow through the hole in the fence, and Vivian held the boards in place while Trey nailed them across the gap.

Mira breathed a sigh of relief and looked at the mangled garden. It was a mess, but the damage wasn't as bad as it had first looked. A lot of the plants were broken or trampled, but the potatoes and corn appeared to be all right, and the tomatoes still had a few red globes that hadn't been squashed.

Melody went back to the house to clean up and Mira walked over to join the others. Brenda glanced up when she approached. "Look at that. The boards are cut. Someone turned these pigs into our garden."

"Jean-Marc's work." Mira couldn't contain her sadness. "You know he did it. This is all my fault."

She turned and walked away, blinded by her sudden tears. He had taken their meat, milk, and eggs. Now he had tried to destroy their vegetables. Jean-Marc wouldn't be happy until he drove them out. How long could she continue if it meant the other women, as dear to her as sisters, had to suffer even more deprivation?

Brenda cut through the garden, heading back to the black-smith shop. The other women wandered off to various chores.

Mira sensed Trey standing behind her. It was strange how she could feel his presence. She remembered the way the corners of his eyes crinkled when he laughed. The sound of his laughter, carefree and happy when he played with Audrey, was now part of her everyday life.

But the way he sometimes said her name was both comforting and disturbing.

He spoke now, his voice deep and fringed with concern. "Mira?"

She clenched her hands to stop their trembling, willing her tears not to fall.

He turned her to face him. "What's wrong?"

"You know what is wrong. Jean-Marc is behind these attacks." She looked up, her eyes meeting his. "What he is doing to these women is *wrong.*"

He nodded. "It's wrong, but I'm telling you again, it's not your fault. Only Jean-Marc is responsible for his actions."

Mira shook her head. "I have to do something; I can't let this go on forever."

His gaze locked with hers and held her in place as surely as if his hands had been on her shoulders. Her breath caught in her throat.

"I understand why you feel responsible, but not a person here wants you to leave."

"Some may."

Deep down they had to know they'd be better off without her. She also knew they'd never speak the words out loud. The women of Sassy Gap were loyal to a fault. "They will not tell me to leave. It will have to be my decision."

"I still say you and Jean-Marc should sit down and try to

work out your differences. What's done is done and you can't change it. It's not up to us to seek revenge."

"'Vengeance is mine, saith the Lord'?"

"Don't mock, Mira. The man might be willing to settle things once and for all if you ask."

"You are a good man, Trey McAllister. The problem is that you think Jean-Marc Portier has redeeming qualities. You are wrong. The man the world believes to be my father is not capable of love. He only knows how to break those who cross him."

Vivian met the couple at the door of the community building. "There you are. We were about ready to come looking for you."

The women sat in chairs around the table with Grandma Speck seated at the head. Trey's heart jumped. Something was afoot, and he wasn't sure he wanted to know what it was. The women were looking entirely too serious to suit him.

Dee sat with her foot resting in a pan of warm water. The biting scent of witch hazel filled the room.

Vivian chopped comfrey to make a poultice for Dee's sprained ankle. Both of them had stopped bothering Trey, evidently conceding that Melody had staked her claim.

Trey wondered if Grandma Speck was strong enough for this. The woman looked like death warmed over. Her face was so pale he was afraid she was about to faint, and her hands shook like someone afflicted with the palsy.

Mira pulled out a chair and sat down. Trey took a seat next to Jane. She turned to smile at him, but her eyes were anxious.

Grandma called the meeting to order. "It has been suggested that we decide once and for all whether to stay in Sassy Gap or leave."

Mira caught her breath, the sound audible in the quiet room. "There is no need for that. I will go."

Grandma Speck held up a hand. "That's not the subject under discussion. No one wants you to leave. Let's understand that right now. No, we're deciding on the future of Sassy Gap. Now, ladies, what say ye?"

Dee pulled her foot out of the water and rubbed her swelling ankle. "I say we leave."

Viv paused in chopping comfrey. "Where do you think we'd go?"

That stopped them for a minute.

Jane looked down at her hands and murmured, "There's plenty of land out west." She glanced sideways at Mira, her expression apologetic.

Mira nodded. "That is all right, Jane. I understand."

Brenda rapped the table with her knuckles. "This is foolish talk. We can't leave."

"Who's to stop us?" Dee demanded.

"No one, I suppose. But there's no place we can go, and if we went who would build a town for us? There isn't anyone and you know it."

"We don't have any money," Melody said. "How could we buy building materials or pay carpenters?"

Dee shrugged. "I'm so tired of Jean-Marc and his tricks. I'm sorry, Mira. I know he's your father, but he's worse than those pigs he turned loose on us."

By the time the meeting broke up nothing had been decided. They were no closer to deciding what to do than when they started.

Mira woke early the following morning and dressed. She set coffee to brewing and prepared to wake Grandma Speck. A teakettle simmered on the back of the stove and she mixed the cup of ginseng tea Jane had prescribed to help boost the older woman's energy. Jane kept the town's herb gardens, which were in long wooden porch boxes; she also served as the town's doctor.

Mira carried the tea to Grandma Speck's cot, balancing the cup in one hand and pushing back the curtain to the cubicle with the other. The older woman lay on her back with her eyes closed. Mira stepped closer, keeping her voice soft so she wouldn't wake the others. "Grandma? Time for your tonic."

Grandma Speck's eyes fluttered open. "What is it, child?"

"I have brought your tonic. Let me help you sit up."

The older woman sighed. "I don't believe I want any this morning. Just let me sleep."

Mira set the tea down and knelt beside the bed. "What is it, dearest? Are you in pain?"

"Heart pain. Seems like I don't have the will to go on." Grandma lifted one frail hand and then let it drop as if the effort was too much. "I don't have a lot left to live for."

"You have us." Mira clasped the cold hands. "I cannot bear for you to speak this way." Grandma Speck had filled the void left by her mother's death. She could not give her up. If there was any way to save this blessed woman who had given so much to others, she must find it.

"We have fresh milk now that Trey found our cows; would you eat some lovely cinnamon milk toast if I prepared it?"

Grandma Speck turned her face to the wall. "I couldn't eat a bite. I keep thinking of Fred and Lois out there somewhere. Are they hungry or afraid? I can't sleep nights for worrying about them."

Mira stood up. "I will find your pets and bring them to you. Then you will not worry and you will eat and grow strong."

A flicker of hope shone in Grandma Speck's eyes, then faded almost immediately. "You're talking about something that won't happen. They've been gone too long. I'll never see them again."

Mira placed her hand on Grandma's Bible, which usually lay open to the last passage she had read. Now it was closed because the devout woman who treasured its words no longer had the strength to hold it. "Look at me," she commanded. "I promise by God's Holy Word I will find your cats and return them to you."

Grandma didn't smile. "I wish you could do that, but I'm awfully afraid they're already dead."

"I will go and I will find them. I promise you I will not return without them."

"You're determined to look for them?"

"Very determined."

Grandma nodded. "Then go with God. I'll be praying."

Mira stepped out onto the porch and walked toward the

funeral parlor, unable to face any of the other women. *Lord, what have I done?* She had made a promise she had no hope of keeping. The sight of Grandma Speck, so fragile, so surely dying, had caused her to say things she had no right to say. How could she have given even a frail thread of hope to someone as desperate as that lonely woman grieving for her closest friends? When she returned without them, Grandma Speck would lose all hope and she would surely die.

Mira sank onto the steps of the funeral parlor and buried her face in her hands, letting the tears fall as steady and as unrelenting as the Louisiana rain.

Hands pressed against her shoulders. Trey pulled her up to stand before him. "What's wrong?"

"It's Grandma Speck. She will not eat this morning, and if she does not, she will die."

"Listen to me, Mira. No one wants her to die, but if she does, you'll go on. You're strong. Grandma is old and tired, and the Lord knows she doesn't want to struggle anymore."

"That is not all. I promised her I'd find Fred and Lois and I know I cannot. I never should have promised, and when I fail she will give up completely and she will die and it will be my fault."

Mira buried her face against his shoulder, letting the tears flow. His arms were warm and sheltering, holding her close. She raised her head to look at him, drinking in the compassion in his eyes. Trey's lips lowered to meet hers and even though she knew he was only comforting her, she felt the blood surging through her veins.

A startled gasp broke them apart. Mira turned to see Melody watching from the street in front of the funeral parlor.

Trey didn't seem to notice the shocked young woman. "You're not going alone." Trey moved Mira aside. "Come with me."

Trey saddled Buck and another horse for Mira. If she was determined to look for the cats, he would go with her. He wasn't about to let her go wandering around the woods alone with Jean-Marc's band of ruffians on the prowl. He knew they didn't have any hope of finding the cats, but they would do their best.

Mira twisted around in the saddle to look at him. "Where are we going?"

"We'll try the woods where Curt had his pen built. Maybe he turned them loose around there." He guessed it was as good a place as any to waste an afternoon. He figured the cats were dead by now, but Mira had gotten herself into this mess and he'd do what he could to make her feel better.

Grass and weeds had grown almost six inches since the cattle had been released from the pen. This was fertile soil, and the rain and muggy Louisiana weather had sent the abundant foliage on a growing spurt. He figured you could throw a dead branch down on the ground and a week later find a young tree growing out of the dry wood.

Mira dismounted and looked around the cleared area. "Where do we start?"

Trey tried to look like he had a sensible thought, which

would surely have been stretching his mental capacity at the moment. "Why don't you try calling them?"

"That is a good idea." Mira strolled to the edge of the woods, calling, "Fred? Lois? Come to Mira."

The silence mocked them. A hawk circled overhead, and Trey watched it in trepidation. The cats had lived with people for too long. Could they survive in the wild?

Mira turned and walked back, her face a study of misery. "They are not here, are they?"

Trey shook his head. "I'd say not."

Mira caught his hands. "Let us pray."

That would be their only chance, he guessed. He bowed his head.

"Dear Father, please help us," Mira prayed. "They are only cats, but they are Grandma's cats."

Trey added his own petition. "God, I know they're just animals, but there's a sick, old woman who loves them. If You can find it in Your heart to do it and if they're still alive, would You send them our way?"

He felt better after they finished, but he still figured the cats were gone for good.

Mira sat down on a large rock and waved him to another. "Let us sit and wait for a moment."

"You giving God time to work?"

She smiled. "A good idea, no?"

"A very good idea." If they couldn't find the cats at least he could spend an afternoon in Mira's company without someone coming along to interrupt them.

"Tell me about your sisters."

Trey chuckled. "I doubt if I can do them justice. There's four of them and they raised me. Made my life miserable. I owe them a lot."

"Yet you are lingering here instead of going to see them. I wonder why."

He didn't figure he could tell her the truth. "I'll have to be going home before long. They need me."

"We will miss you when you leave."

He noted the sadness in her voice and hoped it meant *she* would miss him. He liked the others, but he was being forced to realize he loved Mira Dupree. Somehow he had to find a way to take her with him when he left.

He took her hand. "Let me tell you about Kansas. It's even flatter than the ground here—or at least it is out where I live. Not a lot of trees, nothing to block the view."

"If there are no trees and no hills, what is there to see?" Mira asked.

"Grass, long enough to brush Buck's belly, rippling in the wind like waves on the ocean. In fact, I've heard it referred to as a sea of grass."

"I can almost see it!" Mira exclaimed. "It must be very lovely."

"It is, and the sky stretches out overhead like a curtain of silk." He guessed that sounded sort of fancy, but it was the way he felt. "I'd like to show it to you sometime."

Mira pushed to her feet, her expression sad. "I wish to see it, but that is not likely. We should be going."

Trey stood, knowing he should not have said what he had. She was not ready to accept the words that he wanted to say; maybe she never would be. He leaned on the fence and stared at the surrounding trees. Before he could claim the hand of the

lovely Mira Dupree, he had to defeat Jean-Marc Portier and free
Mira from the chains that bound her to the past.

A strange bird called in the distance. Trey absently noticed
that it didn't sound like any bird he was familiar with. The
sound came again. He stiffened. "Mira, call them again."

She stared at him, questioning.

"Just do it—call the cats."

She did as he asked and looked at him, as if seeking further
directions.

He held up a hand. "Listen."

From her expression, he knew she heard it too: a cat's
demanding cry. Trey held his breath as the sound came closer.
A black-and-white tomcat cowered in the shelter of an over-
hanging bush. Mira made a sudden move and the cat vanished.

"Walk out into middle of the cleared spot," Trey said. "Go
slow."

She did as he instructed, kneeling a few feet from where the
cat had been. "Fred? I know you are there. Grandma wants you
to come home."

The black-and-white cat moved slowly toward her, then
stopped to crouch as if ready to run.

Mira inched her hand toward him, crooning, "Good Fred.
Good kitty. Come to Mira."

He hunched his shoulders as if sensing danger. Tail twitch-
ing, eyes narrowed, the cat watched as if daring her to move
closer. A rustle of underbrush, a swirl of movement, and Lois
bounded past him, running directly for Mira.

Trey realized he'd been holding his breath. *I'm sorry I
doubted, God. Shouldn't have prayed if I wasn't going to believe.*

Mira caught up the cat, cuddling it in her arms. Fred moved

closer, until he was near enough to touch. Mira sat on the ground, holding the cats and crying. Trey felt like shedding a few tears himself. He took a deep breath and relaxed, leaning against the fence. This was going to make all the difference in the world to Grandma Speck.

Mira got to her feet, still holding the cats. She smiled up at him. "Oh, Trey, God answered our prayers."

"He certainly did. Now let's get them back to Sassy Gap and to Grandma Speck. She's waiting for them."

He didn't add that the older woman's prayers probably had more to do with finding the cats than his, but he figured that was the truth. Granny Speck and God had been on good terms for a long time. The good Lord took care of His children.

Trey held the cats until Mira was safely mounted, then gave them to her while he climbed aboard Buck. He took Fred from her, figuring Lois would be the easier to hold. What he hadn't counted on was the way Buck would react to having a cat on his back. The horse crow-hopped across the clearing with Trey yelling "Whoa!" and Fred digging his claws into whatever he could find to hold on. What he found was Trey's leg. He'd come through the war without a scratch and here a cat had drawn blood.

They rode into Sassy Gap and dismounted at the smithy. Brenda came to take the horses' reins. "Bless me, you found the cats."

"We're going to take them to Grandma Speck right now," Mira said.

"Think I'll go with you. This is something I want to see."

They carried the cats into the community room, and everyone stopped talking at once. The other women gathered around as Brenda drew back the curtain separating Grandma's cubicle from the rest of the room. Mira approached the bed and set Lois down beside the older woman.

Trey placed Fred on the gaily patterned quilt and stepped back. Grandma's mouth dropped open, but no sound came out. Lois snuggled against her, a loud purr rumbling in her throat.

The older woman lifted a hand to touch the cats as if she couldn't believe her eyes. She smiled up at Mira. "You found them."

"God sent them to us." Mira said.

Trey figured that about covered it.

Morning dawned bright and full of sunshine, a perfect day. The woman scurried around completing tasks neglected because of the rain. Helen and Melody were in charge of filling the two big iron kettles with water from the spring. Brenda kept a fire under them, heating wash water. Grandma Speck sat in a chair in the shade, watching Fred and Lois loll in the grass. Mira and Jane hung wet clothes on the lines while Brenda, Dee, and Viv aired out the community room and took care of the animals. Trey helped carry water and filled in anywhere else they needed a strong pair of arms. He tipped the tubs, letting the used water pour out on the ground.

Jane stepped out onto the porch of the community building. "I thought a picnic might sound good. Got lunch ready if you'd like to help carry it up to that big shade tree by the spring."

"Good idea." Trey lifted the two full baskets, sniffing appreciatively. Fried chicken. His favorite. Some of the chickens had drifted back home, including Audrey's pet banty, Mr. Peepers. They were enjoying fresh eggs again. He figured they were gaining on Jean-Marc. Nothing more had happened since the incident with the pigs. Maybe the old goat had given up and decided to let the women live in peace.

They spent a lazy two hours at the spring, eating and laughing and talking. Trey got a glimpse of what the women would be like without a threat of another attack hanging over them. They were good women, good friends. He wished he could take them home with him. His sisters would welcome them to Tyrone. In fact, the entire town would benefit from their presence.

Brenda glanced at the sun. "I'd better be getting back. Got a couple of horses to shoe this afternoon."

Jane repacked the baskets. "I suppose we all need to get busy, but this has been nice."

"It sure has," Trey said. "We needed a break."

He picked up the baskets and led the way down the hill.

Mira had lingered behind the others so she heard their angry cries before she saw the reason. Now she looked at the source of distress in disbelief. Every clothesline had been cut. All of the laundry done so laboriously this morning lay on the muddy ground, even dirtier than it had been originally. Each piece would have to be rewashed, and the lines would have to be restrung.

She balled her hands into fists. "That man will not let up!"

Trey pulled her close. "This isn't your fault."

He seemed to be saying that a lot. But she didn't believe him.

She whirled, cutting him off. "What if someone dies because 'it isn't my fault'? What if Audrey gets sick because she cannot have the proper food? How long can we go on pretending that if we just ignore him he will go away? He will not stop until he destroys us all."

She pulled her arm out of his grip and ran to the funeral parlor, slamming the door behind her.

Trey helped the women gather the dirty wash, and then he carried water to be heated in the large cast-iron wash kettles.

Brenda brought an armload of wood to stoke the fires. "Mira blaming herself again?" she asked.

"Yes. Guess I can understand why."

Brenda sighed. "That poor woman is caught between a rock and a grizzly. He won't ever let her go, and she can't live under his iron thumb. I know that man. He's pure mean through and through."

Trey waited until the laundry was flapping in the breeze before heading off to the funeral parlor to talk to Mira. She was sitting dry-eyed on a back pew, but one look at her reddened eyes and it was easy to see she had been crying.

He sat down beside her and took her hand. "You okay?"

She nodded, not speaking.

He stood and pulled her upright. "Let's take a walk."

She let him lead her out of the building and toward the woods. He looked down at her, walking beside him, and it felt right. A fat, bristly worm crawled across the path, and he stopped and pointed at it.

"See that? Back in Kansas we look at wooly worms and determine what kind of winter we're going to have."

She glanced at him inquiringly, and he was happy to see a spark of interest in her eyes. "If that little worm is black on both ends, we say the first and last parts of winter are going to be bad and the middle will be mild. If it's all black then it's going to be a long, hard winter."

She halfway smiled. "Does it work?"

"Well, nothing works all the time, but it hits often enough to give it credibility."

"I have never heard of predicting the winter by a worm."

He grinned. "Sounds silly to you, I guess, but some of those old folk sayings have a lot of truth to them. Take the persimmon seed."

She tilted her chin, glancing out of the corner of her eyes at him. "A persimmon seed?"

"A little old seed. We cut that seed open and if the inside has the knife pattern it means a mild winter because the knife will cut the length of bad weather. But look out if it has a spoon or, as some folks call it, a shovel."

She was showing interest now. "And what is the shovel for?"

"Why, to shovel snow, of course. You get much snow down here?"

She shook her head. "Winter here is different. We have hard freezes followed by warm spells. It can be bad if things start growing and then are frozen back."

He held her hand, swinging it gently between them. "Someday I'd like to take you to Kansas."

She nodded, tightening her grip on his hand. "Someday I would like to go."

Trey cut enough wood to last out the week and stacked it inside the back storage room of the community building. At least Jean-Marc's men couldn't get to it there. He could smell venison pot roast simmering on the cookstove. The women never ceased to amaze him. No matter how much Jean-Marc took away from them, they soldiered on. He believed they could scratch a living out of a rock if they had to.

He shut the storage-room door and started down toward the spring, passing the outhouse on the way.

The two-holer sat back from the path, far enough away from the water supply to be sanitary but close enough to the community building to be convenient. A bird trilled its song from somewhere out in the woods. It was so quiet and peaceful a lizard crawled up on a rock and sat there blinking at him.

Trey reflected on the outhouse, a civil invention. A man could sit there and ponder great thoughts without anyone intruding on his thinking time. There was usually a catalog, and if you got tired of thinking, you could look through the wish book and dream about all of the things you couldn't afford.

As he passed the small building he heard someone crying. Jane? Sounded like her. Trey stopped, listening to the muffled sobs and muttered words. Before long the problem became clear. Someone had rubbed stinging nettle on the paper pages of the catalog, maybe mixed with a little poison oak. Jane would know soon enough.

This was the last straw! Portier had gone too far.

A lady had a right to answer the call of nature without some worthless, no-account scoundrel putting itch weed on the pages of the outhouse catalog.

Trey marched back to the stable and then rode the six miles to Mignon, reaching town fifteen minutes before the telegraph office closed.

He sent six wires. One to Ohio, one to Oklahoma, two to Missouri, and two to Kentucky. He prayed the men remembered the pact. "If you ever need anything . . ." Well, he needed something and these men were the best.

Jean-Marc Portier was about to have the rug pulled out from under him.

CHAPTER 11

That evening Trey walked into the funeral parlor and settled into the podium seat. Once more the women of Sassy Creek had been told there would be a meeting, only this time the velvet gloves were off. It was an open declaration of war!

And war, Jean-Marc would soon recognize, was never a pleasant thing.

The women filed in, both anxious and excited, openly wondering what he had in mind. Well, his first sensation of anger had faded.

It had been replaced by vengeance. And by the agony on Jane's face, she was ready to do battle.

His emotions were much the same as the day Sharon had refused to fight to keep their love alive. He wanted to hurt somebody. He wanted to do some serious harm to Jean-Marc, and not with some juvenile stinging-nettle prank. He was going to beat the man at his own game. There was no need to pull his punches because he realized there was no limit to the man's inhumanity.

Did Portier lay awake nights thinking up absurd plots to antagonize the women? What if Mira had used the privy? Or Audrey? Would he have cared?

It didn't matter. The battle was now joined.

Mira came into the building looking fresh and windswept. Her eyes found his in a silent token of friendship.

Brenda seemed to have taken over. She perched next to Grandma Speck's chair, her jaw tightly clenched. When all were accounted for, the blacksmith called for order. "Pipe down! McAllister has something to say." She nodded to Trey, who gazed down at the compassionate faces.

"Ladies." He paused, glancing at Jane. This was an extremely delicate subject. The last thing he wanted to do was embarrass anyone.

The front door opened on a gust of wind and banged back against the wall. The women twisted in their chairs, peering over their shoulders at the disturbance.

Filling the doorway stood a tall, lanky stranger. His hat was pulled so low it hid his eyes. A long duster hung to the top of his worn, mud-caked boots.

Trey's hand went automatically to his hip, but the stranger was already in the room.

The group had gone as silent as a tomb. The gathering waited for the stranger to announce his purpose.

From the corner of his eye, Trey focused on the heavy candlestick that sat at the end of a casket. A couple of steps would take him within reach.

The stranger's hand came up and Trey tensed, ready to lunge.

But the stranger merely removed his hat and let a crop of

dark curls fall to his shoulders. Trey squinted, barely making out the man's features in the dim lighting, but something about the new arrival looked familiar.

He spoke. "Howdy, folks."

Trey recognized the husky voice as belonging to young Pastor Daniel, from over in Mignon.

A relieved hush fell over the women when Trey stepped off the dais and made his way to the back of the room. The two men shook hands.

"What brings you this way so late?" Trey asked.

The young man grinned affably and knocked mud off his coat. "Heard there's been some trouble up this way. Thought I'd ride over and see if I could help out with a little prayer . . . and maybe even more."

"The 'even more' is what we need." Trey latched on to the man's arm and urged him toward the front of the room. Daniel's Adam's apple bobbed when they turned to face the women.

Trey introduced him and stepped back, giving him room to state his purpose.

"You're a preacher?" Helen asked

"Yes, ma'am. Heard that Grandma Speck was ailing and—" he glanced at Trey—"thought you folks might need someone to hold Sunday morning services."

"We need more than services," Dee declared.

The others spoke up, all talking at once.

Trey finally held up both hands. "Ladies! One at a time!" He could sense Daniel's rising confusion.

The women took their seats and one by one raised their hands for permission to speak. Grandma Speck claimed the floor. "I'm getting better, Daniel, but it was right neighborly of you to come by, and we'd be honored to have you speak. I'm sure the Lord will lay a message on your heart we need to hear."

Trey went down the line, allowing each one a turn. To a woman, the message was the same. "We need help. We need *men* to help."

With each heartfelt petition Daniel's features turned sicklier. Trey could see that as the extent of the women's plight began to sink in, the young man was having second thoughts about coming.

Trey took over. He explained Jean-Marc's continuing vandalism campaign to bring Mira home. He outlined in detail the dire circumstances the women were in.

Daniel listened, shaking his head. "I had no idea he'd gone to such lengths."

"His men smeared stinging nettle on the catalog in the outhouse today," Jane told him.

Daniel's youthful features had slowly grown more serious. Now he looked as solemn as a gravedigger. "I'm afraid there are other rumors circulating—one in particular that you should know about. I managed to escape Portier's thug, who has been trailing me everywhere I go, so I could warn you, although I hate to be the bearer of bad news."

Mira stood up, eyes anxious with inquiry. "Please, what is Jean-Marc planning now?"

"Well, I don't want to worry anyone needlessly—"

"What is it?" Trey interrupted. "We'll know soon enough."

Jean-Marc would see to that.

"Yes. Yes, you will." Daniel cleared his throat. "Portier is planning to build holding pens outside town."

"Holding pens! Cattle?" The women's high-pitched voices raised in protest.

"The stench will be unbearable!" Brenda said.

"That's exactly what he wants! If he can't drive us out one way, he'll find another."

Trey turned back to Daniel. "Can he do that?"

Daniel nodded. "He owns about every square inch of land around here except for Sassy Gap."

"We have to fight him." Trey's forceful tone quieted the room. "We have to fight him," he repeated.

Brenda crossed her arms. "We tried to fight him; it doesn't work. Walnuts only make a man's skull smart, not stop him."

"We need men. Lots of men," Viv said. "And you know yourself that there isn't a man around here willing to help."

"Then we outsmart him."

Trey had sent for help without the women's knowledge. If help couldn't come he didn't want to upset them. But, if they came, would they be able to stop a man from building on his own land?

"How?" Mira bit her bottom lip. "We cannot fight him or outsmart him. He is too resourceful."

"Then we'll be more imaginative." Trey paused, and then looked back at Daniel. "You say stock pens? Exactly where does he plan to build them?"

"Somewhere outside town. Don't know as I've heard exactly where, but near enough that the smell will create a stink."

Grandma Speck curved her hands around her beloved pets. "Only one place to build it. That cleared five acres east of town. They could drive the cattle to the creek to drink."

"Which means they'll pollute the creek as well as the air," Viv said bitterly.

Brenda spoke up. "I've smelled bad things before."

"But stock pens." Dee wrinkled her nose. "Come summer we won't be able to sleep for the cows bawling. And the black flies will eat us alive."

"Well," Jane said, "he can't start immediately. The weather will keep the ground so wet nobody can build fences."

Rain. Wet. Trey motioned for silence.

He pointed to Jane. "You're right. No one, not even Jean-Marc, can build fences until the ground dries out."

She nodded.

"So. What's the one commodity you do have, ladies?"

The room fell silent. The women thought, eyes rolled toward the ceiling, forefingers on temples.

"Water," Mira said. She grinned. "We have lots of water. We cannot drink it, or cook with it, but we can use it to block Jean-Marc's plan."

Brenda frowned, then Helen and Melody.

"Use it? How?"

"We use that polluted pool to keep every square inch of that five acres saturated. With any luck, the rains will keep up for a while. When the weather changes, we use the water to keep the grounds flooded."

"Good, Mira, good," Trey praised, encouraged that they were beginning to think for themselves. "But how? You can't carry that much water. You don't have the horsepower to pull tanks in a wagon."

Trey saw the light burning in Jane's eyes, and he wondered if she would find the courage to speak her mind. She was smart;

he'd seen her juggle what little money the women had and manage to make both ends meet. She could stretch a pound of sugar into two. She read books to Audrey and taught Brenda how to take a cord of wood and burn it low, extending the heat for hours. And Portier had dealt her a mighty blow this afternoon in that outhouse.

Still, Jane didn't speak.

"Come on, ladies. Think. If you can't carry the water, how are you going to use it? "

Jane finally spoke up. "We use gravity."

Trey leaned back, crossing his arms, smiling. These were his ladies. He was proud of them. "That's right. We bring it to them."

"Of course." Mira caught the idea. "We dig trenches, letting the water trickle slowly but steadily out to the field. We put the channels where they cannot be seen, cover them up with debris so that Jean-Marc's men will not suspect."

Dee laughed. "The ground will stay muddy and impossible to work even though the rains will have stopped."

"But what if Jean-Marc won't allow the rains to stop him? What if he decides to set posts in the rain?" Trey asked.

Jane spoke first. "Then each night we take them out."

"He'll have guards."

"We've had guards," someone pointed out, "but the men have slipped by undetected."

"Aren't we as sneaky as a bunch of thugs?" Dee asked.

The women thunderously agreed.

"If Jean-Marc sets posts we'll tear them down!" Brenda declared.

Trey appreciated the newfound fortitude, but he cautioned,

"It won't be easy. Digging is hard work. But the trenches don't need to be deep—just deep enough to move a little water. And since I figure Portier is watching our every move, we'll have to disguise our actions."

Jane grinned. "Maybe we have to enlarge the cemetery."

The group gave it some thought. Trey scratched his chin thoughtfully. "You mean pretend we're opening graves?"

"Why not? This town sets on rock. More than once we've had to dig a couple of places before we found dirt soft enough to bury someone."

"She's right." Mira got up and started to pace. "Last month Grandma Speck and I dug one whole day before we found a spot to put Lucy Wagner. We could pretend to have trouble, dig here and there. Shake our heads and move on."

Trey was all for the idea, but he had some doubts. Jean-Marc's men weren't ignorant. No graves had been dug lately. Canvas-wrapped pine boxes set staked to the ground. Still, if they played it right, acted the drama like a well-directed play, they might pull it off.

"It might work, but, again, it's not going to be easy," he warned. "We'll start at first light and work all day, which means we'll have to work during rainstorms. We furrow trenches from the spring, allowing the water to seep instead of run its usual course. Daniel," Trey addressed the pastor, "can you lend me a hand? We'll have to dam up part of the stream to supply and control the flow."

The young man nodded. "I'd be glad to do what I can. I doubt if I could slip back into town without getting caught anyway."

"Safer for you here," Grandma Speck said. "We'd be real

proud to have you join us. You can sleep in the stable with Mr. McAllister."

Melody got up and came over to stand beside them. Daniel automatically reached to take a sleeping Audrey from the weary mother's arms. Melody smiled up at him, and the thought skimmed through Trey's mind that they would make a fine couple.

He set about quieting the women. "Do you have plenty of picks and shovels?"

Brenda nodded. "We have a few at the livery. We can take turns digging."

Trey nodded. "Then we have our plan. We start first thing tomorrow morning."

"Digging. Walnuts. Apples and turnips," Brenda grumbled under her breath. "What next? Spitballs?"

Some of the women hung around to talk more, but most headed for their beds. Daniel carried Audrey and followed Melody out the doorway.

Trey moved slowly to leave, searching for Mira, but she was gone. He wanted to talk to her, to see how she felt about the plan. Deep in thought, he stepped out of the building and felt someone touch his arm. Rain pelted the yellow rain slicker, but he recognized the eyes. Beautiful, dark, haunted eyes.

"I was looking for you earlier."

She nodded. "I also want to speak with you. Can we walk?"

He took her hand and they started off toward the cemetery.

"What do you think of the plan?" he asked.

"I pray it will work."

"It will work. For a while." Tightening his hold on her hand, he glanced down at her. "But only for a while, Mira. Jean-Marc will catch on to what we're doing."

She nodded wordlessly.

They walked in silence, holding hands. Trey realized they didn't need words, and he was surprised that they'd come so far so quickly. Lately they were of one mind, one heart. Both were powerless to change the course of the relationship, even if they wanted to.

And Trey knew he didn't want to.

"Have you ever been in love?" Even as he asked it, the question seemed unnatural to him, but he knew that she had not loved Paul Dupree. Had she ever given her heart to a man?

She nodded. "Only once."

"Someone you knew when you were young?"

She shook her head.

"Someone you loved prior to marrying Paul?"

Again she shook her head. "Enough about me. What about you? You have never married. Have you never been in love?"

He nodded. "Twice, actually."

"Twice. And you did not ask either woman to share that love?"

"I asked the first one. Sharon. We were planning to be married in the summer, but her father objected. He thought she was too young and he wanted her to go East to school."

"And she wanted that too?"

"More than she wanted me. She left in the spring. She was gone over three years."

"And you were waiting?"

He laughed. "No ma'am. By then I had been called up to fight."

"Then you have not been back? You have not heard from her since you last saw her?"

"My sister Ellie wrote last year and said she'd married some guy from the East. Met him at school. He's a Kansas City lawyer now."

Her hand tightened in his. "I am so sorry."

"Why? The union would have been a mistake."

"Yes," she murmured. "A marriage born of misery is not a good thing."

"Would you have stayed with Paul if he had lived?"

She paused, and then spoke softly over the sound of the falling rain. "Perhaps. Yes. I would have remained with Paul. I spoke vows 'till death do us part.' But it would not have been a happy life for me."

"You don't know. People change. They grow up. Maybe in time you would have fallen in love with him."

Yes, she would have stayed with Paul. He knew Mira Dupree did not give her word lightly.

It was dark, but he felt her smile. "Perhaps, but I do not think so. Since I have experienced the love I now feel in my heart, I doubt I would ever have shared such emotion with Paul."

Needing a name, needing to know every aspect about her, Trey said quietly, "So are you going to tell me who it is?"

It would have to be someone from her recent past, and he knew it would not be one of Jean-Marc's thugs. Yet there were no other men around and none who had stayed long enough to fall in love.

"He is just a man, nosy person."

"Nosy?" He turned, playfully catching her ribs and tickling her. She dissolved in laughter.

"No—stop! Please!"

He relented and they walked on. Rain fell but he didn't seem to notice. Lately when he was with her he didn't notice much of anything except the way her damp hair curled around her face, the way her eyes reflected her emotions, the way her hand fit in his. Tiny. Perfect. The way he enjoyed being with her.

Had he ever felt this way about Sharon? He didn't think so. Not exactly. This time it was different. Newer, actually. This was more tense—more real.

They reached the end of the cemetery and stopped. Trey drew her into his arms, holding her, shielding her from the blowing rain. She didn't try to break his hold.

For the first time in a long time, Trey experienced peace.

Holding her felt right. And good. As if God had this moment in mind all along.

She needed someone to love her, to give her the security and family and sense of belonging that had eluded her most of her life. Was he the man to do that? He now fully admitted to himself that he loved her. He didn't know the exact moment he'd gone from protecting to loving. He wasn't sure—maybe as recently as an hour ago or maybe the first day he'd laid eyes on her. But it didn't matter. Should he act on his feelings? Jean-Marc was a formidable force, and if he were to ask Mira to marry him it might goad Portier into still further cruelty.

Trey stood in the rain, eyes closed, holding her and wondering if he was up to the fight of his life. It would be easier to emotionally release her, but he sure wasn't man enough to do that.

His heart told him that what he had experienced in these last few minutes had taken the choice away from him.

He would stay. And he would fight. He only had to hold out until reinforcements arrived.

Please, God. Let the reinforcements come soon.

Jean-Marc stared with hooded eyes at the man sitting across from him. He had decided he must share his plans with Hi Yates, who had taken over the band of ruffians after Curt Wiggins' defection. Not that Hi was any improvement. Jean-Marc suspected Yates would be even harder to control. Let the scum lead a couple of forays and they got the idea they had leadership qualities.

Hi leaned back in his chair, tilting on the delicate legs. The front legs came off the floor, and Jean-Marc heard the creak of overstressed wood. Fine furniture wasn't intended to be used this way.

"Let it down."

"Huh?" Hi raised a brow. "What?"

"Put all four legs of that chair on the floor before you break it." Jean-Marc spoke precisely so the idiot could understand. Pearls before swine. Undoubtedly the man was unaccustomed to fine surroundings. Was it any wonder that he had no idea how to behave?

Hi shrugged and lowered the chair legs to set level. "As I was saying, building cattle pens out there is a good idea. You come up with that all by yourself?"

Jean-Marc squinted at him. Was this cretin trying to butter him up? As if he needed Hi Yates's approval.

"Where you planning to get the cattle?" Hi asked. "Not that many left in these parts after the war and all."

"We will talk to the cattlemen in Texas and persuade them to drive their cows here. It will only be a variation of the trail drives they make now."

To Jean-Marc's surprise, Hi appeared doubtful. He wasn't accustomed to people doubting what he said. Perhaps he should educate this man about the penalties issued to those who questioned Jean-Marc Portier. The war may be over and his grip on the area loosened, but he still had enough power to take care of his enemies, real or perceived.

Hi shook his head. "The trail's already established and Louisiana's settled. Most people aren't going to want a herd of smelly, noisy cattle trailing through town."

"You leave that up to me. I can make it work."

"Maybe so, but seems to me that while you might know a lot about Louisiana, you don't know much about Texas."

The blood surged to Jean-Marc's head, burning hot. "You question me? Are you not aware I can wipe you off the face of the earth with one spoken word?"

"Are you not aware I can do the same to you?" Hi mocked. "We both got guns. No reason to get hot. I'm just saying what it looks like to me. Trying to cover all the details, so to speak."

Jean-Marc realized the fool was not afraid of him. The realization brought a grudging respect. Obviously Hi Yates was no Curt Wiggins. Perhaps the man's strengths could be used to his advantage. Every man had his weakness and Yates was no exception.

Hi leaned back, tapping his fingers on his boot. "You'll need a contact man, someone to get in touch with the cattlemen and make arrangements."

"Am I to understand you have someone in mind?"

"Of course. I can do that. What are you going to do with the cattle after I get them here?"

"We're going to ship them out on the railroad."

"Railroad? I've been here six months and I've not heard a train whistle yet. What railroad you got in mind?"

Jean-Marc smiled. "The railroad that's going to run through Sassy Gap as soon as we get rid of the women."

A faint movement caught his attention. He jumped to his feet and strode to the door, easing it open. The hall was empty.

Trey spread his bedroll in the stable loft. Daniel threw his down at the other end. Trey shucked his boots and stretched out full length, thinking how tired he was. Riding herd on a bunch of women was harder work than driving cattle. For one thing, the cows didn't insist on talking back.

Daniel eased down on his pallet. "I've never slept in a hayloft before."

"It's not bad," Trey said. "I've spent my nights here, but I can't say I've done much sleeping."

He'd done more worrying than resting.

Rain dripped through the holes in the roof. Someone had emptied the containers set to catch the water, so that the drips made a tinny musical sound striking the bottom, the notes depending on the type of vessel: the metal ones ringing high and true, with the raindrops hitting crockery providing the bass notes.

Trey snuffed out the candle Brenda had provided. He'd have liked to keep it burning, but supplies were tight in Sassy Gap and money even tighter. They didn't have the luxury of letting a candle burn all night, even to ease the shadows.

Daniel spoke into the darkness. "Do you think the women can stop Portier?"

"Not for good, but they can slow him down."

"What's the good of that? He'll win in the long run."

Trey debated telling him about his friends, but stopped short of promising real help. "I've asked some friends to come, but I can't be sure they'll make it. I pray they will."

Daniel was quiet for a minute, and Trey thought he had gone to sleep until he spoke again. "Melody seems like a nice woman."

"She is," Trey said. "Fine woman, and Audrey is a sweetheart."

"You've been here for a while. Is she spoken for?"

"Not that I know of. I'd say it's a wide-open field for the right man."

"I wondered."

Trey grinned. Melody *was* a fine woman. Not the woman for him, but she and Daniel would make a good match.

He dropped off to sleep thinking of dark hair and eyes and a fetching French accent.

CHAPTER 12

Long after Trey retired to the stable, Mira remained in the cemetery. It was peaceful here; she could think. Clouds were rolling in from the west. More rain would come before morning.

She hugged her shoulders against the chilly night breeze. The plan the women had worked out sounded good and it might serve the purpose for a time, but she knew Jean-Marc. He wouldn't rest until he won the war. If the holding pens didn't drive them out, he would come up with something worse. They were outnumbered and too stubborn to admit it. She couldn't allow the women to dig channels to keep the ground saturated. The work would be backbreaking, too difficult for women who were already worn down by months of constant harassment. In the end the gesture would be useless because Jean-Marc would only find another way to torment them.

Her gaze shifted to the barn loft, where Trey was sleeping. In the community building the women were getting ready for bed. They would respect her desire for privacy. They were good people. She knew they hadn't missed her growing relationship with Trey. Although Melody had been hurt at first, even she had accepted what she couldn't deny.

Mira felt she and Trey belonged together, yet they would never share a bond. Her heart ached at the thought of what she was about to do and what she would be leaving behind.

Did she have the strength to leave Sassy Gap and the life she had built here?

What else could she do?

She examined the questions, already certain of the answers. She had absolutely no choice. Jean-Marc would continue to make her friends pay for her rebellion. A light still glowed in the women's building, and she knew they would leave it burning for her until she came in for the night. A sob broke through the iron control she had imposed on herself. She wouldn't be going inside. Tonight she would leave Sassy Gap. And her heart was breaking.

She took a final look around the cemetery and the familiar buildings and then started walking. Her gaze lingered on the barn. *Good-bye, mon cheri.* A sullen rumble of thunder warned her that time was wasting. She turned and set her feet on the path that would take her back to the plantation. Back to Jean-Marc, to a life she abhorred and to dreadful secrets she would never reveal.

He had won.

Mira trudged through the darkness. Never had the road to Belmonde seemed so long. Every step she took, every hour, brought her nearer to the confrontation she dreaded. Her heart was bitter with defeat. She had vowed to never give up, but she couldn't let Jean-Marc destroy Sassy Gap. The women had no other place to go.

Just before daylight, the gates of the Portier plantation came into sight. She stopped and studied the big house in the gray dawn. It was a beautiful house, the home of her ancestors, but for her it had been a prison. She drew a deep breath and continued on, putting one foot in front of the other, feeling she was marching to her doom. From now on every waking moment of her life would be under her enemy's control.

Halfway up the driveway a black-and-tan hound ran to meet her, tail wagging. She stopped to scratch his velvety ears and murmur words of greeting. "Good Sam; good boy." The dog padded beside her as she approached the steps that led to the front door.

She lifted the knocker and let it fall. Footsteps sounded in the hallway. Unseen hands fumbled with the lock, and then the door swung open and Macon stood there, his white hair standing out like a halo. His face split in a grin.

"Miss Mira. If you ain't the sight this old man's been longing for." He glanced at her empty hands. "You home to stay, girl?"

She followed him inside, struggling to remain calm. "Yes. It appears that Jean-Marc has won."

Macon shook his head. "His kind don't lose. That man don't have no give in him."

She stopped in front of the large vase of garden flowers standing on the carved mahogany hall table. "You've known him for many years. Has he ever loved anyone?"

Had Jean-Marc ever experienced the elations, the taking-of-breath emotion she had when Trey looked at her?

Macon's voice dropped to a murmur, and he looked cautiously over his shoulder. "He love Jean-Marc. More than that I don't know."

Mira accepted the truth. The man did not know the meaning of love. She suddenly felt sorry for him, this arrogant man she so despised, realizing that a life of selfishness and bitterness had stolen away the joy of living for him.

God could not work in an evil heart.

Once she had heard that the devil loves to cut the weak one out of the herd, then when the weakling is alone, take the fallen sheep down. *Pity, Jean-Marc, that you—of all people—have fallen for the devil's oldest ploy. You and my mother could have had so much more were it not for your belief that you lived alone. That you and you alone shepherded your life. I—even I—had much love to give, but you wanted no part of it.*

Macon's dark skin gleamed in the glow of the candle he held aloft. "Master Jean-Marc, he's like an old mud turtle. Got a hard shell all around him and he don't know how to break out."

Mira considered his words. Macon had been a slave here before the war. Freed by proclamation, he had chosen to stay on, claiming he was needed. She found that impossible to understand. Jean-Marc Portier had never needed anyone.

"You hungry, girl? I'll rustle up some food if you want me to. You thin as a willow branch."

"No. I will go to my room. Do not tell Jean-Marc that I am here. I will speak to him after I have rested."

"All right." He shuffled up the stairs ahead of her. "Going to be a glorious morning in this old house for sure. Our Miss Mira done come home."

Mira stepped into her old room and closed the door behind her. Macon had given her the candle, and she held it aloft, looking around. Funny, nothing had changed. Even the porcelain figurines her mother had brought from New Orleans sat in the same space on the corner desk.

The bed was made up with fresh sheets, turned back, waiting for her. The sight brought bile to the back of her throat. Had Jean-Marc been so certain that he'd win? Had he known that this latest threat was her breaking point? For a moment she toyed with the idea of walking down the stairs and running as hard as she could back to Sassy Gap, but reason won out. She had come this far; she would stay.

She crossed to the window, pushed it open, and leaned out. A subtle fragrance—jasmine—wafted on the early morning breeze. She could picture the gardens in her mind, the white iron bench where Paul had proposed. She remembered her frantic demand that they be married before telling her father. Dear, sweet, innocent Paul had complied.

She closed the window, then turned and faced her room. There were so many memories here. The strongest was her mother coming in to say good night. Mira could still smell gardenia, her mother's favorite perfume. She sank into a rose-silk chair and closed her eyes. When she'd made the decision to come back she hadn't realized how difficult it would be.

Finally she got up, put on a white cambric gown with hand-crocheted lace, and climbed into bed to cry herself to sleep.

Trey walked into the community building ready for breakfast. He sniffed the air. Fried bacon. He'd shot a stray shoat in the woods the other day, probably one of the hogs that had trampled the women's garden. No telling who it belonged to, but he figured it was payment for the damage done.

Helen turned to face him, her expression somber. "Mira's gone."

Trey's heart hit bottom. "Gone?"

Helen shrugged. "Back to the plantation, I'd guess. We should have known she wouldn't let that rotten man build those holding pens."

"She left without saying anything to anybody?"

He reached for a chair and sat down, struggling to believe she had left, refused to stay and fight not only against Jean-Marc, but for him. First Sharon and now Mira? He should have known. All women were alike.

"She knew we wouldn't let her go." Helen bit her lip and turned to look away. "Mira did what she thought was right. Some of the things her father did hurt deeply, and Grandma Speck getting so sick she almost died hit her hard."

"It affected all of us," Trey argued.

"Yes, but Mira blamed herself."

Dee handed Trey a cup of coffee. "Guess you've heard."

Trey nodded, numb from the news of Mira's leaving.

Dee sat and propped her chin in her hand. "We left a light burning for her and went to bed. Should have stayed up and waited for her to come in. Maybe we could have stopped her."

Vivian joined them. "Couldn't anyone stop Mira from doing what she thought was the right thing. She wouldn't let that black-hearted villain put us through any more misery." She blinked back tears. "I wish she hadn't done it though."

He realized Dee had said something and was waiting for an answer. "What?"

"I said, are you going to let her go or are you going after her?"

"Go after her?" Suddenly white-hot anger filled him. For a second time he'd let a woman steal his heart and then walk away, putting someone else's wishes before his. Go after her? A man could only be so much of a fool.

"I'm not going after her; she's a big girl. Obviously she's made her choice, and in case you haven't noticed, she didn't choose us."

"Now, Trey, that's your hurt talking," Brenda soothed. "She did what she thought she had to." She shrugged. "It wasn't the smartest thing she's ever done, but she had our best interests at heart."

She stopped when the door slammed behind Trey.

Mira woke late in the morning, blinking at her surroundings. She had dreamed she was back in her cubicle at Sassy Gap. Morning sunlight streamed through the windows, brightening the room. Pink roses climbed cream-colored wallpaper and were repeated in the Aubusson carpet. Dusky rose-satin curtains hung at the windows, and the furniture, carved and delicate, was made of rosewood and mahogany. Nothing had been too good for Jean-Marc's pretend daughter. Everyone in their social set had envied her. She'd had everything money could buy.

But money could never buy love.

Money could never buy a mother's care, or the love of a father she'd never known.

A discreet knock sounded at the door, and when Mira called, "Come in," a smiling young woman pushed the door open and entered. She carried a heavy tray, which she placed on the bedside table.

Her dark skin was made even darker by the snowy turban she wore. "Morning, Miss Mira. I'm Daisy. I brought your breakfast."

Mira sat up and looked at the tray. "I did not order breakfast."

"Macon did. He said you'd like to eat in your room this morning."

"Most thoughtful of him."

Macon would have guessed how much she dreaded confronting Jean-Marc. It was like him to send her nourishment before she bearded the lion. Macon and his wife, Lillybelle, had made life bearable for the lonely, motherless little girl she had been years ago.

She swung her legs off the bed and stood up. "Is Lillybelle still here?"

"Yes, ma'am. She in the kitchen. But she say she looking forward to seeing you again."

"Tell her I will be down directly. I am looking forward to seeing her, too."

Daisy left, and Mira sat down at the table and lifted the covers off the dishes. Ham, coddled eggs, toast, bramble jelly, and grits. She closed her eyes, willing herself to remain calm when she remembered the way the women at Sassy Gap had been forced to scramble for food. She started to push the tray away but then stopped. She would need all of her strength to stand before the tyrant of Belmonde. Starving herself wouldn't ease her friends' hunger pangs. She filled her plate and choked down the food.

After breakfast she washed in the water Daisy brought and donned one of the dresses she found hanging in the closet. There, too, nothing had been altered. Her clothing hung where she had left it when she fled with Paul. The room was clean and fresh. It had been consistently aired out and cared for. On Jean-Marc's orders? Of course. Nothing happened at the plantation unbeknownst to him. No effort would have been spared to present himself as a loving father grieving over a wayward daughter too stubborn to appreciate her father's goodness.

She brushed her waist-length hair and walked downstairs, one hand sliding over the polished wood banister. The hall clock struck ten, and she turned her steps toward Jean-Marc's study, knowing he would already be at work plotting more underhanded schemes.

He looked up from his desk when she opened the door. "Ah, Mira. I heard you had joined us. Welcome home."

"Home? When was it ever a home?" She entered and closed the door behind her.

He shook his head. "Defiant as ever, I see. I had hoped absence had made your heart fonder for home and hearth."

"I am here for one reason only. To stop your persecution of my friends at Sassy Gap."

He raised his eyebrows. "Friends? People who kept you away from your rightful place? People who defied me? Strange behavior for friends."

She sat down across the desk from him. "I am back. Whether I stay depends on you."

He spread his hands in an expansive gesture. "Ask and it will be yours. I will be happy to buy you anything you wish. After all, you are Linette's daughter."

"You dare to speak of my mother?" She didn't try to keep the scorn out of her voice. "The woman you abused until you finally took her life? When will you learn the most important things in life can never be bought?"

Jean-Marc was silent for a moment, looking down at his desk. "What do you want, Mira? You are here for a purpose."

"I want you to stop persecuting the women at Sassy Gap."

He shrugged. "But of course. There is no reason to continue the battle." He smiled. "I have won."

Mira left the room and Jean-Marc smiled. Poor, gullible Mira. So trusting. She had come home, believing she could save her friends. Let her believe her sacrifice had purpose. By the time she learned different it would be too late.

Jean-Marc walked to the window, looking out at the well-manicured lawn, the bright beds of flowers. No matter how he had come by the plantation, he had poured his lifeblood into it. If it hadn't been for him, Bellmonde would have been destroyed during the war, like many other fine plantations. There were those who would call him traitor, like that fanatic, Tom Addison, and his cronies. Let them think what they pleased. He had only done what was necessary to save what was his.

The war had brought many changes, but he, Jean-Marc Portier, had survived the war. Now he had plans for the future.

Those plans involved Mira. She would not find it so easy to escape again.

Trey was in the stable when Melody came in. The women were working at their respective chores. He'd shot a deer yesterday and had caught a whiff of braised venison when he'd passed the community room half an hour earlier. He had a hunch the young woman had lost interest in him. Daniel had stolen his thunder, and Trey couldn't be happier. He liked Melody and he was crazy about Audrey, but Mira had taken his heart and run away with it. He'd be leaving for Kansas as soon as his friends arrived. If they arrived. He had summoned them for nothing, but he couldn't leave without seeing them and explaining the reason for his summons.

Melody sat down on an upended bucket. "You miss Mira."

It wasn't a question and he didn't deny it. "I miss a lot of things." He swung a saddle over a rail.

"We all do. You're like the rest of us." She reached out to put her hand over his. "Mira loves you, Trey. I guess I knew it all along, but I tried to convince myself that you loved me."

He started to speak and she put a finger to his lips. "I realize now that you didn't. You loved Audrey."

"I'm fond of you, Melody. Consider you a good friend."

"I know and I feel the same." She grinned. "It's just that you were the only man in town, and I think we all became a little bold."

He laughed. "And now there's a second man in town?"

She blushed. "Yes. I guess there is."

He patted her shoulder. "You couldn't pick a better one. Daniel would make you a fine husband."

She smiled. "He really is a good man, isn't he? And Audrey likes him."

"I've noticed. Fickle woman," he teased.

"Oh, she loves you, Trey. She really does. It's just that Daniel is so good with her."

"I know, Melody. I couldn't be happier for the two of you."

She nodded, smiling. "Daniel sent me to tell you something."

He waited.

"They're having a big party at the Portier plantation. It's Jean-Marc's birthday, and they're celebrating Mira coming home."

Why was she telling him that? "What am I supposed to do about it?"

"Well, Daniel thought you might be able to slip in, mingle with the guests without getting caught, and maybe have a chance to talk to Mira."

He turned to give her a sour look. "And why would I do that?"

Melody got to her feet. "How much do you love her?"

He shrugged. Now she was getting too personal.

"Answer me," she demanded.

"I love her! All right!"

He slapped a pair of reins over the railing. Pesky woman.

She grinned, squeezing his shoulder. "Daniel said he had a nice waistcoat and britches you could borrow."

"No."

She drew him around to face her. "Yes. You're stubborn. She's stubborn. When is this going to stop?"

Trey spun on his heel and left the stable.

The garden was beautiful in the early morning light. Mira sat on the white wrought-iron bench where Paul had asked her to be his wife. How could either of them have imagined the changes that would come to them? Paul dying on a battlefield, one of many where good men had fallen, and Mira locked in a battle every bit as deadly—one she could never win.

Jean-Marc approached, wandering down the path, stopping to cup a blossom in his hand, stooping to sniff the mignonette. Mira smiled in derision. As if his being here was so much coincidence. She would learn soon enough what he wanted.

"Ah, there you are, Mira. Enjoying the fresh air?"

"Of course. It is such a lovely day." Two could play this game. "And what of you? No duty calls for your attention today?"

He shrugged. "There are many things I need to do, but none of them as important as spending time with you."

"You make a mockery, sir. When have you ever wanted to spend time in my company?" She snapped a fan open.

"Ah, perhaps, my dear, I have changed, or perhaps it is seeing you with that pretty bloom on your cheeks, languishing in a setting that must hold precious memories for you. It was here the young man, Paul, wooed and won you; was it not?"

Mira inclined her head, not bothering to answer so obvious a taunt.

Jean-Marc smiled. "Actually I am the bearer of good news. I believe I mentioned that the staff is having a celebration honoring the humble day of my birth and now your happy homecoming. You will be expected to attend, wearing your prettiest dress, of course."

Mira plucked a pink rosebud and held it to her nose, sniffing delicately. "I am not interested in attending a social event, whatever the reason. Surely you realize I am still in mourning."

Technically speaking, she'd never had a mourning period so she would have one now. Not for Paul, but for Trey and what they'd lost.

"Still?" His eyebrows rose in mock amazement. "I believe the prescribed time is one year. Is it possible you were more in love with the young man than I supposed?"

"The depths of my feelings do not concern you."

"Perhaps not, but this does concern me." The smile faded. "You will present a smiling face to our guests, and you will be as gracious and as well mannered as your mother before you."

"Is this the ultimatum you gave her?"

He frowned. "Do not argue with me. You will do as I say or you will regret it."

"And if I refuse, will you push me down stairs also?"

"No, my dear Mira, I will confine you to your room."

"For how long?"

"Forever." His voice took on a tone of deep sorrow. "Poor Mira. The horrors of the war and of losing her husband have overwhelmed her. She is so confused we must guard her carefully so she will not hurt herself."

She felt cold inside. "You would not dare."

He grinned. "Of course I dare. You put yourself in my hands when you came home."

Jean-Marc walked back to the house confident and satisfied. Mira had fallen for his bluff. Of course he would not confine her to an upstairs bedroom. She was essential to his plans. It never hurt to give her reason to be afraid of him, though. All of the talk about ruling through love was a laugh. Nothing inspired a man or woman to fall into line faster than a good dose of pure, unadulterated dread.

Mira was included in preparations for the celebration as though she'd never been away. Every detail was brought to her for attention, and each decision was like a knife in her heart. Everything she loved had been taken from her. She had nothing to celebrate.

Daisy found her on the wide veranda, sitting with her hands in her lap, too downhearted to do much more. "There you are, Miss Mira. Lillybelle say do you want Lady Baltimore cake for dessert, or do you want something else?"

"Whatever she likes," Mira said, feeling as listless as she sounded.

Daisy nodded her expression sympathetic. "Miss Mira, would you like some fresh mint tea? I can brew you a batch."

"No, Daisy, that is all right, but thank you."

The young woman went back into the house, and Mira let apathy wash over her. Her days consisted of nothing. She who had worked for a living in a funeral parlor, helped with the cooking, cleaning, and gardening, sat like a log. A useless log. She had learned to milk a cow and cook over a woodstove, but now servants catered to her every whim. Even the most minor tasks were done for her. She didn't have anything to do with her time. Someone else did the cooking and cleaning. She had everything money could buy. Her home was the most imposing, most beautiful house in the parish.

And she was miserable.

Finally she went to the kitchen to give instructions about the coming dinner. If she had to do this, she would do her best, not for Jean-Marc, but in memory of the mother who had once been the chatelaine of this house. No one would be able to say Linette Portier's daughter was lacking in proper social skills.

Lillybelle's agile fingers worked dough for her cloud-light

dinner rolls. "Your face is gloomy enough to sour milk. What's wrong with my lamb?"

"Oh, Lillybelle. I am so miserable. I hate it here."

"Then why you come back? You got away, Miss Mira, and then you walk back into the lion's den. Why you do that?"

"Jean-Marc gave me no choice. I had to stop his persecution of my friends."

Lillybelle shook her head. "Laws, child. He ain't going to stop until they all leave. He wants the town and the ground it sits on."

Mira sat down at the table, frowning. "Why would he want the town?"

Lillybelle gave the dough a hearty slap and flopped it over. "Macon say there's a railroad coming through where the town be and Massa Jean-Marc needs the land so he can sell it to the railroad folk."

Mira slumped in the chair, the breath gone out of her. Her sacrifice, all she had given up, had been for nothing. The persecution would never stop. She hadn't realized the scope of Jean-Marc's plans. It had never been all about her; he had only let her think so in order to get her back under his thumb. In that case, his promise of ceasing to harass the women was worthless.

"Macon is sure about this?"

"Oh, he sure all right. You see, Miss Mira, people like Jean-Marc is so used to having servants around they don't notice us no more than they would a piece of furniture. Macon knows a lot more than people think."

Mira sat with her head bowed, overwhelmed with questions she wanted to ask. She supposed Lillybelle was correct. It was so easy to overlook a servant simply because he was there. Dedicated. Loving. Working selflessly to make others comfortable.

She raised her head. "Lillybelle, did you ever see my father?"

The woman's hands stilled for a moment. A frown furrowed her brow. "You know about your father?"

"I know Jean-Marc killed him."

Lillybelle stiffened. "Now how you know that?"

"He admitted it."

Lillybelle nodded. "We thought as much, Macon and me. Many's the time we talked about it after we'd gone to bed and we was sure we wouldn't be overheard. But we never knew for certain."

Mira leaned forward. "Tell me about him."

"His name was Benjamin Logan. Strapping young man, big, brown hair and eyes, crazy about your mamma. Miss Linette, she be crazy about him, too."

Mira listened, treasuring every word. She wanted so much to believe her mother had been loved. And had loved.

"The day they run off to New Orleans and got married, she was fairly twittering she was so excited."

"Married! She married him?" Mira sat, mouth open in surprise. Had she heard right?

"Of course they got married. What you thinking? My Miss Linette some kind of tramp?"

"No, it's not that. . . ."

Lillybelle put the dough to rise in a well-greased bowl, covering it with a soft white cloth. "Let me guess." She shrugged a contemptuous shoulder. "He told you that."

Mira nodded, so overcome with surprise she couldn't speak.

Lillybelle touched her shoulder. "They went to New Orleans to get married because Miss Linette begged him to and he couldn't say no to her. He was going back to Texas to take care of business and then he would come here and get her."

"What happened?" The words escaped as a whisper.

"We never knew. They come home and Ben went out to check the lower pasture and he never came back. My poor baby was almost crazy with grief."

"Why didn't anyone know about him?"

Lillybelle stopped to think. "We was a lot more isolated back then. Wasn't so many people out this way. Weeks went by without us seeing anyone else and then they got married so quick and so secret. No one knew about it 'cept Massa Jean-Marc."

"How did he happen to know?"

"'Cause he was here every time you turn around. He knew Miss Linette was in love with Massa Benjamin, but it didn't make him no never mind. He never give up."

"Why did she marry Jean-Marc?"

"Why, she didn't have no choice. Miss Linette was all alone after her daddy die. There wasn't anyone to stop that Jean-Marc from forcing her to marry him."

Mira nodded, tears welling to her eyes. "And then he murdered her."

After breakfast Sunday morning the women trooped to the funeral parlor for worship service. Daniel had taken over the preaching and he was doing a fine job. The funeral parlor was closed now. Without Mira Grandma Speck couldn't carry on alone and the other women refused to work with the ritual of death. Now the folks in the surrounding community had no one to help them bury their dead. Holding wakes was their only choice.

Trey settled on the back row beside Brenda. Melody led them in a hymn, but he missed Mira's clear soprano.

Daniel opened his Bible, reading from the one-hundred-fortieth Psalm, "'Deliver me, O Lord, from the evil man: preserve me from the violent man.'"

It was like God was singling out Trey.

He jumped, barely restraining himself from a startled yelp when someone jabbed him with an elbow.

Brenda raised an eyebrow. "Pay attention."

Thoroughly chastened, he settled back against the pew with his arms crossed. But his mind was on Mira and the coming party. Did he go after her, make a fool of himself a third time? He wanted to. He missed her like he'd miss his right arm. And he had company coming—six men. What was he going to tell them when they got here? *Sorry about the ride. I'm mad at a woman and changed my mind about helping her.*

Afterward, the women trooped to the community room for a dinner of venison and dumplings. Jane had outdone herself this time. One of these days some man was going to eat her cooking and realize this was a woman in a million. Trey remembered what his grandmother used to say. "Cuddling don't last; cooking do."

They had finished eating when Brenda shoved back her plate and rapped her spoon against her water glass. "This meeting is now called to order."

Trey glanced up from his plate. "What meeting?"

Brenda gave him a straight look that brooked no compromise. "We have talked this over, and we want you to go after Mira."

Before he could tell her the hundred-and-one reasons why he shouldn't, Dee interrupted. "Sassy Gap isn't the same. We've lost our heart."

"And our spirit," Vivian said.

Audrey leaned on his knee. "And my Mira. I miss my Mira, Trey."

Trey reached out and ruffled the head of curls. "So do I, Punkin."

The door to the community house opened, and a man stepped in, stopping just inside. Trey recognized the butler from Belmonde. Mira? Had anything happened to her? He half stood.

Macon looked around the room until he came to Trey. "Mr. McAllister, sir?"

"That's me. What's wrong? Is Mira all right?"

"She just fine. She don't know I'm here. I've got some information you need to hear."

Trey motioned to a chair. "Have a seat. Are you hungry?"

Macon shook his head. "Thank you, Mr. McAllister, but it be better if I don't sit down at the table like white folks. It might go hard on me later."

Trey nodded. He knew what the man meant, but it really burned him. He'd just spent three years trying to change this very situation. Even though the war was over, he knew it would take a long time for change to come.

"The thing I come to tell you is that Miss Mira leaving won't make no difference to you people. Jean-Marc needs this town and he won't stop until he gets it."

Trey's gaze met the man's grave dark eyes. "It's not much of a town anymore. Why would it be so important to him?"

Macon turned his hat around in his hands. "It's valuable property. A railroad is coming, and they want to run the line straight through here."

"A railroad?" Grandma Speck asked. "Here? In Sassy Gap?"

"That's right," Macon said. "Mr. Richard Holman is with the company, and he been coming to Belmonde to speak to Master Jean-Marc. He wants to buy this town something awful."

"What if we won't sell?" Brenda asked.

"Then the railroad won't come," Trey said. "They'd have to detour around and probably miss Mignon altogether. Leave Jean-Marc out."

"That right, Mr. McAllister," Macon said. "And that's not all. That Jean-Marc wants to marry my Miss Mira off to Mr. Loyal Moore."

"Loyal Moore?" Grandma Speck exclaimed. "The man's old enough to be her daddy!"

"And he owns the plantation adjoining Belmonde," Brenda said grimly. "That's why that black-hearted sorry excuse for a man plans to marry her off."

"Why would that benefit Jean-Marc?" Trey asked.

"Because Loyal Moore has a lot of business connections in New Orleans and on the coast." Jane stood. "He doesn't spend much time at Linwood, which would give Jean-Marc a free rein with running it and skimming the cream off the top. Loyal won't have any idea how much money he'll lose if that comes to pass."

"Jean-Marc can't make Mira marry anyone she doesn't want," Viv argued.

"Of course he can," Daniel said. "Jean-Marc Portier rules his little corner of the world. Mira won't have a choice."

Trey closed his eyes to shut out the vision of Mira married to anyone but him. He didn't like the picture.

CHAPTER 13

The door to Jean-Marc's dressing room opened, and he swung around to face the newcomer. "Loyal? To what do I owe this honor?"

"Something I want to talk to you about."

Jean-Marc eyed the portly older man, letting his expression show his irritation. "Was Macon not on duty downstairs?"

"Of course. Told him I could find my way. Figured we could forget about formality since I'm going to be your son-in-law."

"Ah. I see."

"That's right, isn't it?" Loyal pressed. "I believe we had an arrangement."

"Yes, of course," Jean-Marc murmured. "No doubt about it."

He'd take the fat old fool for a son-in-law, as long as it rid him of the troublesome woman. Mira was rapidly becoming more of a problem than she was worth. If he didn't need her in order to get his hands on Linwood Plantation, he'd send her to join her mother in the family cemetery.

Loyal flicked a speck of dust off his coat. "Fact is, Mira isn't always courteous. Seems to almost dislike me most of the time, although I'm at a loss as to why."

"Mira is an innocent in many ways," Jean-Marc said, keeping his tone sanctimonious. "Perhaps I have sheltered her too much, but she always seemed such a delicate creature."

The "delicate creature" had just heaved a porcelain box at his head when he had suggested she spend the evening flirting with Loyal, but no need to go into that here. He believed he had been stern enough with her that she would curtail any further displays of temper.

Loyal frowned, wrinkling his brow. "Innocent? The girl's been married. Surely she has some experience in the ways of the world."

"No matter. You can deal with an unwilling wife." The old man's reputation was well-known in the community. Mira would not have an easy time fending off the rakish Moore.

Loyal grinned, revealing discolored teeth. Jean-Marc stifled a grimace of distaste. Did the man know nothing about baking soda and water?

"No, you're right on that. Breaking a woman's spirit and breaking a horse have a lot in common. Each fine sport, and fortunately, I'm experienced at both."

"Of course," Jean-Marc murmured. "If you'll excuse me, I must finish dressing; my guests will be arriving soon."

"Certainly." Loyal opened the door. "Just so you know: I expect you to carry out your end of our bargain."

"What an impatient bridegroom. Don't worry; Mira will be yours."

Loyal left and Jean-Marc stared at his reflection in the mirror, letting his jubilation show. Everything was going according to plan. The price Loyal would pay for Mira would be Linwood Plantation. He picked up gold cuff links with emeralds embedded in the twisted design. Loyal hated the plantation. He'd give Jean-Marc a free hand in managing the land, and best of all, he would take Mira so far away that she would be among strangers and no longer a threat to him. She wouldn't have an opportunity to cause trouble. She would be too busy bearing Loyal's children.

Mira dressed carefully, not too elaborately, but nice enough that Jean-Marc could not complain. She went downstairs to the kitchen to check on last-minute details.

Lillybelle sat in a rocker in the large kitchen, tears streaming down her face.

Mira knelt beside her. "Lillybelle? What is wrong?"

The woman wiped her eyes on her apron. "Nothing, Miss Mira, just me being silly."

"I do not believe this. Silly would not make you cry. Tell me, please."

Lillybelle sniffed. "It's just that talking about Miss Linette brought it all back. I guess you don't know about the baby since she hadn't told no one yet, but it hurt to lose both of them. Seems like it made it twice as bad."

Mira grasped the chair arm. "What are you saying? My mother was in the family way?"

"She was, Miss Mira, and real happy about it too. Miss

Linette always was crazy about children. You know how much she loved you."

"Yes, Lillybelle, I know. She hadn't told Jean-Marc?"

"She was planning to. They went to dinner and something went terrible wrong. I don't know what it was but that was the night she fell downstairs."

Mira's mind raced. "Jean-Marc always wanted a son."

"He sure did," Lillybelle said. "That's what he wanted most, someone to carry on his name."

"I wonder if that baby was a boy or girl."

Lillybelle blew her nose. "We'll never know."

Mira nodded. "And neither will Jean-Marc."

He would have to live with that as well as the other deeds he'd performed.

The Portier mansion blazed with lights Saturday evening. Carriages filled the large courtyard. Impeccably dressed servants assisted ladies clad in billowing silk gowns while handsome gentleman sporting top hats and gloves walked proudly beside them.

Jean-Marc stood at the entrance to the ballroom, with Mira standing beside him, receiving his guests. Hundreds of candles twinkled overhead in glistening crystal chandeliers while white-coated servants moved through the crowded room, carrying trays of exquisite cut-glass goblets.

"Somer Avent. My daughter, Mirelle."

Mira dipped courteously, recoiling at the feel of Avent's sweaty, flaccid hand around hers. The older man squeezed her fingers suggestively, and Mira quickly broke the grip. She snapped open her fan, drawing in a breath of fresh air.

Addressing her from the corner of his mouth, Jean-Marc rebuked her. "Try to show a little more interest in potential suitors. The man owns a fleet of ships."

"And may they all sink the moment they leave port." Mira snapped her fan closed and smiled at the next man in line.

The mansion was insufferably stuffy tonight. She longed to refute Jean-Marc's words, desired to call out to the assembled guests that she was no daughter of this man, that he had indeed murdered her rightful parents. Her gaze roamed the packed room, and she caught sight of a flash of red hair. Instantly her heart flew to her throat, but when the throng parted and the form moved closer she recognized Peter Willit, a son of one of her father's acquaintances.

The tempo of her heartbeat slowed, and she fought back a rush of hot tears. She'd left Sassy Gap three weeks ago, and she had neither seen nor heard from Trey. What had she expected? For him to follow her like a lovelorn suitor and demand that she return to Sassy Gap? She caught tears at the corners of her eyes before Jean-Marc noticed and questioned her mood. Had she expected a man—a stranger—to ride to her rescue and face Jean-Marc's rage by openly declaring his undying love?

Did she expect Trey McAllister to announce that she was his and that he would fight to the death for her?

The idea was ludicrous and whimsical, but the wish constantly tormented her. Day and night every tear, every prayer, centered on this man of the saddle, the stranger from Kansas. Love poured through her veins, pumping the sheer exhilarating feeling through her heart until she thought she would scream with frustration.

When she was younger she used to wonder what love felt like. Was it warm? Was it cool? Did it have a color? Or was *love* merely a term used by ninnies and fools? Now she knew. Love felt awful when it wasn't returned. It ran hot sometimes and icy others. Love had as many colors as the rainbow—yellows, blues, pinks, and greens of bright intensities.

But sometimes it was a dark shadow just out of her view.

Once when she was very young, Jean-Marc had taken the family and sailed to the Hawaiian Islands. Mira recalled little about the voyage except the beautiful, breathtaking arches that filled the island's skies. Rainbows, some double arched, appeared everywhere. They reached for miles and miles. Mira had pleaded with her mother to climb the hillsides and touch the wonderful colors because they looked as if they melted into the earth. She remembered so little about Mama, but ever vivid in her mind was the one special afternoon when her mother had taken her by the hand and together they had climbed to the top of a hill, chasing the vibrant hues. First they sat. Then they lay down at the bottom of the arch, laughing with delight as the pretty colors seeped through their dresses. Mira had lain completely still, letting the colors saturate her heart.

That's how she felt about Trey. She wanted to lie down on the grass, look up in the sky, and let the colors of his love fill her.

Jean-Marc had not encouraged her to keep such memories

alive. This she resented even more than she resented his interference in her life.

Now he had won again. Love would never be a part of her
life. Not now. Not ever.

"Loyal Moore. My lovely daughter, Mirelle."

"Ah yes." The man's beady eyes skimmed her. "Most unfortunate about your late husband, my dear."

"Yes. Most unfortunate."

Mira curtsied and the cur moved on. Jean-Marc had him
pegged for her husband; Jean-Marc and Loyal Moore would be
disappointed. She would never marry now.

The evening was endless. Servants announced the evening
meal would be served in the dining hall. Mira accepted Mr.
Moore's arm, repulsed by the smell of mothballs and strong
drink. Together they preceded Jean-Marc and Lady Paula
Lemour to the dining room.

Over dinner Mira watched while Moore swilled hard liquor
and talked incessantly of his vast business holdings and
imported-cloth empire.

Guest's voices faded and she found herself thinking back to
simpler times in Sassy Gap. She recalled how hard the women
worked simply to survive. She thought about Grandma Speck,
Brenda, Viv, Dee, Helen, Melody, and Jane. What were they
doing tonight? Was Grandma feeling better?

And little Audrey, precious child of God. How she loved the
imp with the dark, shiny curls.

Her heart cautioned her, *Don't think about Trey*. She would
be awash in fresh tears if she let her mind dwell on him. This
was to be her future: this endless, inane round of parties and
people who had never experienced any of life's hardships, who

had no idea what it was like to go to bed at night and wonder if a new day would bring enough food and fresh milk to feed a child of three.

God had been faithful. There had been times when the women had no milk, but Audrey always did.

Trey paused in the shadows on the portico, watching Mira. The long windows and the blazing chandeliers allowed him to see as well as if he had been seated at the table with the invited guests. Mira turned her back on the man seated beside her. Trey eyed him with contempt. Old, fat, looking none too clean. Was this the businessman Macon had mentioned? the man Jean-Marc planned to marry Mira? He clenched his fists. Not while there was a breath of life in his body.

Moore's coarse voice drew Mira back. ". . . about to make a toast, lovey."

The dining hall grew quiet when Jean-Marc rose from his place at the head of the long dining table. Lifting his glass to Mira, he spoke. "To my daughter, the lovely Mirelle. May your life be long, your happiness unending, and my grandchildren forthcoming very soon!"

"Hear, hear!" A shout went up. The plink of crystal hitting crystal filled the long dining hall.

Mira unceremoniously sat her glass down without drinking.

Moore's eyes sparked with merriment. "Always the rebel, aye, Mira?"

"Always, Mr. Moore. Always." How could Jean-Marc make such an odious toast and carry it off as if he really were a doting father? The man's hypocrisy had no bounds.

Loyal leaned closer, his foul breath heavy as he laid a meaty hand across hers. The liquor had glazed his eyes and slurred his speech. "Why do you fight the inevitable? I have asked Jean-Marc for your hand. I can make you very happy. I am rich beyond your wildest imagination, and if you will marry me you have only to speak your desires and they will be fulfilled."

Her gaze met his and she said calmly, "That is not possible."

Her heart pounded. Marry Loyal Moore? Even a sheltered woman like her had heard of his reputation. Living with him would be even worse than being under Jean-Marc's control.

Loyal threw back his head and laughed, revealing uneven, tobacco-stained teeth. "Ah, but you are a saucy wench! I have sufficient money to buy you the world! You have only to speak the word, and you will have whatever you desire."

"I desire love."

He blinked. "Love?" The word seemed foreign to him.

"Yes. Love."

His smile faded and he fumbled for his glass. "Love, she says." He tossed back a drink.

For the moment he seemed nonplussed, but she knew it wouldn't last. Was this the destiny Jean-Marc had in store for her? She had been a fool to come back. Now there was no escape.

After dinner the men retired to Jean-Marc's study. Since there were few women her age in attendance, Mira slipped out of the stuffy parlor and walked along the veranda. The air had cooled. Overhead a brilliant full moon lit the vast Portier grounds. In the distance, she heard the voices of servants talking as they sat on boxes and played a friendly game of cards, waiting until the festivities were over and the carriages could be brought around.

Mira strolled along the pillared terrace, taking in the pleasant evening. When the rains slackened this part of the South was pleasant.

"Pretty fancy place." The voice came from behind the porch pillar against which she was leaning.

Her heart jumped. Though she had hoped and prayed she would someday hear that voice again, she was hesitant to believe it was real. She closed her eyes and said a quick, sincere prayer of gratitude. Trey. He had come.

"Pretentious. Overdone," she agreed lightly.

He stepped from the shadows, looking so strikingly handsome that her heart nearly stopped. He could easily have passed for one of the dapper men who earlier had been whirling spoiled, overprivileged ladies around the Portier ballroom. For a moment she had trouble breathing. She stood motionless, soaking in his nearness.

"You are taking a great risk by being here," she reminded in her soft accent.

His eyes held hers. "One I am finding I don't mind if it involves you."

Oh, how she longed to go to him, to hold him, to kiss and embrace him. But she didn't dare. Jean-Marc's men were everywhere; the barest whisper that Trey was here and he would not be allowed to leave.

They stood apart in the cool moonlight, gazes locked in mute longing.

"Do you know how beautiful you are?"

She looked down, overcome with desire. "And you are most handsome, *mon cheri.*"

He strolled casually to a nearby rock wall, lifted a booted foot to the edge, and appeared to be gazing at the heavens. To an observing eye the meeting was casual, unforeseen. Only Mira's erratic heartbeat gave indication that the encounter was anything but chance.

She snapped her fan closed and leaned against the wall, also gazing up at the stars. "Why are you here?"

"You really need to ask?"

"You took your time, you know."

"I know."

She bit her lower lip, desperately needing him to say why he had come. Was he here to bring news of Sassy Gap? Had something happened to one of the women? Had Audrey taken ill? Her heart tripped faster.

"You will forgive me, sir, but my constant prayer the last week has been that you would come, and that you would come because of me."

He appeared to admire the clear night. "Perhaps God has seen fit to answer your prayers."

She was being outrageously bold. Maybe he was here for nothing more than to carry a message. "Do you bring news?"

"I bring good wishes and prayers for your well-being."

Sighing, she said softly, "I am well." Did he have nothing more to say? So near, and yet so untouchable.

Trey stared up at the moon. "Macon came to visit us. Had some interesting things to say."

Mira's hand went to her throat. "Macon? What did he tell you?"

"That a railroad is coming to Sassy Gap. That Jean-Marc Portier knows about the railroad and has been talking to the company, telling them he will soon own the town."

"I, too, have heard this," Mira acknowledged bitterly. "It seems I have made my great sacrifice for nothing. I might as well have stayed with the women."

"He won't give up," Trey agreed. "But now that we know we can take steps to defeat him."

"You think we can defeat Jean-Marc? You do not know him well."

"No, that's true, but no one is unbeatable, Mira. Sooner or later, no matter how big the man, he takes a tumble."

"And you think Jean-Marc is ready to tumble?"

"I don't know, but I'm going to do everything in my power to stop him if I can."

They fell silent when a laughing couple danced from the ballroom onto the portico. Amid a flurry of greetings, the couple moved deeper onto the veranda. Mira risked a brief glance into the overheated room and located Jean-Marc at the punch bowl, conversing with friends. For the moment they would remain undetected.

"How did you get in?"

He turned to smile. "I am a man of many resources."

She blushed, averting her eyes. "I am sure that is true."

His voice dropped. "Your father's servants are easily diverted. I entered with a large group and was barely noticed."

"You should not take such risks. I fear for you."

She was afraid of what Jean-Marc might do if he was to find Trey here. He knew Trey represented all he'd fought against. The day she'd come home Jean-Marc had thrown down the gauntlet: she was not to see this tall, redheaded stranger again. At the best he would feel Trey was beneath her social standing and at the worst a troublemaker.

"You cannot do this!" she'd spat back.

Jean-Marc's eyes had turns to shards of steel. "I think we both know that I can do whatever I choose, Mirelle."

She had turned, about to leave his library when she suddenly stopped and whirled back to confront him. "I will stay, Jean-Marc, and I will give you no further trouble, but you must allow me to see my friends. The women of Sassy Gap are family to me. I will not forfeit the right to spend time there on occasion."

Jean-Marc had not readily agreed, but he addressed her demand over breakfast one morning. "You will be allowed one visit a month."

"Only one a month! That is not enough! I want to go once each week."

He hesitated, clearly upset that she questioned him. "Once a week it is. See, my dear? I can be a reasonable man." Then his voice hardened. "But they will be brief."

She'd crossed her arms over her chest. "An afternoon a week."

"Two hours a week."

"Four," she countered.

He threw up his hands and left the table while she sat back and sipped her tea, smiling behind the cup. Four hours.

One afternoon.

At the time she'd thought she had won; now she was not so certain.

Mira eased closer to the line of fragrant heirloom roses. Here they would be completely hidden from sight.

Trey straightened and slowly followed her. When they reached the privacy of the hedge she stepped into his arms.

The kiss was hungry and wild and exciting, like nothing she'd ever known.

Showering his face with stolen kisses, she whispered, "I have missed you so."

His hold tightened and he kissed her again and again. The embrace would have gone on forever, but Mira knew there was little time.

"Brenda and Viv and Dee and Jane and Helen—"

He shushed her with a soft chuckle. "All fine, all missing you. Audrey asks about you every day."

"And Melody," she asked, praying that her envy didn't show.

"Melody's been cooking a lot of suppers for Daniel. The three are becoming quite the little family."

Relief left her faint. "Oh, Trey, I thought you might have gone back to Kansas."

"Not without you."

His bold declaration was sweet and frightening. Both knew their love was destined to failure, but the bittersweet thought that he cared would help her exist through the coming lonely months.

He pulled her to him possessively. "Who was that lout you were eating beside tonight?"

She laughed, lovingly tracing his features with the tip of her finger. She wanted to memorize every crook, every angle. "My future husband—if Jean-Marc has his wish."

"Over my dead body." He pulled her tighter and kissed her soundly.

"You are not angry at me for leaving," she whispered when their lips parted. She laid her head on his broad chest, drinking in his clean smell. Soap. Fresh air. The wind.

"Angry as any one man can get, but I know why you did it."

"You did not think I had betrayed you?"

"A hundred times a day."

"And yet you have still come to me."

He drew back, holding her gently by her shoulders. She could barely see the outline of his face in the deep shadows.

"I am deeply in love with you, Mira. I've been a fool. I've known for some time, but I let my past decide my future."

"The woman that you once loved—"

He shushed her with another long kiss. Later, he whispered, "I was bitter for a long time. Sharon coupled with my sisters, who cluck over me like an old mother hen, I'd pretty well decided I was through with women. Until I met you."

She smoothed the collar of his waistcoat—or one belonging to Daniel, she suspected. Smiling up at him she said, "You are now ready to admit that you love me?"

He nodded, lowering his mouth to take hers.

Long moments passed before she said softly, "Our love—you know it is and will forever be forbidden."

"I know Jean-Marc will not willingly hand you over to me."

"No, *cheri*. He will not." They stood in the embrace, drawing strength from each other. Moments were passing. They must part soon or be discovered.

"Marry me, Mira."

She caught her breath, so tempted. Then hope failed her. "I cannot. You know I cannot."

"Don't say that. If you don't marry me that blackguard will see you married to that old man. I couldn't bear that. You braved his anger once to marry Paul; won't you do the same for me?"

"I married Paul because I had no other choice!"

"Now you do have a choice." His tone moderated. "Marry me. Let me be your family, your husband, the father of your children."

She shook her head, "Jean-Marc is—he could and *would* make our life unbearable. I love you too much—"

"Is your life happy now?"

Her arms crept back around his neck. "I would spend my life here, in your arms, *mon cheri*, if only God would make it possible."

The ballroom doors opened and two couples emerged. Trey pulled Mira deeper into the shadows.

"Then you will marry me if we can find a way to do it without your father's knowledge?"

"You cannot talk foolish, my darling. There is no conceivable way to fool him again. He is too watchful—"

He put his fingertip to her lips. "I asked if you will marry me if I find a way. Listen to me, Mira. If we are married he can't force you to marry Loyal Moore."

Mira knew he could. Jean-Marc had forced her mother to marry him. A man like Jean-Marc Portier, with no conscience, had no compunction about using the vilest tactics to get what he wanted.

She paused, biting her lower lip. She loved Trey more than life itself, but loving her could ruin his life.

"Yes," she whispered, giving in to her selfish nature for the moment. "Yes, but it cannot be—"

"That's all I need to hear." He kissed her one final time and then gently nudged her back onto the veranda before she could question his intent.

Trembling, she drew her light wrap closer, tremulously smiling at the couples that now stood taking in the moonlight.

Marry Trey. It would be her wildest dreams come true. Her heart beat a staccato cadence.

But how? Only a miracle would allow their love to grow and survive.

Trey walked the lane back to where he had tied his horse. Even though the guests at Belmonde were congregated at the house and weren't likely to notice him, he kept to the shadows. Warmed by Mira's love and encouraged by the memory of her kiss, he knew he could never give her up to Loyal Moore, or to anyone else.

Somehow he had to find a way to marry her. It wouldn't be easy, but if this was God's will for their lives, then nothing would stop him.

CHAPTER 14

Deception, Mira learned, could be simple. And Satan's tool.

As easy as a walk in the afternoon to gather berries.

As simple as a brief duck into an oak grove.

As wonderful as a redheaded Kansas man and a country preacher waiting for her.

As pleasurable as exchanged wedding vows in that same oak grove. The country preacher supervised the nuptials before an imaginary altar decorated by wispy moss draped over spreading branches.

The ceremony was over in two minutes.

Afterward Mira had stepped out of the grove with a basketful of berries, supplied by Viv, Brenda, and Dee. She slowly made her way back to the mansion, no longer Mira Dupree. The name was now Mira McAllister.

Mrs. Trey McAllister.

One problem solved; one to go.

Someone had to inform Jean-Marc.

Trey watched his bride walk away with a heavy heart. He would have fought Jean-Marc with his bare hands rather than be separated from her, but this was the way she wanted it. He had yielded to her request to keep their marriage a secret for now, but it was a secret that would have to come out someday. In the meantime, they were over one hurdle but there were larger ones to come. God had smiled on them so far. Trey would have to trust that in time they would be together forever.

The women climbed into the buggy for the return trip to Sassy Gap. He knew from the sympathetic glances sent his way that they were commiserating with him. Just married and alone. It shouldn't happen to a nice, God-fearing man like Trey McAllister. For once he was in complete agreement. He climbed into the saddle and followed the buggy back to Sassy Gap.

Mira approached the study on Saturday morning, anxious about the coming confrontation with Jean-Marc. He had been duped; he had no idea she had married Trey, and at her insistence they had decided to keep it that way for now. However, she would manage to be with her new husband at least once a week by executing the agreement that allowed her to visit the women in Sassy Gap one afternoon a week. Jean-Marc still hated the concession but had consented, and she planned to hold him to the bargain.

She tapped on the door before entering. "You wanted to see me?"

He looked up. "I've been thinking that we need more social life for you. I'm sure you are bored easily these days. What would you think about visiting New Orleans? We could see friends, enjoy what the city has to offer. Loyal has invited us to stay at his house. I think you would enjoy it."

Her heart stopped. She pulled a chair away from the desk and sat down, primly crossing her hands. "Why, I don't know." Her mind raced. *Think, Mira.* She couldn't bear to miss even one visit with Trey.

"I am quite content. New Orleans would be exciting, but shall we wait until cooler autumn weather? I am sure the journey would be ever so much nicer."

By then she would have come up with another excuse.

He frowned. "I would have thought you'd be eager to get away. "

"No. Not at all." She smiled and picked up a paper knife and ran her fingers over the carved ivory handle shaped like a lion. "There is one thing though. I do so enjoy my visits to Sassy Gap. Seeing my friends is important to me. I would sometimes like to go two or even three days a week?"

She braced for the explosion.

He made a dismissive gesture. "The women of Sassy Gap? Hardly in your class."

She raised her eyebrows and tried for a haughty expression. "Who in our immediate area would be in my class?"

His shrewd eyes searched hers, but she forced herself to

meet his direct gaze and keep smiling. Could he detect the blush of womanhood on her cheeks? Could he see in her eyes the undiluted love for Trey McAllister?

After a moment he shrugged. "I would think three visits excessive."

"Two then. But on occasion I do need to stay overnight. The women are busy during the day. At night they sit around the fire and talk. I miss those chats."

He frowned. "I don't understand you, Mirelle."

"Am I such a mystery? I am asking your permission to sometimes stay the night and come home the next day. The trip is dreadfully tiring, going both ways in one day. It's dark before I get home. You have made it clear that my life belongs to you. Only you decide where I can go and when I go and how long I stay."

He waited and she let him wait. Two could play this game. He looked directly into her eyes. "And if I say no?"

She tilted her chin, meeting his questioning gaze head-on. "Then I am afraid I may be indisposed the next time you have a social event." She made a pretty pout. "That would be such a shame."

"A shame indeed. I enjoy showing you off, and Loyal is most appreciative of your beauty. Surely you enjoy the gatherings of your peers more than a visit to the riffraff of Sassy Gap."

She let that pass, suspecting that he wanted to rile her into giving up her request.

"I suppose in the future I will have less in common with those women, but at the moment I am going through a transition. Surely I am not asking for anything unreasonable."

"Unreasonable? No." He glanced at the papers on his desk.

"And if I grant your request you feel your health will allow you to attend the social events I choose for you?"

"That is a very good possibility."

"With Loyal Moore?"

She swallowed. "Perhaps."

"Very well, Mira. You drive a hard bargain: one day a week and overnight if you please. At least for now. No more."

Mira rose, trying not to show her elation. "Thank you. I appreciate your kindness." She hoped he did not hear the sarcasm.

She started toward the door when he stopped her. "Just 'thank you'? Your manners have deteriorated since you've been away, Daughter."

She turned to face him. "Thank you, sir."

"You're welcome, Daughter."

"I am not your daughter."

"Ah, but we digress."

She resisted the urge to say that Macon and Lillybelle knew the truth; he would only make their lives miserable. Maybe even dismiss them, and then where would they go?

She left, also resisting the urge to slam the door behind her.

Jean-Marc sat down when the door closed, thinking how little it mattered what she did. Let her go to Sassy Gap and spend time with her friends—although he was surprised a woman like Mira, born to the aristocracy, could enjoy mingling with common women like those in the town. But then her father was a Texas cattleman, and it was truly said that water found its own level.

The trip to New Orleans would go as planned, except Mira would not come back to Belmonde. She would remain in New Orleans as the wife of Loyal Moore, and Jean-Marc would be finished with her. Grandchildren—her children—would not be true blood, so he could get by with one courteous call a year.

Now there only remained the problem of Sassy Gap. The railroad crew had hit a snag. High water had halted the construction of an important trestle. Bad luck for Richard Holman III; good luck for Jean-Marc Portier. He marveled at the way the breaks always went his way. He had at least three more weeks to get rid of those pigheaded women.

Who would have believed the lower classes could show so much tenacity?

"Come, we have something to show you."

Trey yielded to Vivian and Dee pulling him up the steps to the funeral parlor. What could be so important in the old building? It hadn't been used since Grandma Speck died and the women stopped handling burials. He missed Grandma. He didn't much like to come into the building. The long talks they used to share, sitting beside her at supper. He knew Grandma was in a far better place, but still the memories left him feeling unsettled.

Once they were inside Dee proudly led him to a curtained alcove that hadn't been there the last time he'd been in the room.

Vivian pulled back the curtains. "Ta-da."

A bed fitted out with fresh sheets and a hand-woven coverlet filled most of the space. An oak dresser with a mirror had been added, and a bouquet of wildflowers was arranged in an old white ironstone pitcher. A woven rag rug lay beside the bed, and his shaving things had been laid out on the dresser with the few personal items Mira had left behind.

He indicated the furnishings. "What is all this?"

Dee grinned. "Mira's coming today and she's spending the night."

"Here?" He felt the grin building up inside him. "She's spending the night here?"

She had promised to find a way to spend time with him, but knowing the odds against her, he had doubted she'd be able to pull it off. He never should have doubted her. He knew how persistent she could be. She might not be Jean-Marc's daughter, but she had his grit.

Mira drove her carriage down the main street of Sassy Gap, noticing the improvements the women had made since her last visit. The community building sported a coat of fresh white paint. New curtains hung at the windows. The pink rambler across from the blacksmith shop was loaded with blooms, and there was an air of hope where only depression had previously been. Sassy Gap had a new lease on life. She wondered what effect the coming railroad would have on the town and the women who lived here. It could only prosper the well-deserving, hardworking ladies.

Trey lifted her from the carriage and kissed her soundly. "I hear you're staying the night."

She smiled up at him. "One night a week. Not enough, but something."

"We'll be grateful for what we have." He released her to the women, who immediately suffocated her with hugs.

"Oh, Mira. It's so good to have you back, even if it's for only a day." Helen released her and stepped out of the way so Jane could have a turn. "Guess what we're having for dinner."

Mira laughed. "I have no idea."

"Fried chicken and fresh apple pies," Helen said.

"A real feast." Mira stooped to greet Audrey. "Hello there, little sister. Miss me?"

Two grubby little hands patted Mira's cheeks. "I missed you this much." Audrey stretched out her arms as far as she could reach. "A lot."

"A lot, indeed." Mira let her friends pull her inside, laughing and talking, secure in the knowledge that later she would be alone with her husband.

Her husband. The words sent a delicious shiver through her. She had never expected to feel this way. God had been good to her. He had answered her prayers and through supernatural divine strength allowed her to escape Jean-Marc. He didn't know it, but her days of fear were over.

Jane echoed her thoughts. "God has been good to us, Mira.

Now that the terror is over we can live a normal life. With Trey's help we're improving the town more every day."

"God is always good," Melody said. "He blesses us when we least expect it."

"He knows our every need," Dee echoed.

Mira nodded assent, but inside her heart was aching. God had been good to the women of Sassy Gap, and she had been blessed by being able to marry Trey, but what kind of marriage could they have when she had to sneak around to be with him for only one night a week? She wanted a bigger blessing and she wanted it now. She wanted Jean-Marc Portier to pay for what he had done to her and to her parents. He lived in luxury in a mansion to which he had no right. His wealth had been built on the shedding of innocent blood. Surely God would turn His head when Jean-Marc left this earth.

The day was spent sitting and talking. There was a lot to catch up on. Everyone had a story to tell about how conditions had improved in town. They went to Mignon freely now to buy groceries and sell garden products. The townspeople were friendly since Jean-Marc had ended the oppression.

Mira watched as Melody ran back and forth, waiting on Daniel. She apparently had forgotten her earlier attraction to Trey, which was good since he now had a wife. Mira had to admit they made a handsome couple. The young preacher was gentle and even tempered. He appeared to be as interested in Melody as she was in him.

Audrey climbed up on Mira's lap. "I love you, Mira."

She hugged the child. "I love you, too. It is good to be here."

Audrey's face puckered in a frown. "Can you stay?"

She shook her head, forcing out the words. "No, I cannot. I am only visiting."

The little girl shook her head. "I don't want you to visit. I want you to *stay*."

Mira kissed the top of Audrey's head. "I want that too. Maybe someday."

"Tomorrow?"

"No, not tomorrow. But someday."

She saw Melody lean closer to Daniel, her hand resting on his arm. He smiled down at her and said something so low no one else could hear, but it brought a light blush to Melody's cheeks.

A dull ache filled Mira's heart. She knew coming here one night a week wasn't enough to satisfy her, but she also knew any more would arouse Jean-Marc's suspicions. She couldn't let him know she was married. Not until she had a solid plan. But she needed time. Trey must be patient. Should Jean-Marc learn of her marriage, his anger toward the women and Sassy Gap would know no bounds. She wasn't sure even she would be safe.

Audrey climbed down from Mira's lap and ran to stand by Daniel. Her hand patted his knee.

He looked down and smiled. "What is it, child?"

She grinned up at him. "I love Daniel."

He hugged her. "I love Audrey, too."

Mira looked away. Melody and Daniel were a family now. It was obvious Audrey had stolen his affection the way she had Trey's. She bit her lip to keep from crying, recognizing the fire burning in her heart. Jealousy. Daniel and Melody were free to follow their hearts, letting their relationship develop openly and naturally. She couldn't be with her husband in public, except here in the sheltering buildings of Sassy Gap.

Trey thought supper would never end. Mira sat beside him, laughing and chatting with her friends. He knew she was happy to be back. If only she could stay. He reached for her hand, holding it under the table. Tonight. They had tonight, even if she had to leave in the morning.

Finally the meal ended and the women gathered around the fire. Trey rose and stretched. "I think I'll get some fresh air."

Mira glanced up and blushed.

He held out his hand and she took it, rising to stand beside him. "I will join you," she said.

Brenda smiled. "You two go on. We've got things to do. We'll see you in the morning. Sausage and eggs for breakfast."

The door closed behind them and Mira turned to look up at Trey. "Sassy Gap seems more prosperous now."

"Things are going well. The people in Mignon are willing to trade since your father has called off his dogs."

"This is nice. The women seem to be doing well."

"Better than I am." He brought her hand to his lips. "I've missed you, Mira."

Her breath caught on a sob. "Oh, Trey. I have been so lonesome without you."

He slid his arms around her then bent his head, his lips

seeking hers. For a minute he could forget the vicious man who wouldn't hesitate to destroy their love if given the chance.

They wandered slowly toward the old funeral parlor. Once they were inside, he lit the kerosene lamp Jane had provided.

Mira's gaze roamed the familiar surroundings. "This room holds so many memories. Grandma Speck . . . the others. I know a funeral parlor doesn't seem like a happy place, but this was. We were happy working together, and we were performing a service the community needed."

Trey drew her close. "It's going to be put to a different use now."

She looked up at him, her eyes questioning.

He led her to the alcove, pulling the curtain aside. "A wedding present from your friends."

Mira stepped inside the alcove, her eyes going from the bed to the dresser, lingering on the wildflowers. Her lips trembled. "A bridal suite?"

"For us."

She leaned against him, her heart in her eyes. "No one could ask for a better one."

Trey lit the lamp and lay on the bed to watch Mira brush out her hair. *Mira McAllister*. He tried out the name, liking the sound of it. She belonged to him now.

She bent from the waist, brushing her hair forward until it hung in a shining curtain almost touching the floor. Then she straightened up in one swift, smooth movement, flinging her hair back out of her face.

"Why do you do that?"

"It's good for my hair. Stimulates the scalp." She placed the brush on the dresser. "Trey, do you think Jean-Marc has given up the fight for Sassy Gap?"

He laced his fingers behind his head, relaxed and comfortable. "No, I have a feeling this is the calm before the storm."

Mira sat down on the end of the bed, her eyes clouded. "The women are so happy and they have done so much to improve the town. I would feel very bad for them if they are forced out now."

"I've been thinking about that. When you go back to Belmonde, I believe I'll see if I can find Richard Holman and find out what's going on with the railroad. These women own the town. If it's valuable property then they deserve to get the money."

"Do you feel that is wise?"

"Maybe not, but I'll be discreet with my inquiries." He held out his arms. "Come here and give me a kiss, Mrs. McAllister." She turned toward him and smiled. Beautiful, so beautiful. *Thank You, God, for giving her to me. I'll try every day of my life to be good enough for her.*

Later they lay in the dark, whispering.

"Trey?"

"What, darling?"

"Jean-Marc wants me to go to New Orleans."

He sat up in bed. "He wants what? Why?"

"I am not sure, but we would stay at Loyal Moore's house."

"You are *not* to go with him." Trey spoke each word with emphasis.

"No," Mira agreed. "It would not be wise, but I must think of an excuse to delay the journey."

Trey's heart contracted. If Jean-Marc Portier harmed one hair of Mira McAllister's head, he would personally put an end to that blackguard's career of misery and destruction.

Two days later Mira's new husband stood before the broad-shouldered man dressed in shabby but good-quality clothing. His brown hair and eyes were commonplace, but he wore an air of authority that said he was a force to be reckoned with. "You say you represent the owners of Sassy Gap?"

The tent canvas flapped gently in the breeze. "That's right," Trey said. "We have just learned about the proposed railroad line that is to run through the town. I'm here to discuss the specifics, if you know them."

Richard Holman frowned. "I understood that Jean-Marc Portier was acting as the women's go-between."

Trey grunted in disgust. "Jean-Marc has done everything he can to drive those women out of Sassy Gap so he can steal the town and claim the property."

"That is a serious charge."

"It's a serious crime. Portier has done everything from stealing their livestock to poisoning their water supply to get rid of them."

"I see. And what do you want from me, Mr. McAllister?"

"I want you to come to Sassy Gap and talk to these women, answer their questions, and deal directly with them."

"That seems reasonable enough." Holman stacked the sheets of paper he had been working on. "I will notify my foreman and be ready to go with you in an hour."

An hour later they were on their way, riding side by side through the verdant Louisiana countryside. Richard Holman glanced up at the sky. "At least the sun is shining today. Does it always rain like this, or are we in the rainy season?"

Trey shook his head. "Don't know. But I've had about all the rain I want for a while."

"You're not from here then, Mr. McAllister?"

"Call me Trey. No, I'm from Kansas. I was on my way home from the war when I rode through Sassy Gap and saw what the women were going through. I couldn't turn my back and ride away."

Holman was quiet for a minute. "I understand. I don't like the idea of making war against women either. Tell me, what do you get out of this?"

"Absolutely nothing. I've recently married, and when I get things straightened out in Sassy Gap I'm taking my wife and going home."

Home. He welcomed the sound of that word. He was looking forward to introducing Mira to his sisters.

The sun had shone for the past two days—a record for Louisiana, he guessed. It would be good to get home and let the heat bake the damp out of his bones.

Holman shifted in the saddle, his gaze taking in the landscape. "This long, flat valley is perfect for a railroad. Once we get that trestle built we'll rip right along through Sassy Gap."

"Another reason to deal directly with the women," Trey said. "This valley continues straight through the town."

When they reached Sassy Gap they stopped at the black-smith shop. Brenda's eyes were full of questions, although she remained quiet. Trey knew she would think it bad manners to be overly interested, but a strange man in town was something to wonder about.

"Call the women to a meeting," Trey said. "This is Richard Holman the third—"

"Call me Richard," their guest interrupted. "I have a hunch we're going to be seeing a lot of each other."

Trey grinned when Brenda's expression changed to acute bewilderment. She nodded and left the stable, but he watched her break into a run toward the community building. He took care of their horses, pleased to see Richard step in and help. His admiration for this man was growing with every passing hour.

When they reached the parlor, the women were already gathered in chairs facing the podium. Trey kept the introduction short. "Ladies, this is Richard Holman. He's building a railroad and he wants to talk to you."

Richard stepped up to take Trey's place. His gaze slid across to the coffins stacked neatly against the far wall, but to his credit, he didn't miss a beat. "I understand you ladies own this town. I want to run a railroad through it. Let's talk."

Mira's days fell into a pattern. Reading, approving meal plans, counting the hours until Friday afternoons when she rode to Sassy Gap and stayed the night. At first she had tried to vary the days of the week, but whatever schedule she chose the time apart from Trey was far too long.

She marked time at the plantation, praying for strength and patience. Every time she made the trip to Sassy Gap it was like she and Trey renewed their vows. Every time she left it seemed like her heart broke all over again. Still she found no viable way to tell Jean-Mare about the marriage. She had no plan. She prayed constantly for an answer but none came.

She knew the forced separation was difficult for Trey, too. He hadn't said as much, but she realized it was only a matter of time before they could be together. Once she had come up with a way to thwart Jean-Marc, the guise would be over. Then they could live openly as man and wife.

Today, after the initial greetings, he pulled her aside and suggested a walk down by the creek.

They strolled hand in hand, but he seemed to be wrapped in his own thoughts. He stopped at a cluster of large rocks beside the swiftly flowing stream. "Let's sit here."

Mira sat down on one of the rocks and watched the rippling water. A minnow darted in the shallows. She pointed at it. "Look, a fish. Life is coming back to the pool again."

"Nature has flushed the poison out; we've had a lot of rain. We've noticed deer drinking here again."

She watched a wren hop from one branch to another on a young willow tree. "I guess everything heals in time."

"Even hearts?" He sat down beside her.

"Sometimes," she said cautiously, feeling her way in this sudden turn in the conversation.

He reached for her hand and looked down at it. "I want the world to know that you're my wife."

"I would love that, darling, but I understand why that is not possible."

He bent forward, speaking so low she almost missed what he said. "I want you with me all the time. I hate it when you ride away. Don't go back this time, Mira."

She drew away, unable to hide her hurt. "You know I cannot do that. Why even say such a thing?"

Sighing, he let her hand drop. "How long, Mira?"

She bit her lip, refusing to answer. She knew what he wanted from her, but she was unable to say the words. The time she spent under Jean-Marc's roof had hardened her anger and contempt for him. Every time she walked to her mother's grave her heart filled with bitterness all over again, like a never-ending stream flowing through her. And yet her courage failed her; she was terrified to let Jean-Marc know of her marriage.

"How long are you willing to continue this deception?" He turned to confront her. "It's almost like you enjoy the sparring and fight."

"That is most certainly not true," Mira protested.

"It is, Mira. Accept it. For whatever reason, you are as intent on besting Jean-Marc as he is in ruling you. The way we're living now isn't a long-term answer; you know that. Neither of you will win. I'm begging you to give it up. We'll tell him together that we're married and that we're moving to Kansas."

When she tried to look away he caught her shoulders and turned her to face him, his features sober. "It's time to start our own family, our own life. You say it's what you've always wanted—a family and children. So do it. *Now.* Don't let this go on another day."

What he proposed sounded so wonderful that for a moment she believed it could happen. Then reality set in. "No. I want him to pay for what he has done to me. He killed my mother, my father. Surely you see he cannot be allowed to go free. I have to find a way to expose him to everyone."

"I've said it before, Mira. You have to forgive him. Only then can you be free."

Mira didn't want to talk about forgiveness. She turned away to look back at the town. "What about them? Can you promise he will not hurt these women we would be leaving at his mercy?"

"I can't promise anything about him, but with the railroad coming and Richard Holman dealing directly with the women, it has shut Jean-Marc out of the negotiations. With you gone he would have no reason to harass them."

"But I cannot be sure."

Was she only delaying? Was it possible that somewhere deep in her heart she really did not want to end this madness on a peaceful note? She could not accept that. Once she forced Jean-Marc to be held accountable for what he had done, she would be content. Trey had to be patient.

"I do not think Jean-Marc knows he has been shut out. Otherwise he would be raging, and he has been relatively calm the last few days."

"He will know in time. There is nothing more he can do to the women. Nor anything he can do to you. Jean-Marc has lost."

"No, he has not lost. He can still build the cattle pens. He owns the land surrounding the town, and he can still make it so miserable the women will have to move."

"How, Mira? How do you plan to stop him, to expose him, make him pay for his transgressions? Give me a plan."

She shook her head, tears welling. "I have none. I pray—"

"For what? For God to strike the man dead? I hardly think He will do that." Trey tried once more. "Don't we have a right to make a life together?"

She spoke softly, trying to ease the sting of her rebuttal. "I—I will have to pray about this. You are asking much of me."

Mira bit her lip, watching him walk away through a veil of tears.

What did you hope for?

A miracle.

The next Friday, Trey was ready for Mira. He didn't say much, simply ate the supper of fried squirrel and Jane's biscuits smothered with gravy. Afterward, he took Mira's hand and they walked along the spring. It was the long-shadows time of day. The sun provided back lighting through the pines. It was peaceful. But it wasn't Kansas, and Trey missed home.

Mira grasped his arm and pressed close against his side as they walked the path. "It has been a beautiful day."

"Gets even prettier when you show up."

She smiled up at him and his heart constricted. He was about to do something that would bring turmoil back into their world. But he had no choice. Peace without freedom was still prison. He would never rest until he and Mira were free to live openly as husband and wife.

"Have you given any thought to our last conversation?"

She sighed. "*Mon cheri*, let us not ruin the day."

He paused and turned to face her. "If it means getting our real life under way I'm going to ruin it." When she started to protest, he laid a finger across her lips. "I haven't said anything, but I've been waiting. . . ." His voice trailed off.

"For what?"

"For some of my old fighting unit to show up. I wired six of my closest friends from Ohio, Oklahoma, Missouri, and Kentucky. I asked them to come and help me fight Jean-Marc."

Her eyes brightened. "You did? You did that for me?"

"I figured if he knew he was up against men, rather then women, he'd be more likely to end this fight and he'd realize that you were determined to make your own decisions about where you live and who you marry."

She gazed expectantly up at him, but he shook his head negatively. "They haven't come. I don't know. They just got home from the war, back to their families. Maybe the roads are too washed out. Maybe they can't come. Whatever. They're not here, and we can't put our lives on hold forever."

Mira slipped her arms around his waist. "Oh, darling. I know you grow tired of waiting."

They turned when they heard Audrey's voice calling.

"Mira! Trey! Brenda says for you to come."

Mira turned to face the child. "Why? What is wrong?"

"Nothing. You just come."

Trey slid an arm around Mira's waist. "All right, we're coming. Tell her we're on our way."

Audrey skipped away, humming a ragged tune that didn't appear to have a melody.

"What could this be all about?" Mira asked.

Trey shrugged. "I suppose Brenda will tell us when we get there."

Inside the community building the women were waiting, seated around the table. Brenda sat at the head. Trey pulled out the two vacant chairs and motioned for Mira to sit down.

Brenda called the meeting to order. "We've been thinking. Life is a lot more pleasant than it used to be since Mira's father has stopped harassing us."

Mira leaned forward. "Again, I am sorry I put you all through that. I should have left before it went as far as it did."

Dee patted her arm. "Sit back and relax. We're got some things to say."

Melody, who didn't usually speak out in these meetings, colored and got to her feet. "I like the peaceful air the town has now, and I like to be able to come and go as we please without being persecuted, but I think we've paid a very high price for this peace."

She sat down and Jane got up. "We used to have some spunk. We were willing to fight for what we believed in but we're getting soft, used to waking up to no problems. Life usually doesn't stay that way for long."

Helen got to her feet. "We got our peace at Mira's expense. Can any one of us actually say we feel comfortable knowing that because of us Mira and Trey can only be together one night a week?"

Mira turned accusing eyes toward Trey, and he smiled and ran one finger down her cheek. "Just listen. Please."

He watched her struggle to control the tears brimming in her eyes, but she firmed her lips and turned her attention back to the women. They meant what they were saying. They didn't want peace if it came with the price of hurting Mira. They were good women, all of them.

Viv stood. "I don't like the idea of Jean-Marc or any other man ruling us. At least we had our pride before. We were strong and we fought back."

Brenda caught Mira's eye. "What we're trying to say is that we want you to be with Trey. We want you to be free to come and visit us whenever you please."

Mira stood and faced them. "You know what this means? It will no longer be about me or the town. Nor about the railroad. He will not be defied. No matter how long it takes, he will not stop until he destroys all of us. If you will only be patient, let God work, we will find a way to beat him that won't endanger us."

Brenda nodded. "And we'll be doing our best to keep that from happening, but we're ready to fight until we win."

Trey held his breath. What would Mira do? He knew this wouldn't be easy for her. She would never willingly put her friends in harm's way, but if she crossed Jean-Marc again after he thought he'd won, his anger would know no limits.

Conflicting emotions raced across Mira's face. She looked at Trey with longing in her eyes, and he could see the battle raging within her. She placed a hand on his shoulder and offered a quivering smile.

"You will never know how much I appreciate this," she said. "But before I let you make this kind of sacrifice, I must pray about it. The consequences are too great to rush into it without God's leading."

"Fair enough," Brenda said. "Just don't wait too long to let us know. We're getting antsy."

The meeting broke up, and Trey wondered if Mira recalled their earlier conversation about leaving. If she did she didn't mention it. He loved her, but he couldn't tie his life to her obsession with revenge. If she wanted to stay and spar with Jean-Marc until she was a bitter old woman, that would be her choice. As for him, he was leaving for Kansas soon, regardless of her decision.

Two days went by and Mira had not notified the people of Sassy Gap what she had decided. Trey was starting to think he really might have to leave without her. He wasn't going to force her to make a decision, but they both knew the present situation was intolerable.

He was working in the stable, repairing the stalls, when he heard Dee calling his name. He dropped his hammer and hurried to the stable door to see what she wanted.

She scurried toward the building, followed by Viv. One look at their faces and he knew something was wrong. Mira? She was supposed to come tomorrow. Had something happened to her?

Dee reached him and paused, one hand pressed to her chest. "Wait a minute," she gasped. "Got to catch my breath."

"What is it? What's going on?"

He wanted to grab her by the shoulders and shake the answer out of her. From the way she was looking at him, it had to be something bad.

"Oh, Trey," she said. "We never meant to do it. I'm so sorry."

"What? What did you do?" What was wrong with the woman? She needed to get to the point.

"Me and Viv, we were talking in the mercantile in Mignon."

"Yes? Get on with it, woman."

"And we sort of let it slip that you and Mira were married."

Trey felt like he had been hit in the stomach with a two-by-four. "You did?"

That was a lame response, but his mind was so occupied with all the implications of the news that he couldn't think of anything else to say.

"And that burly, black-haired man that works for Jean-Marc was in there. He left like a scalded cat scratching for higher ground." Viv shook her head. "I'll bet he's carried the word right to Belmonde."

"It's going to break loose after this," Dee predicted.

Trey agreed. "Get the women together." Now they were going to have to do something and do it fast. Jean-Marc wasn't known for letting the grass grow under his feet. His men would retaliate immediately, and the women of Sassy Gap had to be prepared.

But how could they prepare themselves when they didn't know what to expect?

Macon passed the summons on to Mira. Jean-Marc wanted her in his office. Immediately.

"What does he want? What's wrong?"

Macon shrugged. "I don't know, Miss Mira, and that's for sure. He be one powerful angry man."

"I will go immediately."

She'd turned down an invitation to travel to New Orleans with a group of his friends. She knew he was trying to force her into a marriage with Loyal Moore, and she had outsmarted him. He was angry.

She descended the stairs and opened the door to the office. "You wanted to see me?"

"Indeed I did, Mira—or should I say 'Mrs. McAllister'?"

She stopped inside the door, pinned by the fury in his eyes. Her heart hammered against her ribs.

"How did you—?"

"Find out? I have my ways." He dismissed her with a glance. "You've had your chance, Mirelle. The holding pens go up tomorrow."

"Jean-Marc, no. You cannot let my rebellion influence your actions against the women—"

Portier turned on his heel and a moment later the door closed.

Closing her eyes, Mira knew with a sinking sensation.

The false truce was over.

CHAPTER 15

"I can't stop him, Mira. God help us; other than shoot him, I can't stop him."

Trey stood behind Mira, watching the activity. Wagons, as far as the eye could see, poured into the fringe of Sassy Gap. Rough-hewn oak posts and rails filled their beds. The sun was barely over the rise, but already the solid whack of hammers driving nails filled the air. Jean-Marc had wasted no time in resuming the battle.

As Trey and Mira stood watching out the parlor window, her arms were crossed and her jaw set. She seemed to be shrinking, drawing into herself. Her face was pale and drained.

Trey realized the resumption of hostilities was taking its toll on his wife. He wondered how long she would be able to fight the onslaught this time.

He drew her close, nuzzling the sweetness of her neck. He would fight for her until there's wasn't a breath left in him, but in the end his efforts would be useless. Only she could determine her life. Bitterness or love. What would she choose?

Sighing, she rested against his chest and closed her eyes. He could feel her body trembling with unspoken emotion. Yes, she had come back to him this time, but at what cost?

"He has not won," she whispered vehemently.

Holding her closer, he murmured, "I can't stop him from building those pens, and if he builds the pens Sassy Gap will turn into a rowdy border town. There will be fighting, drinking, gambling, and worse. It will be a cattle town, somewhere for drovers to let off a little steam. The women could never survive that kind of living, and I won't let them try. We'll pack up and move them, every last one of them, to Kansas. "

She patted his arm absently and then stepped out of his embrace, leaning closer to the open window. Before he knew it, she was leaning out on the sill, screeching.

"Stop it! Stop that hammering this minute!"

"Mira—"

"I mean it! Stop it!"

They could see Jean-Marc overseeing the activities from atop his large stallion. Trey wanted to take a bullwhip and wipe the smirk off his face.

He hooked his arms around Mira's waist and pulled her back into the room. She squirmed, struggling to break the hold.

"Mira, listen to me."

"No! He cannot do this."

"He can and he is." He caught her by the shoulders and turned her around to face him. "Mira, listen to me. End this fight; end it right now. Make your peace with the situation. Accept it. You can't spend your life fighting a man you can't beat. Forgive him and move on before he destroys you! Destroys us!"

Calming, she sagged against him, her breath coming in short

gasps, too worried about the latest turn of events to rest. Neither one had slept last night. Now the sound of hammers beat into their brains, reminding them of the forces they faced.

The relentless *whack, whack, whack* was maddening. Taking his hand, she pulled him up. "He has not won. Come with me."

"Come where?" Pouring rain. What was she up to this time? "Mira. Will you listen to common sense?"

"Just hush and come with me." She took his hand and they slipped out of curtained alcove. The sounds of hammers continued to fill the early morning air. As they rounded the corner of the livery Trey saw Jean-Marc's imposing height perched erect in the saddle. Even in the rain he was a commanding figure. The pens were his last resort, and he'd gotten up plenty early to watch the progress.

Mira waded through the thick mud, crossing the two hundred feet from the funeral parlor to where Jean-Marc sat tall in the saddle watching her halting progress.

"Ah, Mrs. McAllister. I am overseeing my new business enterprise. You will be happy to know that the holding pens will bring much business to your town. I do hope you will be able to accommodate it all."

Mira smiled. "Oh yes, the holding pens. Well, you must do what you have to do. What a shame, though, that you have no son to whom you could leave your 'business enterprises.'"

Jean-Marc's face darkened with anger. "You mock me, Mirelle. That is not wise."

Mira ignored Trey's startled glance, her attention centered on the man on horseback. "Is it possible you do not realize that my mother was with child when she fell down those stairs?"

Oh, Mother, I will not betray you, but I will uphold you.

"The child was your own, Jean-Marc. Perhaps the son you wanted so badly."

Jean-Marc's features remained carved of stone, a statue of a man on horseback. He forced two words out through tightened lips. "You lie."

"Oh, but no. She had planned to tell you that night after dinner, but something went wrong, did it not? What happened, Jean-Marc? Why was my mother running from you?"

Jean-Marc stared at her as the set expression on his face gave way to one of dawning incredulity. "She *was* often ill."

"In the morning?" Mira asked. "You never thought it might be morning sickness?"

"No." His expression closed. "This is foolish. You are only saying these things to draw my attention away from the work at hand, which is building my new holding pens. How do you think you will enjoy having cattle for neighbors?"

Mira shrugged. "I will not be here. I leave soon with my husband to go to his home in Kansas."

"To live in what?" Jean-Marc jeered. "A Kansas farmhouse? A sod hut dug into the side of a hill? You who have lived at Belmonde? Surely you jest."

"Belmonde," Mira repeated. "The plantation you stole from me? It is not what sort of house in which one lives that matters; it is only important that love lives there too. Has love ever lived in your house, Jean-Marc? Or did you destroy all hope of love when you killed my father, Benjamin Logan?"

Mira was aware of the people gathered around. Their voices had caused a stir. Daniel and Tom Addison had arrived a few minutes after Trey and Mira. The expressions on the women's faces were grave.

Jean-Marc glared at her. "Lower your voice."

"Poor Jean-Marc," Mira sighed, shaking her head. "Perhaps the baby—your baby—was a boy, the son you always wanted," she repeated. "How sad that you will never know for certain."

Jean-Marc's face turned mottled. "I will not listen to this."

"Perhaps not," Mira said. "But you will remember; in the dark of the night you will lie awake and wonder and there will be no answer."

She realized the man before her didn't sit so tall in the saddle now. For once the mighty Jean-Marc Portier didn't look so mighty. Mira's heart exalted at the way she had brought him low. She had laid his secret out in the open for all to see, but when she looked at Trey and the women some of the joy faded. Their expressions spoke louder than any words, and she knew what they were thinking. Forgive? Not yet. Not until she had wrung the final drop of satisfaction out of making this evil man pay for what he had done.

Trey listened to the exchange between Mira and Jean-Marc, wondering if she spoke the truth or if she simply meant to hurt the man who had mistreated her over the years.

She must have sensed what he was thinking, because she stretched out her hands as though appealing for his belief. "I have told the truth. My mother was with child."

The sincerity in her voice could not be denied. She believed what she said. Even Jean-Marc appeared to sense the truth in her accusations. Trey watched the man shrink into himself.

Hoofbeats rattled against the road's hard surface, signaling the approach of a band of horsemen.

At the head of the group Trey made out Bill Trotter, still sporting his wiry beard. Just behind him were the two Claxton brothers, Cole and Beau. Following them were the Cox brothers, Elmer and George. Dallas Ewing brought up the rear. His old fighting unit had finally arrived.

Jean-Marc pulled himself together. "Who, pray tell, is this scroungy-looking group?"

Grinning, Trey crossed his arms, smiling up at him. "They're your worst nightmare, Portier."

Trey McAllister's friends were a little late, but still dependable. The promise between war-weary comrades was as steadfast as the day it was made.

"If you ever need anything . . ."

"You got a problem, Trey?" Bill Trotter asked, his gloved hand resting on the saddle horn. "We're here to do what we can to help."

Trey glanced at Jean-Marc. "Do I have a problem?"

The plantation owner shrugged. "I do not see how you can prevent a man from building on his own land."

Dallas Ewing's eyes roamed his surroundings. "What are you building, friend? Looks like a lot of activity going on."

Trey indicated Jean-Marc. "He's building cattle holding pens outside of town so he can drive these women from their home by making it so miserable to live here they will have to move."

"That so?" Beau Claxton asked. "I don't hold with fighting women. Only a knuckle-biting, full-fledged coward would do that."

"Now, Little Brother, don't go jumping to conclusions." Cole Claxton rested easy in the saddle. "We don't know this gentleman. What's his name, Trey?"

"Jean-Marc Portier," Trey supplied, enjoying the encounter more than he should.

"Well, Mr. Portier, you tell me: are you the kind of knuckle-biting, full-fledged coward who would fight women? Because if you are, you'll have to go through us." A slow grin spread across Cole's rugged features. "Why, if they'd have turned us loose sooner, we'd have won this war single-handed."

Bill Trotter leaned from his saddle to spit. "You better believe, Portier. Claxton speaks the truth."

"And then you can do a little explaining to me as to how Belmonde is still standing and prospering and my house got burned to the ground." Tom Addison, who had been silent, joined the conversation. "Been wanting to get your story on that little detail for some time."

Jean-Marc glared at the men, the silence growing. Then he turned to his foreman, who had joined the group. "Pack it up and move it out. We will not be building holding pens today."

"Or ever," Trey said. "Or at least, not here."

Jean-Marc reined his horse to leave, but Mira stepped forward, holding out a hand to stop him.

He looked at her, his face impassive, waiting.

She paused within touching distance of him, staring up at

the man she had hated for so long. *Lord, help me to do this;
I cannot do it on my own.* But she knew that God would provide
the strength if she'd take it.

She reached out and placed a small hand on Portier's.
"I forgive you."

Jean-Marc frowned. "What?"

"I forgive you for all you have done to me and what you
have done to my family. I will pray that God forgives you also."

His shoulders drooped. For a moment she glimpsed something akin to sorrow in his eyes, and then the arrogant expression returned. "You forgive me?"

"I forgive you." She met his eyes evenly. "Can you not
forgive yourself?"

Without another word, he turned his horse and rode away.

Trey stored the last of the bags in the back of the wagon and
then leaned against the wooden side, waiting for Mira. The
horses stood patiently. Buck was tied to the back, and they were
ready to ride as soon as his wife finished saying good-bye to her
friends.

Jean-Marc had sent Mira's clothing and personal possessions
with no message. She had not been back to Belmonde nor had
she been invited. Included in the items were photograph
albums, one of which held the wedding picture of Linette and
Benjamin, along with their marriage license.

The sun shone warm on his shoulders and all was right with

Trey's world. The railroad line would run past Sassy Gap, not through the town as originally planned. Richard Holman had agreed to build a station, and the train would stop here on its daily run. The women, at Holman's suggestion, would establish a restaurant and hotel to accommodate the railroad passengers and employees. Sassy Gap was on its way back.

The funeral parlor would reopen and Bill Trotter was set to help. Deciding they liked the town, Bill and Elmer Cox planned to stay in Sassy Gap. They joined Trey now.

"Waiting for the little woman?" Bill asked.

"Get used to it," Elmer advised. "Your troubles are just beginning."

Trey grinned. "Seems to me like the two of you are thinking of starting down the same path."

"I wouldn't be surprised," Bill said. "That Brenda is my kind of woman. You don't find them like her very often."

Trey suddenly turned serious. "She's a fine woman. They all are. A man would be lucky to have any one of them for his wife."

"Got a feeling you're right," Elmer said. "And I've got my eye on Jane. The way that woman cooks, why, it would make the angels in heaven sing."

Bill laughed. "You gain any more weight and your horse will go on strike."

Elmer grinned good-naturedly. "I'm going to be busy converting the community building into a restaurant. Before I get all the work done Jane has planned for me, I'll be a mere shadow of my former self."

Elmer Cox had packed on ten pounds since Trey had last seen him. The large gold buckle on his belt seriously strained against his middle. He claimed the weight was the result of going home and being content, but the other men said it was probably all the fried chicken he'd been eating.

A loaded wagon traveling the main street of Sassy Gap drew Trey's attention. He recognized the driver: Macon, the butler at Belmonde. The wagon drew up beside him.

Macon tipped his hat. "Mr. McAllister, sir."

"Macon. What brings you this way?"

Had Jean-Marc thrown them out? It looked like he was going to have to whip the man in spite of all he'd done to avoid the confrontation.

"Iffen you would have us, we'd be honored to go to Kansas with you and Miss Mira." He indicated the woman beside him. "This my wife, Lillybelle. We took care of Miss Linette's baby from the day she be born and we want to go with her now."

Trey stepped closer to the wagon and held out his hand. "We'll be honored to have you with us. Mira will be pleased you've decided to go along."

Pleased? She'd be elated.

The remainder of the outriders rode up, looking fresh and relaxed after a hearty breakfast. The women of Sassy Gap had rolled out the welcome wagon for the men to show their appreciation for their help, digging deep into their meager stores to provide bountiful meals.

"We'll ride a spell with you." Beau Claxton grinned. "Then I'm heading back to Missouri to get married. Bets has waited long enough. McAllister, you've got the worst timing; you know that."

Trey grinned. "So Cole reminded me."

Cole was still officially on his honeymoon, and he'd good-naturedly told Trey more than once what a sacrifice he was making to come here.

The men had talked late into the night. Cole had met and married Wynne Elliot; Beau was scheduled to marry Betsy next month. Their willingness and commitment to the band of brothers bespoke how they would drop everything and come when a brother was in need.

They'd accomplished the job. No one had seen or heard anything about Jean-Marc since he'd ridden out of town after Mira's declaration that she forgave him.

Mira came out of the funeral parlor, trailed by the women of Sassy Gap. "Are you sure you won't change your minds and come to Kansas with us?"

Brenda shook her head. "Like it right here, thank you. Without Jean-Marc to bother us, we'll be just fine."

Melody echoed the sentiment, standing beside Daniel, who was holding Audrey.

Sighing, Mira stared at the group. "I am going to miss you so much." She hugged each of the women, pausing when she came to Melody. "At least I was here to see you two get married."

Melody smiled winsomely. "We couldn't be happier."

Jane, Viv, and Dee all offered something for the long trip to Kansas. Colorful blankets, food, crocheted doilies.

Mira approached the wagons. "Oh, Macon, Lillybelle! Someone just told me you were here! Are you really going with us? I thought you stayed at Belmonde because Jean-Marc needed you."

Lillybelle sniffed. "That man don't need nobody but hisself and a mirror. We stayed for you and we going to Kansas to take care of you. Mr. Trey—do they have Indians out there in Kansas?"

"They do, Lillybelle, but I'll protect you."

She grinned. "That's right nice of you, sir, because I don't know how we going to get along out there on that old prairie. But if Miss Mira going, then we going too."

Trey lifted Mira up on the wagon seat, kissing her in midair, and then settled her comfortably. There was sadness in her eyes that hadn't existed in the old Mira. Life didn't come in a neat bundle. There were knots and snags throughout the fabric, some beyond repair. But one thing Trey had learned from all the fighting: for the most part, life was what a man made it. Sow bitterness and pride, reap pain and loss. The results were as old as Adam and Eve.

Mira had learned things about her past that hurt, but she had also learned about the healing power of forgiveness. With God's help they would build a new life together that would be stronger and richer because of what they had gone through. A life built on love instead of greed, on forgiveness instead of revenge.

George Cox shot a stream of tobacco juice on the ground, tipped his hat politely to the women, and then climbed atop his roan. The others followed. At the edge of town the men and women shouted their final good-byes and promises to stay in touch.

The buckboard carrying the young bride and groom set off for the plains of Kansas, to new life, new hope, and fresh dreams.

Mira looked up at Trey. "I never believed this day would come. It seemed that only a miracle would allow us to be together."

He looked at his bride and winked. "I believe in miracles."

She sighed, laying her head on his shoulder where it seemed to fit just right. "As do I, *mon cheri.* I have you, don't I?"

A NOTE FROM THE AUTHOR

God speaks of forgiveness over and over in His Word. Maybe He mentions it so often because He knew that it would not come easy to most of us.

A few years ago I had (as we say in Missouri) a "fallin' out" with a very dear friend. I doubt that she ever realized the depth of my hurt, and I reacted in a way that I'm sure the Lord would find shameful. Because of my inability to get past the problem, I lived in constant turmoil, resentment, and hurt. I prayed for God to open her eyes, for her to realize that *she* was wrong. For over a year I lived with these hateful emotions, and each painful day was a lesson in disobedience. I knew I should forgive, but I wouldn't.

To this day I don't believe that she knows how profoundly she hurt me, but I carried the grudge to the point that we eventually lost contact with each other. I'd see her name and it was like a knife ripping my heart. I missed her. I loved her. When she showed no signs of returning my sentiment my misery would grow . . . and grow and grow until it turned into bitter bile in the back of my throat. There was a very simple—almost too easy—way to alleviate my pain, but I refused to choose the path of forgiveness. In my failure to obey God's Word I allowed the situation to make me ill. I allowed resentment to fester in my soul until it became an oozing, seeping cancer—one God had told me how to cure, but with a method I chose to ignore.

Thank God that even while we're in our rebellious mode, He's at work in our hearts.

Eventually, through God's abundant grace, I began to work through my feelings. As the anger began to fade into poignant memories, my prayers turned from "God, get her" to "God, forgive *me*." Now I can see that the problem wasn't her; it was me. Who am I to judge others when I have so many faults myself? How could I judge someone for doing the exact thing that I was doing?

Today I am healthy and whole again. Today I enjoy this person's friendship and thank God daily that He opened my eyes to the truth.

Someone once said, "Bitterness is like lacing your coffee with strychnine and expecting the other person to drop over dead." Mira and Jean-Marc learned this lesson at a high price. I pray today that if you need to forgive someone that'll you run— *run*—to do just that. Before another hour passes. *You* can't do it, but God can.

Until we meet again,
Lori

ABOUT THE AUTHOR

Lori Copeland, Christian novelist, lives in the beautiful Ozarks with her husband and family. After writing in the secular romance market for fifteen years, Lori now spends her time penning books that edify readers and glorify God. She publishes titles with Tyndale House, WestBow, and Steeple Hill. In 2000, Lori was inducted into the Springfield, Missouri, Writers Hall of Fame.

Lori's readers know her for Lifting Spirits with Laughter! She is the author of the popular, bestselling Brides of the West series, and she coauthored the Heavenly Daze series with Christy Award–winning author Angela Elwell Hunt. *Stranded in Paradise* marked Lori's debut as a Women of Faith author.

Lori welcomes letters written to her in care of Tyndale House Author Relations, 351 Executive Drive, Carol Stream, IL 60188.

Turn the page for an
exciting excerpt from *Faith,*
the first book in the best-selling
six-book Brides of the West series.

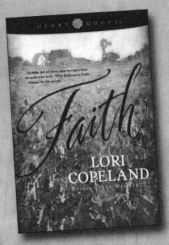

ISBN 0-8423-0267-0

*All six Brides of the West books are available now
at a bookstore near you.*

Faith

Deliverance, Texas
Late 1800s

"She's late." Liza Shepherd slipped a pinch of snuff into the corner of her mouth, then fanned herself with a scented hanky.

Nicholas checked his pocket watch a fourth time, flipping it closed. Mother was right. His bride-to-be was late. Any other day the stage would be on time. He poked a finger into his perspiration-soaked collar, silently cursing the heat. He'd wasted half a day's work on Miss Kallahan, time he could ill afford. Fence was down in the north forty, and ninety acres of hay lay waiting to fall beneath the scythe before rain fell. He glanced toward the bend in the road, his brows drawn in a deep frown. Where *was* she?

Calm down, Nicholas. Work does not come before family obligations. Why did he constantly have to remind himself of that?

A hot Texas sun scorched the top of his Stetson. Fire ants scurried across the parched soil as the town band unpacked their instruments. Tubas and drums sounded in disjointed harmony. He wished the town wouldn't make such a fuss over Miss Kallahan. You'd think he was the first man ever to send for a mail-order bride—which he wasn't. Laymen Snow sent for one a year ago, and everything between the newlyweds was working out fine.

Horses tied at hitching posts lazily swatted flies from their broad, sweaty rumps as the hullabaloo heightened.

High noon, and Deliverance was teeming with people.

Men and women gathered on the porch of Oren Stokes's general store. The men craned their necks while womenfolk gossiped among themselves. A few loners discussed weather and crops, but all ears were tuned for the stage's arrival.

Nicholas ignored the curious looks sent his direction. Interest was normal. A man his age about to take a wife fifteen years his junior? Who wouldn't gawk? Running a finger inside the rim of his perspiration-soaked collar, he craned to see above the crowd. What was keeping that stage? It would be dark before he finished chores. He stiffened when he heard Molly Anderson's anxious whispers to Etta Larkin.

"What is Nicholas thinking—taking a wife now?"

"Why, I can't imagine. He owns everything in sight and has enough money to burn a wet mule. What does he want with a wife?"

"I hear he wants another woman in the house to keep Liza company."

"With the mood Liza's in lately, she'll run the poor girl off before sunset."

"Such a pity—the Shepherds got no one to leave all that money to."

"No, nary a kin left."

Nicholas turned a deaf ear to the town gossips. What he did, or thought, was his business, and he intended to keep it that way.

A smile played at the corners of his mouth when he thought about what he'd done. Placing an ad for a mail-order bride wasn't something he'd ordinarily consider. But these were not ordinary times. In the past two years since his father had died, he and Mama had been at loose ends.

Eighteen years ago he'd thought love was necessary to marry. Now the mere thought of romance at his age made him laugh. He'd lost his chance at love when he failed to marry Rachel.

Looking back, he realized Rachel had been his one chance at marital happiness. But at the time, he wasn't sure he was in love with her. What was love supposed to feel like? He'd certainly been fond of her, and she'd gotten along well with Mama—something not many could claim, especially these days. Rachel was a gentle woman, and in hindsight he knew he should have married her. He had come to realize that there was more to a satisfying union than love. Mama and Papa's marriage had taught him that love of God, trust, the ability to get along, mutual respect—those were the important elements in a marriage. Abe Shepherd had loved Liza, but even more, he had respected her. Nicholas knew he could have built that kind of relationship with Rachel if he had acted before it was too late.

Well, water over the dam. Rachel had married Joe Lanner, and Nicholas had finally faced up to the knowledge that love had passed him by. He would turn thirty-five in January, and he had no heir. There was no blood kin to carry on the Shepherd name. No one to leave Shepherd land and resources to.

Mama thought he'd lost his mind when he sent for a mail-order bride, and maybe he had.

He smiled as he recalled her tirade when he told her what he'd done. "Why on God's green earth would you want to complicate our lives by marryin' a stranger?"

Why indeed? he thought. God had blessed him mightily. He could stand at the top of Shepherd's Mountain, and for as far as the eye could see there was nothing but Shepherd land.

Shepherd cattle.

Shepherd pastures.

Shepherd outbuildings.

Some even said the moon belonged to Shepherd—Shepherd's Moon, the town called it, because of the way it rose over the tops of his trees, beautiful, noble in God's glory. God had been good to him, better than he deserved. He owned all he wanted and more, yet at times he felt as poor as a pauper.

The emptiness gnawed at him, a misery that no abundance of material possessions could assuage. Where was the love he should have known? Rachel had walked through his life, then walked out of it. Had he been so busy acquiring material wealth that he let the one missing ingredient in his life, the love of a woman, slip past him? The question haunted him because he knew the answer: he had let Rachel walk away and marry a man who, rumor had it, now drank and mistreated her. He should have seen it coming—Joe was not a godly man. But he'd done nothing to stop her, and now he had to watch her suffer for his mistake.

There were other women in the town who would have given anything to marry Nicholas Shepherd, but he had never loved any of them. Then, after his father died and Mama became so unlike herself—so moody, so irritable, so stingy—he didn't think anyone would put up with her. At the same time, he wondered if what she needed more than anything was another woman around to talk with, get her mind off her grief. He began to think that maybe he should marry—not for love, but for other reasons. To have someone to keep Mama company, help her around the house. Mama wouldn't think of hiring help, though they could afford it. But maybe a daughter-in-law would be a different matter.

Then there was the matter of an heir. What good was all his fortune if he had no one to leave it to? Perhaps a daughter-in-law, and eventually grandchildren, would help Mama and make all his hard work mean something. He had amassed a fortune, and it would be a shame if no blood kin were able to enjoy it.

He had been praying over the matter when he'd come across the ad in the journal for a mail-order bride, and the thought intrigued him. The answer to his problem, and his prayers, suddenly seemed crystal clear: he would send for a mail-order bride. Much like ordering a seed catalog, but with more pleasant results. He would, in essence, purchase a decent, Christian woman to marry with no emotional strings attached.

This marriage between Miss Kallahan and him would not be the covenant of love that his parents had had; this was a compromise. He needed a wife, and according to Miss Kallahan's letters, she was seeking a husband. He had prayed that God would send him a righteous woman to be his help-mate. To fill his lonely hours. Someone who would be a comfortable companion. Love didn't figure into the picture. When Miss Kallahan accepted his proposal, he accepted that God had chosen the proper woman to meet his needs.

Admittedly, he'd grown set in his ways; having a wife under-foot would take some getting use to. He valued peace and quiet. What his new bride did with her time would be up to her; he would make no demands on her other than that she help Mama around the house, if Mama would permit it. And he did like the thought of children—eventually—although he wasn't marrying a broodmare.

Mama didn't seem to care about anything anymore. She still grieved for Papa, though he'd been dead almost two years now. Nicholas's fervent hope was that having another woman in the house, someone Mama could talk and relate to, would improve her disposition, although he wasn't going to kid himself. He couldn't count on Mama's taking to another woman in the house. But as long as Faith understood her role, the two women should make do with the situation.

Removing his hat, he ran his hand through his hair. What was keeping the stage?

"Brother Shepherd!" Nicholas turned to see Reverend Hicks striding toward him. The tall, painfully thin man always looked as if he hadn't eaten a square meal in days. His ruddy complex-ion and twinkling blue eyes were the only things that saved him from austerity. Vera, a large woman of considerable girth, was trying to keep up with her husband's long-legged strides.

"Mercy, Amos, slow down! You'd think we were going to a fire!"

Reverend Hicks paused before Nicholas, his ruddy face breaking into a congenial smile. Turning sixty had failed to dent the pastor's youthfulness. "Stage hasn't gotten here yet?"

"Not yet." Nicholas glanced toward the bend in the road. "Seems to be running late this morning."

The reverend turned to address Liza. "Good morning, Liza!" He reached for a snowy white handkerchief and mopped his forehead. "Beast of a day, isn't it?"

Liza snorted, fanning herself harder. "No one respects time anymore. You'd think all a body had to do was stand in the heat and wait for a stage whose driver has no concept of time."

The reverend stuffed the handkerchief back in his pocket. "Well, you never know what sort of trouble the stage might have run into."

Vera caught Liza's hand warmly and Nicholas stepped back. The woman was a town icon, midwife, and friend to all. When trouble reared its ugly head, Vera was the first to declare battle.

"We missed you at Bible study this morning. Law, a body could burn up in this heat! Why don't we step out of the sun? I could use a cool drink from the rain barrel."

"No, thank you. Don't need to be filling up on water this close to dinnertime." Liza's hands tightened around her black parasol as she fixed her eyes on the road. "Go ahead—spoil your dinner if you like. And I read my Bible at home, thank you. Don't need to be eatin' any of Lahoma's sugary cakes and drinkin' all that scalding black coffee to study the Word."

"Well, of course not—" The reverend cleared his throat. "I've been meaning to stop by your place all week, Liza. We haven't received your gift for the new steeple, and I thought perhaps—"

Scornful eyes stopped him straightway. "We've given our tenth, Reverend."

A rosy flush crept up the reverend's throat, further reddening his healthy complexion. "Now, Liza, the Lord surely does appreciate your obedience, but that old steeple is in bad need of replacement—"

Liza looked away. "No need for you to thank me. The Good Book says a tenth of our earnings." Liza turned back to face the reverend. "One-tenth. That's what we give, Reverend."

Reverend Hicks smiled. "And a blessed tenth it is, too. But the steeple, Liza. The steeple is an added expense, and we sorely need donations—"

"There's nothing *wrong* with the old steeple, Amos! Why do you insist on replacing it?"

"Because it's old, Liza." Pleasantries faded from the reverend's voice as he lifted his hand to shade his eyes against the sun. His gaze focused on the bell tower. "The tower is rickety. It's no longer safe—one good windstorm and it'll come down."

"Nonsense." Liza dabbed her neck with her handkerchief. "The steeple will stand for another seventy years." Her brows bunched in tight knots. "Money doesn't grow on trees, Reverend. If the Lord wanted a new steeple, He'd provide the means to get it."

The reverend's eyes sent a mute plea in Nicholas's direction.

"Mama, Reverend Hicks is right; the tower is old. I see no reason—"

"And that's precisely why *I* handle the money in this family," Liza snapped. She glowered toward the general store, then back to Vera. "Perhaps a small sip of water won't taint my appetite." She shot a withering look toward the road. "A body could melt in this sun!"

An expectant buzz went up, and the waiting crowd turned to see a donkey round the bend in the road. The animal advanced toward Deliverance at a leisurely gait. Nicholas shaded his eyes, trying to identify the rider.

"Oh, for heaven's sake. It's just that old hermit Jeremiah," Liza muttered. "What's that pest doing here?"

Nicholas watched the approaching animal. Jeremiah Montgomery had arrived in Deliverance some years back, but the old man had kept to himself, living in a small shanty just outside of town. He came for supplies once a month and stayed the day, talking to old-timers who whittled the time away on the side porch of the general store. He appeared to be an educated man, but when asked about his past, he would quietly change the subject. The citizens of Deliverance were not a curious lot. They allowed the hermit his privacy and soon ceased to ask questions. Jeremiah neither incited trouble nor settled it. He appeared to be a peaceful man.

"Who's that he's got with him?" Vera asked, standing on tiptoe.

The animal picked its way slowly down the road, its hooves kicking up limpid puffs of dust as it gradually covered the distance. The crowd edged forward, trying for a better look.

"Why—it looks like a woman," Reverend Hicks said.

As the burro drew closer, Nicholas spotted a small form dressed in gingham and wearing a straw bonnet, riding behind Jeremiah. A woman. His heart sank. A *woman*. A woman stranger in Deliverance meant only one thing. His smile receded. His bride-to-be was arriving by *mule*.

Nicholas stepped out, grasping the animal's bridle as it approached. "Whoa, Jenny!" His eyes centered on the childlike waif riding behind the hermit. She was young—much younger than he'd expected. A knot gripped his midsection. A tomboy to boot. Straddling that mule, wearing men's boots. The young girl met his anxious gaze, smiling. Her perky hat was askew, the pins from the mass of raven hair strung somewhere along the road.

"You must be Nicholas Shepherd."

"Yes, ma'am." His eyes took in the thick layers of dust obliterating her gingham gown. The only thing that saved the girl from being plain was her remarkable violet-colored eyes.

Jeremiah slid off the back of the mule, offering a hand of greeting to Nicholas. Nicholas winced at the stench of woodsmoke and donkey sweat. A riotous array of matted salt-and-pepper hair crowned the old man's head. When he smiled, deep dimples appeared in his cheeks. Doe-colored eyes twinkled back at him as Nicholas accepted Jeremiah's hand and shook it. "Seems I have something that belongs to you."

Nicholas traced the hermit's gaze as he turned to smile at his passenger.

Offering a timid smile, she adjusted her hat. "Sorry about my appearance, Mr. Shepherd. The stage encountered a bit of trouble."

"Lost a wheel, it did, and tipped over!" The hermit knocked dust off his battered hat. "Driver suffered a broken leg. Fortunate I came along when I did, or this poor little mite would've scorched in the blistering sun."

Nicholas reached up to lift his bride from the saddle. For a split moment, something stirred inside him, something long dormant. His eyes met hers. His reaction surprised and annoyed him. The hermit cleared his throat, prompting Nicholas to set the woman lightly on her feet. He finally found his voice. "Where are the other passengers?"

"Sitting alongside the road. Stubborn as old Jenny, they are. I informed them Jenny could carry two more but they told me to be on my way." Jeremiah laughed, knocking dirt off his worn britches. "They'll be waiting awhile. The stage sheared an axle."

"I'll send Ben and Doc to help."

"They're going need more than a blacksmith and a doctor." Jeremiah took a deep breath, batting his chest. Dust flew. "You better send a big wagon to haul them all to town."

The reverend caught up, followed by a breathless Liza and Vera. "Welcome to Deliverance!" Reverend Hicks effusively pumped the young woman's hand, grinning.

Faith smiled and returned the greeting. The band broke into a spirited piece as the crowd gathered round, vying for introductions. The donkey shied, loping to the side to distance itself from the commotion.

"Nicholas, introduce your bride!" someone shouted.

"Yeah, Nicholas! What's her name?" others chorused.

Reaching for the young lady's hand, Nicholas leaned closer, his mind temporarily blank. "Sorry. Your last name is . . . ?"

She leaned closer and he caught a whiff of donkey. "Kallahan."

Clearing his throat, he called for order. "Quiet down, please."

Tubas and drums fell silent as the crowd looked on expectantly.

"Ladies and gentlemen." Nicholas cleared his throat again. He wasn't good at this sort of thing, and the sooner it was over the better. "I'd like you to meet the woman who's consented to be my wife, Miss Faith . . . ?"

"Kallahan."

"Yes . . . Miss Faith Kallahan."

Sporadic clapping broke out. A couple of single, heartbroken young women turned into their mothers' arms for comfort.

Faith nodded above the boisterous clapping. "Thank you—thank you all very much. It is a pleasure to be here!"

"Anything you ever need, you just let me know," Oren Stokes's wife called.

"Same for me, dearie," the mayor's wife seconded as other friendly voices chimed in.

"Quilting Bee every Saturday!"

"Bible study at Lahoma Wilson's Thursday mornings!"

Liza stepped forward, openly assessing her new daughter-in-law-to-be. "Well, at least you're not skin and bone." She cupped her hands at Faith's hips and measured for width. "Should be able to deliver a healthy child."

"Yes, ma'am," Faith said, then grinned. "My hips are nice and wide, I'm in excellent health, and I can work like a man."

Women in the crowd tittered as Nicholas frowned. What had God sent? A wife or a hired hand?

"Liza!" Vera stepped up, putting her arm around Faith's shoulder. "You'll scare the poor thing to death with such talk. Let the young couple get to know each other before you start talking children."

Children had fit into the equation, of course, but in an abstract way. Now he was looking at the woman who would be the mother of his children.

"Pshaw." Liza batted Vera's hands aside. "Miss Kallahan knows what's expected from a wife."

When Nicholas saw Faith's cheeks turn scarlet, he said, "Mama, Miss Kallahan is tired from her long trip."

"Yes, I would imagine." Liza frowned at Jeremiah, who was hanging around watching the activity. She shooed him away. "Go along, now. Don't need the likes of you smelling up the place."

Jeremiah tipped his hat, then raised his eyes a fraction to wink at her.

Liza whirled and marched toward the Shepherd buggy, nose in the air. "Hurry along, Nicholas. It's an hour past our dinnertime."

The crowd dispersed, and Faith reached out to touch Jeremiah's sleeve. "Thank you for the ride. I would have sweltered if not for your kindness."

The old man smiled. "My honor, Miss Kallahan." Reaching for her hand, he placed a genteel kiss upon the back of it. "Thank *you* for accepting kindness from a rather shaggy Samaritan."

Nicholas put his hand on the small of her back and ushered her toward the waiting buggy.

As he hurried Faith toward the buggy, his mind turned from the personal to business. Twelve-thirty. It would be past dark before chores were done.

Nicholas lifted Faith into the wagon, and she murmured thanks. Ordinarily, she would climb aboard unassisted. She wasn't helpless, and she didn't want Nicholas fawning over her. She hoped he wasn't a fawner. But she was relieved to see her husband-to-be was a pleasant-looking man. Not wildly handsome, but he had a strong chin and a muscular build. He looked quite healthy. As he worked to stow her luggage in the wagon bed, she settled on the wooden bench, her gaze focusing on the way his hair lay in gentle golden waves against his collar.

His letter had said he was of English and Swedish origin, and his features evidenced that. Bold blue eyes, once-fair skin deeply tanned by the sun. Only the faint hint of gray at his temples indicated he was older than she was; otherwise, he had youngish features. He was a man of means; she could see that by the cut of his clothes. Denims crisply ironed, shirt cut from the finest material. His hands were large, his nails clean and clipped short. He was exceptionally neat about himself. When he lifted her from the back of Jeremiah's mule, she detected the faint hint of soap and bay-rum aftershave.

She whirled when she heard a noisy *thump!* Nicholas was frozen in place, staring at the ground as if a coiled rattler were about to strike.

Scooting to the edge of the bench, Faith peered over the wagon's side, softly gasping when she saw the contents of her valise spilled onto the ground. White unmentionables stood out like new-fallen snow on the parched soil. Her hand flew up to cover her mouth. "Oh, my. . . ."

Liza whacked the side of the wagon with the tip of her cane. "Pick them up, Nicholas, and let's be on our way." She climbed aboard and wedged her small frame in the middle of the seat, pushing Faith to the outside. "A body could perish from hunger waiting on the likes of you."

Nicholas gathered the scattered garments and hurriedly stuffed them into the valise. Climbing aboard, he picked up the reins and set the team into motion.

As the wagon wheels hummed along the countryside, Faith drank in the new sights. She'd lived in Michigan her entire life; Texas was a whole new world! She remembered how she'd craned her neck out the stagecoach window so long the other passengers had started to tease her. Gone were the cherry and apple orchards, gently rolling hills, and small clear lakes of Michigan. She still spotted an occasional white birch or maple, and there were pines and oaks, but the scenery had changed.

With each passing day on her trip, the landscape had grown more verdant and lush. The closer they drew to San Antonio, the more the countryside transformed. They passed beautiful Spanish missions with tall bell towers, low adobe dwellings covered with vining ivory, and bushes of vibrant colored bougainvillea. At night the cicadas sang her to sleep with their harmonious *sczhwee-sczee*. Ticks were plentiful, and roaches grew as big as horseflies!

The elderly gentleman seated across from her had leaned forward, pointing. "Over there is mesquite and—look there! There's an armadillo!"

Faith shrank back, deciding that was one critter she'd leave alone.

"It's beautiful land," the gentleman said. "You will surely be happy here, young lady."

Faith frowned, keeping an eye on the animal scurrying across the road. She would if those armadillos kept their distance.

Deliverance gradually faded, and the wagon bounced along a rutted, winding trail. Faith suspected her new family wasn't a talkative lot. Liza sat rigidly beside her on the bench, staring straight ahead, occasionally mumbling under her breath that "it was an hour past her dinnertime." The tall, muscular Swede kept silent, his large hands effortlessly controlling the team.

Faith decided it would take time for the Shepherds to warm to her. She hoped they would be friendlier once they got to know her. Still, the silence unnerved her. She and her sisters had chatted endlessly, talking for hours on end about nothing. Generally she was easy to get along with and took to most anyone, but the Shepherds were going to be a test; she could feel it.

Please, Lord, don't allow my tongue to spite my good sense.

She might not be in love with Nicholas Shepherd, but she had her mind made up to make this marriage work. Once she set her mind to something, she wasn't easily swayed. Besides, she *had* to make the marriage work. She couldn't burden Aunt Thalia any longer, and she sure wasn't going to marry Edsel Martin without a hearty fight. She would work to make Nicholas a good wife, to rear his children properly, and be the best help-mate he could ask for.

She glanced at Liza from the corner of her eye. Now *she* would need a bit more time to adjust to.

Her gaze focused on the passing scenery, delighted with the fields of blue flowers bobbing their heads in the bright sunshine. The colorful array of wildflowers nestled against the backdrop of green meadows dazzled the eye.

She sat up, pointing, excited as a child. "What are those?"

Nicholas briefly glanced in the direction she pointed. "Bluebonnets."

"And those?"

"Black-eyed Susans."

"They're so pretty! Do they bloom year-round?"

"Not all year."

The wagon rolled through a small creek and up a hill. Rows upon rows of fences and cattle dotted lush, grassy meadows.

"Just look at all those cattle!" Faith slid forward on the

bench. She had never seen so many animals in one place at the same time. "There must be thousands!"

"Close to two thousand," Nicholas conceded.

"Two thousand," she silently mouthed, thunderstruck by the opulent display. Why, Papa had owned one old cow—and that was for milking purposes only. She'd never seen such wealth, much less dreamed of being a part of it.

Nicholas glanced at her. "Shepherd cattle roam a good deal of this area. Do you like animals?"

"I love them—except I've never had any for my own. Papa was so busy with his congregation and trying to rear three daughters properly that he said he had all the mouths he cared to feed, thank you. I remember once Mr. Kratchet's old tabby cat had kittens. They were so cute, and I fell head over heels in love with one. It was the runt, and sickly, but I wanted it so badly."

Sighing, she folded her hands on her lap, recalling the traumatic moment. "But Papa said *no*, no use wasting good food on something that wasn't going to live anyway." Tears welled to her eyes. "I cried myself to sleep that night. I vowed when I grew up, I'd have all the sick kittens I wanted. Mama said, 'Be merciful to all things, Faith'—did I tell you Mama died giving birth to my youngest sister, June?—did I mention that in my letter? Well, she did. Faith, Hope, and June—"

Liza turned to give her a sour look.

"June," Faith repeated, her smile temporarily wavering. "Papa was kinda mad at June when she was born. He took his anger out on that poor baby because he thought she'd killed Mama, but later he admitted the devil had made him think those crazy thoughts. It certainly wasn't the work of the Lord. Lots of women die in childbirth, and it's not necessarily God's doing—but by the time Papa got over his hurt, it was too late to call the baby Charity, like he'd planned to do in the first place. By then, everybody knew June as 'June' and it didn't feel right to call her anything else. Now Mama always said—" Liza's iron grip on her knee stopped her.

She paused, her eyes frozen on the steel-like grip.

"Do you prattle like this *all* of the time?"

"Do you chew snuff all the time?" Faith blurted without thinking. She had never once seen a woman chew snuff. She was fascinated. Perhaps Liza would teach her how—no, Papa would know. And the good Lord.

"Hold your tongue, young lady!" Liza returned to staring at the road.

Faith blushed. "Sorry." She watched the passing scenery, aware she was starting out on shaky footing with her soon-to-be mother-in-law. She vowed to be silent for the remainder of the trip, but she couldn't help casting an occasional bewildered look in Liza's direction. *Mercy!*

What did it hurt to talk about some poor kitten she hadn't gotten in the first place?

BOOKS BY BEST-SELLING AUTHOR
LORI COPELAND

Morning Shade Mystery series

A Case of Bad Taste. . . . . ISBN 0-8423-7115-X
A Case of Crooked Letters . . . . ISBN 0-8423-7116-8
A Case of Nosy Neighbors . . . . ISBN 0-8423-7117-6

Child of Grace . . . . ISBN 0-8423-4260-5
Christmas Vows: $5.00 Extra . . . . ISBN 0-8423-5326-7

Brides of the West series

Faith . . . . ISBN 0-8423-0267-0
June . . . . ISBN 0-8423-0268-9
Hope . . . . ISBN 0-8423-0269-7
Glory . . . . ISBN 0-8423-3749-0
Ruth . . . . ISBN 0-8423-1937-9
Patience . . . . ISBN 0-8423-1938-7

Roses Will Bloom Again . . . . ISBN 0-8423-1936-0

Men of the Saddle series

The Peacemaker. . . . . ISBN 0-8423-6930-9
The Drifter. . . . . ISBN 0-8423-8689-0
The Maverick . . . . ISBN 0-8423-8690-4
The Plainsman . . . . ISBN 0-8423-6931-7